FIRE & ICE

BLOOD FEUD

JACKIE ANDREWS

SIMON AND SCHUSTER

For Sister Anne Henderson.
My grateful thanks for all your encouragement,
and for inspiring me with your great courage and faith.

SIMON AND SCHUSTER

First published in Great Britain by Simon & Schuster UK Ltd, 2005
A Viacom company

1 3 5 7 9 10 8 6 4 2

Simon & Schuster UK Ltd
Africa House
64-78 Kingsway
London WC2B 6AH

A CIP catalogue record for this book is available from the British Library

ISBN 0 689 87291 7

This book is a work of fiction. Names, characters, places and incidents are either
a product of the author's imagination or are used fictitiously. Any resemblance to
actual people living or dead, events or locales is entirely coincidental.

Typeset by SX Composing DTP, Rayleigh, Essex
Printed and bound in Great Britain by Cox & Wyman Ltd, Reading, Berks

www.simonsays.co.uk

ONE

Much as I enjoy the novelty of role-playing undercover work, most of the time my assignments as a private investigator take me into situations I can really do without. I'm still relatively new to this game, though, and I can't afford to turn any clients down. Take tonight, for instance. I'm at the swish Ambassador Club, pretending to be a waitress so that I can keep an eye on my rather special client. In relative terms, she's a tad younger than I am – fifteen in human years – and she's already lost one parent and is about to say *au revoir* to the other. But there the similarities between us stop. I never knew my parents, and I grew up in the fey district of Ysgard – mostly amongst the street gangs, but later with a foster mother who took me off the streets and generally put my life in order.

My client, however, was born and raised in the Palace of Ysgard, she being the daughter of the reigning monarch. Except "reigning" may be a moot point, since King Vyktor

IV has been on his death bed for the last six months, giving his relatives and enemies plenty of time to plot and conspire against him to take over the kingdom. Still, it's a pretty disgusting wind that doesn't blow *some*body some good, and I have to be grateful to King Vic for driving his daughter to my door.

In case you think I'm being cold-blooded about all this, let me make it clear that the Royal Family of Elginagen have fought like cats and dogs for centuries. None of them has ever liked or trusted the others. It's remarkable really that they have survived for as long as they have done. I'm not a monarchist myself, but at the present time, Elginagen hasn't got much else on offer. The Elginish are generally speaking a stodgy race: they'd rather have the idiots they know than the ones they don't. Their favourite adage is, "If it still works, don't throw it away".

Perhaps I should explain here that I'm not human Elginish myself. I'm mostly Ellanoi. We're a fey people, which means there is elemental magic in our blood that the stodgy Elginish lack, and are generally suspicious of. Unfortunately, persecution and interbreeding down the centuries has meant that the Ellanoi are now a dying race: there aren't many pure-blood Ellanoi left, certainly not in Elginagen. If I still lived within an Ellanoi circle (our word for a family, or clan), I would avoid Elginagen like the pestilence, but being orphaned at an early age, I didn't have a whole lot of choice where I went.

My particular magical gifts, in case you were wondering, lie with fire. I'm an unqualified fire-mage, which means I'm a natural, without formal training. It sounds impressive, but these days there's not much call for fire-mages: we're considered a potential hazard, as if we're likely to self-combust at any moment, or cause the building we're in to go up in smoke (as if we would!) so I don't advertise the fact unless it's crucial to the work I'm doing. Besides, without the proper training, any magic I've done has been largely instinctive and a bit hit-and-miss. When my foster mother, Esther, discovered I could call a fireball from her wall lamps and toss it in the air, she realised at once what I was and set about teaching me to control the power. But she wasn't a mage herself, so the training didn't go as far as it should have done if, say, I was going to go professional one day.

Anyway, to get back to the Ambassador Club. HRH hired me to find out who had been sending her threatening notes and playing rather distasteful practical jokes on her. Poisonous bugs in her water jug, for instance, and small dead animals in her bed. She is convinced it's her twin brother, Vyktor. Myself, I doubt this. Vyktor (like his sister) is not over-endowed with the old grey matter. Both of them might spit and yell at each other, but there's no history of their family members ever actually bumping each other off. Well, it's not practical for a start. There would be bodies to get rid of, and explanations to be made. In Elginagen, the Administration takes a poor view of homicide. Not even the Royal Family could get away with murder.

So here I was, taking orders and carrying drinks and stuff, and all the while keeping an eye on the rest of the room. Let me tell you, if you're not used to it, this waitressing lark is very hard on the feet, legs and back. You can also finish up with a thumping headache. And your face aches with the effort of looking pleasant in front of the customers. I've tried all ways of standing to relieve the pressure on my legs, but at the end of the shift they still hurt like fifteen kinds of torture. I'd been standing beside the royal table with my order pad for at least five minutes, my stubby pencil poised to write down the order.

I pride myself in being able to keep my face expressionless, but the young man dithering over the menu in front of him was beginning to irritate me.

"Shall I give you another five minutes, sir?" I asked, with wonderful restraint. He was frowning at the menu like it was written in hieroglyphics and needed decoding. Perhaps I should have offered to translate it for him.

HRH Veelya, sitting opposite him, was a small, neat girl, wearing expensive-looking earrings and a dress that certainly hadn't come from a charity shop. But then you'd expect that at the Ambassador Club. And besides, Veelya wasn't short of cash by any means.

Now even she began to grow impatient. "Siggy, hurry up, will you?" she hissed at him.

Siggy seemed to have been nudged into a decision. "Sorry, Vee." He looked up at me as I pointedly angled my pencil to take down his order. But there was a new problem. He suddenly seemed to be mesmerised by my appearance. Well, if you aren't used to Ellanoi features, I suppose they might be a bit startling. Especially to an earth-brown human. We all have naturally green hair, for one thing – like verdigris – and our eyes are generally a shade of violet: anything from pale lavender to deep royal purple. Mine are lavender. The two colours look good against our pale skin. We're also quite tall and thin compared to average humans.

"Yes?" I prompted him with a raised eyebrow.

Veelya glared.

Siggy shook his head, trying to remember what he was going to say. "Oh, yes. I think I'll have the escalope, with salad. Do you want any wine, Vee?"

I gave a polite cough. Veelya was underage for public alcohol consumption.

Vee scowled. "What's the matter with you tonight? I don't drink wine. I'll have a fruit cordial." She paused, then felt a pang of guilt. "Thanks." She caught my frosty stare and looked away, as if embarrassed.

"I'll just have a jug of water." He smiled at me.

"One baked fowl. One escalope. Fruit cordial and water. Thank you." I snapped my order pad shut, scooped up the wine glasses and fish knives and forks, since they weren't needed, and left them. I pushed my way through the double swing doors of the kitchen and clipped the order on the rail for the chefs, then went back out to the bar. The business of preparing the drinks gave me a chance to casually check out the rest of the restaurant, since the bar gave me a good all-round view of the room.

The ceiling and walls were decorated with over-the-top gilt work. Alcoves around the walls held massive silk flower arrangements in shades of cream, rust and aubergine, matching the dark rust of the carpet. Crystal chandeliers hung the length of the room. Swags of heavy gold brocade were draped around each of the six huge windows, and the whole place glittered sumptuously, reflecting some bygone era when Oppressive-Claustrophobic was all the rage. Each table was covered in a pristine white cloth, sparkling cutlery and candles, in shades to match the décor. I always felt I wanted to slip on dark glasses when I came into this place: all that golden brightness was much too hard on the eyes. I could also have done without the muted flute and galiol music that was played interminably by a resident quartet of musicians.

It was relatively early for the Ambassador. Only eight o'clock. Most of the guests arrived after ten, when the entertainment centres emptied. So only half a dozen tables were occupied. Siggy and Vee – being royalty – were secreted away in a private corner, surrounded by a gold-painted trellis covered in an artificial climbing plant, which screened them from the rest of the dining room. It was the table reserved for media celebrities and aristocracy: people who for personal and security reasons didn't want to mix with the commoners.

Actually, the table was screened by more than a golden trellis. There was a completely invisible shield between the table area and the rest of the room, made of a special, toughened, glass-like material that was impervious to anything short of a doomspell or atomic bomb. Attempted assassination by explosive projectile probably wouldn't be a problem tonight. It was the possibility of malicious magic that worried me.

Two palace security guards stood ostentatiously against the walls with views of the whole room and the opening to the private area. Their ubiquitous grey suits each had a bulge under the left armpit – they were carrying shoulder holsters and stunners.

I picked up my tray of drinks and carried them over, winking at the nearest security guard as I went past. He smirked.

"One cordial, one jug of water," I said, arranging the glasses and jug on the table.

Vee nodded. Siggy smiled nervously.

I didn't go straight back to the kitchen. Instead, I casually made my way round the tables to number five. It wasn't strictly within my area, but I chose a moment when Annet, the waitress for that table, had disappeared into the kitchen. A young man with fashionably-cut, collar-length hair, which looked expensively streaked and dishevelled, sat at the table, toying with a glass and a dish of nuts. He was wearing a dull-green wool jacket and informal beige trousers. Nothing memorable. Apart from the fact that he was rather gorgeous. His face might not have been sculpturally perfect, like an Ellanoi's, but it was interesting, with good bone definition and a sensitive mouth. And the eyes! He was wearing rimless spectacles with tinted lenses, which gave him a rather *interesting* appearance, but obscured his eyes a little. They looked as if they might be grey framed with dark lashes (hard to tell behind the tints). He was definitely worth a second look. Or two.

"Can I get you anything?" I asked, smiling my best waitress smile.

He looked up and his gaze went right through me. For a second I had a feeling that my hair had just shot straight up into the air. Mercifully this was just an illusion. I felt blood coursing to my ears – an Ellanoi's most sensitive body part. This guy had some kind of power – that much I could sense. He dropped his gaze quickly, as if embarrassed, or concealing something, and adjusted his spectacles on his nose, in a kind of nervous gesture. My instincts told me I was right to check him out. Solitary diners were not unusual in the Ambassador Club, but this one was sitting with his back to a wall, in sight of the door and looking towards the private cubicle. I pegged him as an enforcement agent of some kind, or a cop. Maybe security. Or maybe something else. He looked out of place on his own in this nobby restaurant: his sort generally went to the trendy wine bars in the fashionable quarter of the city, where I'd have expected to see him with a leggy model, or beautiful, aspiring actress. Or even another young man.

"No, thank you," he replied. "Actually, I've already given my order."

Cool. Nice voice that did funny things to my insides. He gave me a slight smile and glanced at me almost coyly from under those lashes as if sharing a secret with me. I felt a ruffle of unease. Paranoia. Could this guy know who I was?

I fixed an apologetic smile on my face. "Fine. Enjoy your meal." I turned away, swirling my short black skirt, and giving him a nice view of my long, straight legs encased in black tights, and strappy shoes. With any luck he'd be distracted enough not to think too hard about what he might have seen in my eyes.

Back in the kitchen, my meals were ready for collection, the order sheet folded and tucked under the plates. I put them on a tray with the dish of salad and backed out of the swing doors. More customers were trickling into the restaurant now. I could see the restaurant manager ushering them to their tables.

"Ah. At last!" said Vee, as I perched the tray on the edge of their table. "Mmm. This looks good, Siggy."

I put the plates in front of them and the salad to the left of Siggy's plate. That was when the folded order sheet fell on to the table.

"I think this is yours." Vee picked up the piece of paper and handed it to me.

"Thanks." I took the paper from her . . . and dropped it on the floor. "Oh." I bent down and, hidden from view, opened up the note. It wasn't a page from my order book: I'd known that immediately from the feel of it. There were only four words written on the paper:

SAY GOODBYE SOON, VEELYA

Great. I tucked the note into my skirt pocket, then stood up.

"Enjoy your meal!" I backed away and glanced round, checking every diner in turn for anything out of the ordinary. Something had changed. Table five was empty. The lone diner had gone.

"Urgin!" I hissed and yanked my head at one of the

bodyguards. He came over and bent his head down to me. "We've had another note. Call the unit and get all the outside doors secured. Be prepared to leave in a hurry."

Urgin gave me a nod and murmured quietly into his lapel button transmitter. I threw the tray on the bar counter and pushed open the doors into the kitchens. I just stood for a moment looking round at the chefs, listening to the noise of pans, spoons stirring, knives chopping and one chef singing an aria from a popular opera. The senior chefs called out to the juniors for more fennel, another saucepan. Stir this! Chop that!

I couldn't see anything out of place. It all looked and sounded very normal.

I went back out and scanned the dining area again. Something wasn't right. I could feel my ears tingling and my hair lifting from my scalp. Then I caught a faint acrid smell carried on a whispery draught. A *firespell!*

"URGIN – OUT!" I yelled. "*RUN!*"

The two security guards pulled Vee and Siggy from their chairs without ceremony and ran with them through the kitchen doors, which swung giddily behind them as they disappeared. The chairs clattered noisily to the floor.

I threw myself over the bar – this was no time for heroics – and landed with a grunt on the other side.

The private dining area erupted with a WHOOSH into a ball of flame. In seconds the table and chairs where Vee and Siggy had been about to start their meal were nothing but charred skeletons. Glasses exploded with the heat. Cutlery blackened and buckled. A black, evil-smelling smoke roiled through the restaurant.

Fortunately, the screening had effectively contained the fire and protected the rest of the room. But that didn't reassure the other diners, who screamed and coughed, falling over chairs, tables and each other in their scramble to leave the dining room.

I didn't stop to see whether the restaurant staff were handling the situation. I raced through the kitchen doors after the security guards and my client, catching up with them in an alley at the back of the Ambassador Club, just as they were bundling the princess and her escort into a palace security vehicle with smoke-glass windows. One guard was standing ostentatiously looking left and right up the alley, a stunner pointing upwards in his hand.

"You won't need that," I told him. "It was a remote conflagration spell. Whoever sent it won't be anywhere near the place."

He grunted, but didn't stop his vigilance. "How can you be sure?"

"I felt it. And the bad smell was a giveaway. It's the aftertaste, if you like, of all the ingredients that went into the spell." I poked my head into the transpo. "Are you OK, ma'am?"

Vee and Siggy sat in shocked disarray on the back seat. "Hardly," said Vee. "Was it really necessary to manhandle us so roughly?"

"What happened?" asked Siggy.

"Conflagration spell. Your dining table went up in smoke. You would have, too, if you'd stayed put."

The Illustrious Lord Sigmund d'Estivrania went paper white. His eyes rolled up into his head and he folded limply back into the soft leather seat.

Her Royal Highness Veelya Sofania Gloriosa clicked her tongue at him impatiently. "Honestly, Siggy. You're such a wimp. Well, I hope you believe me now, Silke."

I nodded. "I know someone wants to kill you, for sure. I don't know who, though." I stood up and shut the car door. "I need to check out a few things. I'll be in touch, Princess. In the meantime, cancel all your public engagements."

"I will not," said Veelya, defiantly. "Go and arrest my brother."

I just smiled and smacked the roof of the transpo, which took off at speed.

"Sorry, Princess. No can do."

I had a sorcerer to find.

TWO

I nipped back through the kitchens, where the atmosphere was now distinctly different. Furious chefs were waving their arms in frustration at their gastronomic masterpieces going to waste. They started to aim their anger in my direction, but I ignored them and pushed through the doors, shutting off their shouting behind me. I needed to check the scene of the fire before the firefighters and Enforcers arrived and began pushing everyone around – they might even decide to take me downtown as well, to ask a few questions. No way. Been there. Done that. I had no desire to repeat the experience. Besides, I'd have a hard time explaining away the coincidence of a fire-mage working in the restaurant at the same time as a firespell threatened the life of one of the heirs to the throne.

The restaurant staff were milling round by the exits, but none of them took any notice of me as I approached what was left of the private dining area.

The fire had been well contained, showing a remarkable degree of accuracy on the part of the mage who had sent it. Careful not to touch any of the charred remains or leave my prints in the soot on the floor, I had a good look around. The fire had burnt itself out quickly, which was another indication that it was magical in origin. Firespells were always efficient: a quick flare for effect, then instant barbecued princess. I closed my eyes, and concentrated on drawing on the power that had come to me down countless generations of fire-mages. I focused on the *smell* of the spell, sucking in the smoky atmosphere like a wine-taster, rolling it around my mouth and licking it from my lips. Tasting it. Yes, I had its pattern now. I'd know when this spell was used again: it had quite a distinctive signature, but not one I recognised. The question was, who had sent it? I knew one or two low-life fire merchants, but couldn't imagine them doing this. It had too much finesse about it. Then I remembered the young man at table five. Although there had certainly been something supernatural about him, I didn't think he was the perpetrator. He may have been working for someone, though. These things were often carried out by teams: one remote working the spell and one on the spot, watching that the event happened as planned. Sometimes they communicated with each other tele-pathically, or, more prosaically, they might use a crystal communicator. I didn't remember seeing table five use a

15

crystal (they were not encouraged in the restaurant) but he could have been a telepath. That would account for the feeling of "otherness" I'd got from him.

I went in search of Annet, and found her sitting shocked and pale in the staff rest room with several others.

"Hey, Annet? Do you remember the guy at table five tonight?" I asked.

"What?"

"Table five. Do you know who he was?"

"You're joking. I can hardly remember who *I* am. Didn't you notice? The restaurant just got hit by a fireball."

I shook my head and left the room. Nothing to be learnt there. Instead, I searched out Cosi, the manager of the restaurant. He was so agitated by the appalling events – "How *dare* anyone vandalise the *Ambassador Club?*" – that he barely heard my apologies and excuses for leaving early, so I took off for the night before he realised what I was saying. I'd only get partial payment, of course, but then this had been a special arrangement so I didn't feel guilty about leaving. There would be no more meals served there tonight, in any case.

My waitress persona was just one of the many characters that I dropped into when I needed to, and the Ambassador was just one of the restaurants in Ysgard that allowed me to freelance in this way.

As I swept past table five, I stopped to give it one last

check in case the young man had left behind any clues. His glass was still where he had left it, and the dish of nuts was half eaten. A small tip lay by the glass. There were no other signs that he had been served a meal: no crumbs on the table, no cutlery removed. I picked the glass up and sniffed it. Water. Interesting.

I grabbed my things from my locker, changed into my comfortable boots and threw a shabby, but warm cloak round my shoulders. Then I left the club by the staff exit. I was in such a hurry, I snagged the hem of my cloak on a splinter and had to yank it free before I could push the door shut behind me. Then I set off through the dark streets of Ysgard, in the direction of the waterfront, and home.

I guess I'd chosen a strange place to live by most people's reckoning. The waterside area of Ysgard was a hotbed of criminal activity: muggings, illegal wheeling and dealing, gambling, brothels; every kind of vice you could think of, and probably some you couldn't. But it had been my home ever since I fled from the bratcatchers at the age of six – those Special Enforcers whose job it was to round up minors living rough on the streets and take them to the state orphanages. No way was I ever going to let them stick me in an institution. After nine years' living rough, working with street gangs and having to hand over the weekly tithe, I'd had a lucky break. Just by being in the right place at the right moment, I got the job of tracing a missing relative for some rich aristo. I successfully traced his long-lost daughter (who had been stolen by river pirates) and after that I found other commissions coming my way. Before long I had quite a thriving private-investigations business and I got a real kick out of it. Running your own business feels good when you've suffered a lifetime of subjugation. My contacts from the underworld proved to be very useful, and although I could now afford a much better place to live, I deliberately kept my old apartment because of its anonymity and useful location.

There were bars and taverns here whose landlords were accustomed to never ask questions, and whose clients – many of them illegal immigrants off the riverboats – valued privacy above all else. These were the kind of haunts frequented by the people I often needed to tap for information, and what's more, they knew me and trusted me – as much as they trusted anyone, that is.

As I walked the familiar streets and alleyways, I automatically clipped my purse on to a belt round my waist to hide it from snatchers, and drew the hood of the cloak over my hair. Not much of a disguise, but enough. If anyone *were* looking for a young woman in a black waitress skirt and white shirt, with distinctive hair and eyes, they wouldn't give me a second glance. Couldn't do much about the height, unfortunately.

I was still in the classy district, however, when I picked up the shadow. We Ellanois have enhanced senses. It would be a foolish human – or else a clumsy amateur – who'd imagine he or she could sneak up behind one of us unnoticed. Furtive movements always stand out much more clearly than natural ones, and boy, was this shadow furtive. I slowed my pace slightly, pretending to study a shop window, and then moved on until I reached a crossing. I turned as if to go over to my right, then grasped hold of a lamppost with my right hand and swung round, my left foot extended. I caught the guy right in the stomach, just as he brought up his hand with a knife. The knife went flying and he doubled up in pain. I flipped my own knife out of my boot scabbard, crunched my foot on to his chest and pushed the tip of the knife under his chin. He was too winded to even complain. His face was partially covered with a close-fitting hood that concealed all but his eyes. I ripped it off.

"Well, well," I said, pleasantly. "Yorgish! Who'd have thought you'd have the audacity – or the brains, come to that – to imagine you could mug me!"

Yorgish wheezed. "Sssilke! Ah . . . your foot . . ." He squinted up at me, his eyes pleading. "Can't breathe . . ."

"Who put you up to it, Yorgish?" I pushed the knife into his scaly chin. I can tolerate most of the outlandish races, but reptilian Taurugs really creep me out.

Yorgish squirmed under my foot. "Missstake . . . Ssssilke."

"Don't lie to me, Yorgish!" His eyes popped disagreeably as his yellow blood trickled down the blade of the knife.

"No . . . no . . . jussst . . . freelanssing, Sssilke!" He tried a leering version of a grin.

"Trying to make an honest buck, Yorgish?" I asked him, a note of sarcasm in my voice. "How much?"

"Aw . . . Sssilke." He tried to wriggle out from under my foot. I pressed harder, and could hear his breath rasp in his throat. His face was turning an interesting grey colour.

"How much and who, Yorgish?"

"Caaan't. Sssahh . . ."

The reptilian head snapped back and Yorgish collapsed under my weight, going completely rigid. It was a trick they had – along with the ability to snap off body parts and regrow them – appearing for all the world to be dead to the point of rigor mortis. I stepped off him and wiped my knife on his coat. I wasn't going to get any more out of him until he stopped playing dead. But I could make life difficult for him. I felt in his pockets and smiled to myself when I found the pair of silver restraint bracelets. Sneak thieves and muggers like Yorgish always carried them, so they could immobilise their victims – chaining them to railings or gates – and take off at their leisure. Silver made them effective against both fey and non-fey victims. I slipped one bracelet on Yorgish's right hand, and looked around. There was a signpost a few metres up the street. I tucked up my cloak and dragged Yorgish over to it, wrapped his arms round the post and clipped the other bracelet on to his left hand. He'd be there until one of the Night Enforcers came across him, or he chose to chop off one of his own hands.

My foot caught against something lying in the road. It was Yorgish's knife. I stooped and picked it up but almost dropped it again. My fingers were sparking blue magefire. "Hey, Yorgish, how did you get this?" I didn't really expect him to reply – in fact I would have jumped out of my skin if he had. This was a very rare weapon. Forged by Taurug smiths centuries ago and imbued with dark magic which was more powerful than poison. If Yorgish had managed to nick me with this, I'd be history now. Hard to imagine how a petty criminal like Yorgish had got hold of it. I weighed the knife in my hand, then tucked it carefully into one of my knife sheaths and went on my way.

Fortunately, traffic was light that night. But although nothing had passed us, I didn't doubt someone had witnessed our scuffle. I passed a few drunks in doorways and the occasional vagrant wrapped up in cardboard and rags, sleeping on the benches beside the footpath, but mostly I used back alleyways in order to avoid the patrols of Enforcers.

Finally, I could smell the river. It was about half nine, so I still had a couple of hours to go hunting. I headed for the

Goat's Beard: a sordid little inn situated among the dockyard warehouses that I knew was frequented by the scum I was looking for.

Being a commercial port in the estuary of the river Swathe, Ysgard played host to a great many different nationalities and species, brought in by ship. Some were simply passengers on their way inland or further upriver, but the majority were sailors of every description: merchantmen, shipmasters, weather-mages, freightmen or simply able-bodied. Nearly all were opportunists, with an eye for a fast bargain and a little under-the-table smuggling, and they would slit your throat in a blink without any remorse. Survival was the name of the game down here.

As I approached, sallow yellow light streamed from the inn's windows. I tossed back my cloak, draping the length of it over my shoulder to leave my hands free. I pushed open the door and nearly gagged on the fug of scented smoke inside the public bar. It was hot and fairly busy. A party of mariners was noisily celebrating pay day with some good-time females over on one side of the room. Alfric, the barman, was pulling pints for a group of frog-faced Marshmen perched up on the high bar stools. He saw me and nodded. I scanned the room carefully and located my quarry, then made my way to the bar.

"Hi, Alfric."

"Silke." Alfric plonked down the last tankard and rang

up the money on the till. He gave some change to one of the Marshmen, then flipped his towel over his shoulder and came over. "What'll it be?"

"I'll have a Red Devil. What's Sarvik drinking?"

Alfric glanced across the room to the lone drinker in a dark corner. "Double Xlactian."

"Come into money, has he?"

"Apparently. You watch that one, Silke." He put the glass of Red Devil in front of me.

"OK. Give me a Xlactian, too."

"Double?"

Sighing, I pulled my purse round to check I had enough cash.

"Why not? Thanks." I put a couple of coins on the bar. Alfric poured out the bittersweet liqueur into a tot glass, and my money disappeared faster than a blink. I picked up the drinks and went over to the dark corner to join the lone drinker.

He didn't look up as I approached, but continued to stare into his drink, his headdress dipping over his face so that his features were hidden from view.

"Sarvik?" I said softly. "Long time. How's things? Here, I brought you a drink for old time's sake."

Sarvik didn't respond. Must have been drunker than I anticipated. I sat down opposite him and sipped my drink. "Sarvik?"

The room went oddly quiet. I resisted turning round, but all my senses were screaming that something was seriously wrong and that everyone else in the room knew it. It felt as if all eyes were on my back, watching to see what I'd do next. Keeping my voice steady, I carried on talking quietly to Sarvik and, shielding the movement from the other customers with my body, carefully slid my hand across the table to touch the fingers curled round his glass.

They were stone cold. I almost jumped out of my skin. I stared at Sarvik, but couldn't see any visible sign of damage. He looked too . . . *still* . . . to have been poisoned. My guess was that an investigation would find a fine wire shot through Sarvik's greedy heart, either from frontal close range, or through the wall behind him. I certainly wasn't going to find out for myself.

". . . I'll just go and get some ice," I announced. "Wait here." *Ha! He wasn't going anywhere.*

I stood up casually and made my way to the bar again with my drink, aware of furtive, sliding looks as I passed other tables. Alfric moved over to me, an unspoken question on his face.

"Can you give me some more ice in here, Alfric?" I asked. Then, lowering my voice, "Sarvik is dead."

Alfric picked up my glass and took his time dropping chunks of ice into it from the bucket under the counter. "Go," he said without moving his lips. "Out the back."

24

He didn't have to say it twice. I turned and walked naturally to the door at the side of the bar, which led to the rest rooms. As soon as I was through it, I ran down the short corridor to the outside door. It was made of leadwood and bolted on the inside. I threw the well-oiled bolts, certain that someone would hear the noise, and dragged it open. Then I was through, pulling the door shut behind me. Time to take off.

Ducking and weaving through the rabbit warren of the dockyards, doubling back and taking fiendish shortcuts, I finally made my way to my own apartment, confident no one had followed me. I hadn't heard any Enforcement sirens, so perhaps the erstwhile Sarvik was still propped up against his table, colder than the drink he was nursing. I wearily climbed the steps up the side of the converted warehouse where I lived, unlocked my front door and went inside, locking it securely behind me. Only then did I sag against the wall and shrug off my cloak.

I made my way into the main room of the apartment, where the couch beckoned to me. My antiquated crystal communicator was blinking at me that I had a message, but I reckoned that at this hour it could wait. I flopped down into the cushions, tugged my boots off my throbbing feet, and spent a few blissful moments lying full length, one arm flung over my tired eyes. I tried to imagine who would have paid Yorgish to mug me. It was likely the same person who

25

had taken out Sarvik, a small-time freelance fire-worker, whom I'd hoped to peg for information. Now he was dead, I had to find another source. I also needed to track down the man at table five. Hmm. That wouldn't be such an unpleasant task. I felt my face crack into a tired smile.

Then I remembered the note I'd put into my pocket at the restaurant. I pulled it out carefully and laid it on a side table. Tomorrow, I'd have to compare it with the others Veelya had received, but it was a safe bet that they were from the same person. Veelya was convinced that Vyktor was sending them, but I wasn't so sure. Leaving threatening notes in obscure places was not something that a prince of the realm would find easy to do: everywhere that Vyktor went, his PBs – personal bodyguards – were sure to follow. They'd have to be in on the act, too, and I doubted loyalty could be stretched that far.

A tinny sound came from the communicator. I looked up and squinted at the luminous face of the clock. Two in the morning. I'd fallen asleep.

"Silke, are you there? It's Veelya." She was speaking in a stage whisper which sounded like someone blowing across the top of a bottle: echoing and hollow. "I can't talk now, but I have some important news for you. Please meet me at the usual place at eight . . . no, make that ten, tomorrow morning. Oh. That would be *this* morning. Sorry, Silke. But it's very import—!" The crystal went silent and blinked its ghostly light. It has a mind of its own and cuts off when it chooses. One day I'll replace it with something state of the art. I wish.

I groaned, rolled off the couch, and padded out to my tiny kitchen to pour myself a glass of water. Then I went into the bedroom, shrugged off my clothes and crawled under the bedclothes. I was asleep in seconds.

THREE

The early morning sun bathed the city of Ysgard in a pale lemon light, which made the galong trees down the central promenade glisten as if covered with diamonds. None of it did much to dispel my irritable mood. Meeting Veelya in the Adamanté Salon in the city's most exclusive shopping arcade was not how I would choose to start my day. I had to be careful about what I wore, for a start. No way could I throw on my comfortable, worn black jeans and leather jacket; the prissy attendants in the Adamanté wouldn't allow me near the pink satin sofas for love nor money.

So, at five minutes past ten, dressed in an inoffensive beige wool skirt and long jacket made of red, patchwork suede, I was flashing my member's card (one of the benefits of working for the Royal Family) at the snooty, suspicious attendant blocking the door of the salon. A small figure on the far side of the room, wearing dark shades and an outfit that probably cost as much as I would make in three years, waved a hand imperiously. Veelya, attempting a disguise.

I smiled benignly at the attendant, who grudgingly stepped aside with obvious distaste, and made my way over to Veelya's table. A pot of kashla was waiting, along with a plate of discreet pastries: small enough to be eaten without too much guilt, and expensive enough to be worth their weight in gold. But if you were royalty these things were of no consequence. Mindful that this was all on Veelya's bottomless expense account, I poured myself a large kashla and tucked into the pastries with gusto, barely offering Veelya a grunt of recognition. Free meals are the perks of the job and not to be turned down.

"Haven't you had breakfast, Silke?" There was an edge to Veelya's voice. Ladies visiting the Adamanté were not supposed to appear hungry. They sipped and nibbled daintily.

"Nope, but this will do," I mumbled, trying not to spray crumbs. "What did you want to tell me, Princess? You know you're not supposed to be out on your own."

Veelya looked round sharply. "Ssssh! Don't call me that *here!*" she hissed. "Anyway, I'm not exactly alone. That one over there having her nails done is Astrid, one of my PBs."

I scanned the aristocratic ladies dotted around the elegant room, studiously ignoring us. At least four were having manicures, but I picked out the familiar face of one of Veelya's personal bodyguards, who was looking extremely uncomfortable about her situation and stood out like a troll at a convention of fairies. The other ladies were in discussion with their beauty therapists or friends. It would have been the height of social indiscretion for anyone here to *notice* that an heir to the throne was actually sharing the same room as them.

"OK." I nodded and sipped at my drink. "So, what was so important? Have you had another note?"

"No, thank goodness. But I think Our Friend has *hired* someone," said Veelya, darkly. She twitched the shades over her eyes.

I swallowed a hot mouthful of kashla and tried to figure out what Veelya was trying to say to me. Our Friend, I knew, meant her brother, Vyktor. "Hired someone? What, like . . . a gardener? A butler?"

Veelya sighed and slid her hand across the table to mine. "*No. An assassin!* I found this in his jacket pocket." There was a piece of paper under her fingers.

I picked it up and opened it out. It was the bill from KleenKwick Laundry for the cleaning of one shirt, gents, white, ready for collection last Tuesday. There was a crystal code and an address scrawled across it in green ink.

"I looked it up," said Veelya with a touch of excitement in her voice.

"What, personally?"

Veelya rolled her eyes. "I sent one of my maids to inquire."

"And?"

"Well, actually I sent her to KleenKwick first, to see if they remembered who brought in a white shirt for cleaning last week."

"You mean, it wasn't Vyktor?" I couldn't resist it. Can you imagine the prince personally taking his shirt to the cleaners?

"We have our own laundry at the palace," said Veelya primly. "Anyway, they were most uncooperative. Apparently they clean about two hundred and fifty white shirts *a day*. So then I used the crystalcomm on that code. It was some strange man. Asked me if I was the *agency*!" Veelya was so triumphant she took off her glasses and had to blink a little in the bright lights of the salon.

"What kind of agency?"

Veelya looked a little nonplussed for a moment. "What kind?"

"Yes. Travel? Literary? Domestic? Employment? Escort? Dating?" I was being rather hard on Veelya. In truth, before the fire in the restaurant, I was convinced that the princess was merely bored with her life and was inventing some excitement in the guise of a threat to spice it up a little. Probably writing the notes herself. Now I had to start taking her seriously.

"Oh. I . . . um . . . didn't ask," Veelya admitted. "I suppose I was thinking of *special* agency."

"You mean, Kill'emKwick: Assassins for Hire? – cheap rates for senior citizens?" I knew I shouldn't, but I couldn't resist teasing her. I chuckled at my own joke.

Veelya turned red. "There's no need to be offensive, Silke. I may have jumped to an erroneous conclusion, but at least I'm trying to be alert and take advantage of opportunities." *Which is more than you seem to be doing*, was the unspoken implication.

"So what did the strange man say when he answered the phone?" I asked. I doubted very much it was anything useful.

Veelya tried to remember. "Well, I was trying to disguise my voice. The last thing I wanted was for him to recognise me! He was rather rude, I thought. Kept saying, 'Speak up. Can't hear you!' Then, 'Is that the agency? If it is, I'm still waiting for my money.' Something like that, anyway. But it fits, doesn't it? He'd be after his money having tried to murder me last night."

I pocketed the bill. "It's not likely. He'd only get paid for actually killing you. Not to worry. I'll follow it up," I promised, and poured myself another cup of kashla. Might as well take advantage of the situation.

"Any news about the *fire?*" Veelya mouthed the last word. She had put the glasses back on and nibbled at a pastry to cover her nervousness. It was miraculous that the broadsheets and government spies hadn't picked up on the attempt on her life: that would have blown everything. She'd never be allowed to leave the palace again.

"Not exactly," I replied. "But someone I wanted to pump for information was taken out last night, which suggests he may have been involved." I didn't tell her about Yorgish – it would have freaked her out even more. Besides, I didn't know that the two incidents were related. Yorgish hadn't exactly been very forthcoming.

"Taken out?" Veelya wasn't quite up on the vernacular of the street. "Taken out" would have meant, for her, a date at the theatre.

"Murdered."

The princess covered her mouth with her napkin. "Oh!"

"Not to worry, Princ— . . . um, I still have a few other leads to follow up." This, of course, was not true, but I have a professional obligation to my clients (especially ones that pay so generously) to give them confidence I am on top of things. Anyway, I still had the young diner to check out. He was my main suspect at the moment. Well, the only suspect as it happened, as the other one was dead.

Veelya looked at me dubiously. "Well, keep me informed," she said primly, trying to sound on top of things as well. She dipped into her micro purse again and brought out another folded paper. "Here, this is Vyk . . . er . . . *Our*

Friend's schedule for the next fortnight. I thought you might find it useful." She handed me a sheet of cream parchment embossed with the palace coat of arms. It listed an itinerary of dates and venues, printed out in colour and surrounded by a heavy, ornamental border.

"Where did this come from?"

"The Palace Press Office. They give this stuff to journalists and tourists."

"So what about *your* itinerary?"

"Oh. Did you want a copy of that as well?"

I rolled my eyes. "Well, it would be helpful to know where you are, but the point is, that if you can get this about Our Friend, then he – or his *agent* – can know all about *you*! The whole world and his wife will know where to find you. How early is this stuff printed?"

"About a week in advance, I think." Light dawned. Veelya snatched off her glasses again. "Oh. I see. Not very secure, is it?"

"That has to be the understatement of the year," I snapped. "I can't bodyguard you as well as track down a would-be killer. You'll have to persuade your Press Office to keep information to a vague minimum. No precise times or venues. And make sure your PBs are on the ball. One's not much good on her own." I glanced across at the muscle-bound Astrid, sitting awkwardly with her hands splayed out in front of her on a satin cushion, waiting for the dark blue lacquer to dry. If there were an attempt on the princess's life in the next few minutes, Astrid would get her fingers stuck together trying to draw a weapon.

"Oh, all right, Silke. But you do fuss sometimes. I think I ought to be given some credit for thinking ahead. After all, I did find and hire *you*, didn't I?"

There wasn't much I could say to that. I couldn't blame Veelya for her sheltered upbringing.

"Anyway," Veelya continued, "I'm at the palace all day today. This evening there's a cocktail party for the Ambassador of Illithgarten. It'll be tedious, but he has a rather delicious-looking nephew who is coming, and I'll contrive to spend the evening with him. So you don't need to worry about me."

I looked at the printed itinerary. "So where's Our Friend? It doesn't say he's at the party." Instead it said *7.30 Sunfire Rooms*.

"No. He's at a literary dinner at the Sunfire Rooms. Some academic bore has written Pa's biography and it's being published tomorrow."

"Fine. Well, take care. I'll . . . er . . . keep you informed." I stood up and brushed pastry crumbs from my jacket. "Thanks for the breakfast. Oh, and let me know immediately if you get any more notes . . . or whatever."

Veelya turned a little pale and touched her throat with her elegant fingers. "Do you think there will be more?"

"Not yet, at any rate. Our guy has to come up with another plan, since the last one failed."

Something else suddenly occurred to Veelya, apparently banishing her momentary alarm. "Silke, why don't you have a beauty make-over while you're here? You can put it on expenses. After all, you need to keep up appearances if you're working for me."

I felt my face blanch and scowled down at her. "I'm supposed to be undercover, remember?"

"Well, at least get your hair dyed," Veelya protested. "It's very *distinctive*, Silke."

I resisted the impulse to make the shape of her nose more *distinctive*. "I know. And that's the way it's staying."

I strode out of the salon, leaving Veelya huddled over her kashla, probably wondering how many of the ladies present had recognised her. I guessed she hoped they all had.

Outside the rarified atmosphere of the salon, the day was hotting up to be a scorcher. I stopped in the doorway and breathed in the noise, smells and sounds of the city. The walkways were crowded with jostling tourists and shoppers of all shapes, sizes, colours and species. I spotted three Narthians working a pickpocket scam, dipping their long, elegant digits into unsuspecting out-of-town pockets. Not my problem, but if they came near me, I'd bust them. I went in search of a public crystalcomm-booth.

Using my crystal card (another palace perk) I made

contact with several old associates, setting up a few meetings to pick their brains; then fished out Veelya's slip of paper and spoke the code number on it.

I was answered almost immediately. Voice only. Public crystal booths didn't offer viewing as well as sound.

"Marcus Stone."

Marcus Stone?

"Good morning, Mr Stone—"

"Is that Scribbins?"

"Scribbins?" I repeated, stupidly.

"I'm due a royalty payment."

Royalties. Books. Agent. Right. I didn't spend much time reading books, but I suddenly remembered the name Marcus Stone. Wrote a blockbuster a few years ago.

"No, I'm afraid I'm not from Scribbins. I'm, er, a journalist, Mr Stone. My name is, um, Silvia Flambard. I wonder if I could have an interview with you?"

"An interview? For whom?" Stone asked. I was having to improvise fast.

"Oh, I'm freelance. I write articles and then sell them to journals. I'd like to do a feature on . . . um . . . writing a bestseller."

There was silence at the other end of the phone. Not for the first time, I wished I had a viewscreen. Then I heard a rustling sound – pages being turned. A diary?

"Oh. Yes," said Stone. "Are you going to the literary

dinner, tonight? I could meet you there and we could have a chat before all the speeches start."

"That would be perfect!" I lied, wondering rapidly how I could get into the Sunfire Rooms legitimately.

"Fine. I look forward to seeing you, Ms Flambard. And when you see Marta, tell her my royalty payment's due."

He disconnected and I shut down the unit. *Marta? Must be his agent.* The man was clearly confused, which wasn't promising. I immediately opened up the unit again and called Veelya's code.

"Yes?" Veelya's voice was muffled. I guessed crystals were frowned on in the Adamanté Ladies' Salon. I doubted they'd throw her out, though.

"It's me. Can you get me an invite to this literary dinner tonight?"

There was silence. "Well, yes, I suppose so. I'm sure the Press Office could—"

"Thanks. And can you send it round to my apartment? Courier?"

"You don't want much, Silke," she hissed. "I'm your *client*, remember, not your secretary."

"I haven't forgotten, ma'am. But you do want results, don't you? And I can't track down Vyktor's contacts without a little inside help, can I?"

"Oh, all right." Huffy. She cut the connection.

I pushed open the door of the booth and immediately felt

as if someone was walking over my grave. I shivered. My ears throbbed. Someone was watching me. I hitched my bag over my shoulder, glanced carelessly about, and began walking down the promenade, gazing into shop windows as I went. I caught sight of an occasional flicker of movement behind me, but couldn't get a fix on the shadow. Whoever it was, they were being very cautious. I went inside a bargain clothes shop I knew, and headed straight for the changing cubicles at the back. I passed a startled shop assistant on her kashla break and slipped out of the rear exit. I grinned and shut the door behind me before the girl could say, "Hey!"

I nipped round the back of the shop, scooted down the dark alley alongside, and crept along the shadowed walls until I had a view of the promenade again. Then I saw my tail. A darkly-dressed figure in a hooded cloak – somewhat overdressed for the heat of the morning – was hovering outside the clothes shop, staring through the window. As I watched, I saw a thin, pale hand emerge from the cloak and point some kind of stick at the shop doorway. There was no way I could allow the shop to go up in smoke. I ran out of the alley.

"Hey, you!" I yelled.

The figure turned in surprise, raising the stick. A bright ball of flame shot towards me.

I threw up my hands and focused my power. The bright

flame, intended to turn me into a living torch, engulfed me but did not burn. It felt almost like a caress; a touch of velvet. I could hear screams from the crowd, but I didn't break my concentration. With slow, measured movements I collected the flame from around me with my spread hands, chanting the ancient commands of Old Magic that came into my head from deep in my genetic make-up. I don't remember anyone teaching them to me. They were just there. As I moved, I compressed the flames: shrinking them smaller, smaller and smaller, until I finally brought my hands completely together and they disappeared.

I shook my head to clear it and quickly scanned the crowd for the cloaked figure.

"Where did he go?" I demanded loudly. The bystanders looked at me blankly: too shocked, I guess, by what they had seen. I could just hear the distant sound of Enforcer sirens. Time to take off.

"Not a mark on her!" I heard one woman say.

"'T'ain't natural," said someone else.

"Went up in flames – whoosh! Never seen anything like it!"

I pushed impatiently through them, ignoring their comments, but my quarry had disappeared. Still, I had learnt something. The cloaked figure had been a fire-mage like myself, but one with a mission to kill. I recognised the spell: it had the same signature as the one used at the Ambassador

Club. Sarvik had probably been murdered because he knew too much, not because he had actually cast the spell.

Before the Enforcers could arrive and ask awkward questions, I decided to look up an old friend, whom I hoped might be able to shed some light on whoever wanted me dead. I still hadn't done anything about the man from table five, but he could wait. People who actively tried to fry me really piqued my interest. Besides, the place where I was headed was roughly on my route home. I badly needed a shower and change of clothes. Firespells may not be able to burn me, but they sure leave behind a pungent stink.

FOUR

The herbalist shop in Lepp Street was run by a witch called Esther. I'd known her most of my life, since she'd often taken me in as a young tearaway and given me a refuge from the Enforcers who would have dumped me in an orphanage. Esther was my nearest equivalent of kin.

It's difficult to explain the relationship between us. I never called her "Mother", since I never thought of her in that way. To me she was just Esther. I guess she saw me as a young fledgling picked up out of the gutter and nurtured to see what kind of creature I developed into. A witch of Esther's talent would always be on the lookout for a useful apprentice and cheap labour, and Esther found my streetwise skills particularly attractive to her needs. For my part, I never wholly let go of my fierce independence enough to trust Esther with my life – or even my back – but I did respect her craft.

Situated in the heart of the Old City, Esther's shop was

well positioned to channel all the underworld gossip. Most of the workers of magic – good, evil or impartial – visited her shop at some time or another for herbal supplies or specialist knowledge. It had been established five generations ago, down the female line of Esther's predecessors. While not a mage herself, she did have a formidable knowledge of organic magic and could advise the most learned practitioners on ingredients and their properties.

Today, I was after information, but I was also long overdue for a "family" visit.

Like any metropolis, Ysgard had a great many different districts that reflected the occupations and living styles of the people who lived and worked in each. I made my way briskly down the narrow walkways of the Old City, taking a slightly convoluted route just in case I was still being followed. I did have a slightly bad feeling in my ears, but put this down to paranoia. A few glances behind gave me no cause for concern.

Halfway down Lepp Street I saw the familiar shop sign of a stylised pestle and mortar, swaying in the light breeze. Two big wicker baskets each side of the door held branches of greenberry and curly witch-broom, and a hand-written sign declared them to be the bargain of the week. I grinned. Esther was not above good marketing techniques.

I pushed open the door, which caused a red-beaked mimic bird to hop along its perch behind the counter and yell "Ding-dong!" I scratched his head and he tilted it for me so that I hit the right place. "Mornin' darlin'," said the bird, in a perfect imitation of Esther.

"Morning Mort," I replied. Mort had been with Esther for at least ten years – the time I had known her – and never showed any sign of senility. He might have been Esther's familiar, except I'd never known him to leave his perch in her shop despite being untethered.

I barely had time to register all the heady smells of drying herbs and pharmacopoeia before a beaded curtain at the back of the shop swished noisily to one side.

"Silke, darlin'!" A short, plump woman emerged and bore down on me, her arms spread wide in welcome, her many beads, charms, necklaces and bracelets jangling and flying about as she moved. Her face was flushed and smiling, framed with long, black braids wound round like a turban. Her eyes glinted bright and dark, like chips of ebonite. "Have you come to see Esther at last? It's too long you are away. And are you not my own sweet flesh and blood?"

I had to bend so that she could engulf me with her arms and give me a smacking kiss on the cheek. The familiar, leafy smell of her assailed me and wrenched me back a few years to when I was younger and wilder. "Well, not exactly, Esther. But I'm sorry I haven't been around for a while." I flinched to realise just how long it was since I last came to see her.

"Pooh!" said Esther, waving aside my niceties. "Does a mother forget her own child?" I decided not to point out that I was only a foster child. Esther was getting on in years: her memory was not so good any more, except when it came to her herbs and spells.

"Come!" she said. "Come inside and I'll get us something special." She tapped her nose conspiratorially. "I've this bottle of Raillian wine I've been keeping for just such a day. This calls for a celebration!"

I followed her through the bead curtain into her dark, fuggy living room that contained far too much furniture and too many animals. Cats, birds, bats and snakes all lounged carelessly in whatever manner suited them, across chairbacks, on cushions, on perches, hanging from the candle sconces or stretched on the carpet in front of the log fire. None of them took much notice of me, except one old moggy who stretched himself into an arching curve and padded across the room to rub his head against my legs. I could feel his purring vibrating through me.

"Hi, Juniper." I rubbed his ears and as soon as I flopped into one of Esther's engulfing armchairs, he jumped into my lap and began kneading my thighs to make a bed. Juniper was remarkably ancient for a cat. He'd been a great comfort to me when, as a young kid, I had wept myself to sleep in the dark, lonely nights.

Esther came back with a tray laden with a jug of dark

wine, plates, two glasses and a plate of home-made fudge cakes, sticky with dark chocolate coating. While she poured the wine, I took a small plate and slipped one of the cakes on to it, reflecting that today was not turning out to be one for healthy eating.

"Mmmm," I said appreciatively as I bit into it. "No one makes fudge cake like you do, Esther!" A little toadying would, I hoped, mollify her so I could get down to the real reason I was here.

She bobbed her head and smiled, acknowledging the compliment, then she clouted me lightly on the shoulder. "But your favourite cakes don't make you come see me more often!" she complained. She eased herself into a chair opposite, pushing out two of the cats first, and sighed as she relaxed into the cushions.

"So, what's the word on the street?" I asked between sips of wine.

Esther took a drink herself, smacking her lips in appreciation before answering.

"Let's see. I don't suppose you know where I could get hold of some silith root?" She shook her head in exasperation and muttered, "Can't get the stuff for love nor money – they want a fortune for it these days."

"Not really," I smiled. I'd never taken much of an interest in her herbology. "Heard anything about the palace?"

"Huh. The *palace*. Well, rumours are *rife* as far as that

place is concerned. That's an unhappy family if ever there was one. You wouldn't get me to live in there for all the money in the land. As like as get me throat cut or worse before the day's out." She took another gulp from her glass. "They do say the royal brats are at each other's throats and like to kill each other. Runs in the blood, don't it, dearie? And that the king won't last the month."

"What do they say is wrong with him?"

Esther tapped her nose. "Ah, now. That's the big question, isn't it? All those fancy *doc-tors* up there, and none of them as knows what's really wrong. They need to ask old Esther, they do. I'd soon have the gent back on his feet."

That may or may not have been true. Esther could certainly find a cure for most ailments, but I suspected that even she couldn't do much for the king. As she said, he had all the world's finest looking after him.

"So, child. You didn't come just to catch up on gossip," said Esther, raising her glass and looking sharply at me over the rim as she sipped.

I pulled a face and took a deep breath. "I'm trying to track down a fire-mage, Esther," I said. "One that I don't recognise. Able to conjure remote conflagration." I held out my scorched sleeve for Esther to "taste".

"My dear, I could taste you in the next street. No need to give me your sleeve. What did you do? Jump into a fireball?"

"No. Someone wanted to put me out of action. They couldn't have known me very well, or they'd never have tried it. Which makes me believe they are out-of-town." I put my empty plate back on the table, sighed, and gave Esther a bland account of my assignment that didn't compromise my client's confidentiality. "Have you heard of any new mages being brought in on contract?"

Esther leaned into the fireplace and picked up a slim clay pipe from a pottery ashtray and tamped it down prior to lighting it again with a spill. She puffed at it meditatively, filling the room with aromatic smoke that smelled like a burning compost heap. She said nothing for a while. Her face registered a shiftiness that I put down to unwelcome information. Then she glanced at me quickly with those little black chips of eyes, before looking down at her pipe. "Word is that Sattine's around," she said very quietly. "He's brought his own retinue of . . . talented assistants, too. Daresay your fire-mage is one of 'em."

"*Sattine?*" I sat up sharply, making Juniper leap off my lap in alarm. My eyes must have looked wild. I stood up then and paced about the small room, my hand unconsciously twitching on the hilt of the knife I kept tucked into my belt. "Who could afford to hire that despicable, filthy, cesspit maggot?" I swore colourfully, forgetting where I was.

"You can keep that language out of my house, for a start, my girl," Esther reprimanded me. "He may not have been hired," she said carefully. "He may have his own agenda. Have you thought of that?"

"He's lived in the Southern Isles for the last thirty years, enjoying all his money. And his consorts!" I spat. "What would interest him here? What would *he* get out of putting me out of action? He's already got his own little kingdom: he'd hardly want another one. Especially not this one. Elginagen has nothing he'd want."

"Stop pacing, child. You're making me dizzy." Esther tapped her pipe out in the hearth and stood it in a pipe-rack on the mantelpiece. "Sometimes it don't pay to get too inquisitive. Specially where that one's concerned. He's got a long arm, Silke, and an even longer memory. You mind you don't get in his way."

"Can you find out where he's based?"

Esther shook her head. "Too dangerous. If I looked for him magically, he'd know it. More than my life's worth, dearie. Even saying his name is unwise. And don't you go meddling!"

I shrugged off that advice. "I have to find out who's trying to kill my client. And me, come to that." I rubbed my face, thinking hard. I realised I needed inside information. Veelya was going to have to get me inside the palace. In the meantime, I needed to find out something about this guy Stone. Oh, and the guy at the restaurant. I made a point of looking at the clock on the mantelpiece. "Gotta dash,

Esther," I said, as I made to leave the room in a hurry. "Thanks for the wine and cake!"

"Don't mention it, I'm sure," I heard Esther mutter as I let myself out of the shop door. "Drop by when you just want to see if I'm still here, why don't you?"

If her sarcastic words aroused any feelings of guilt or remorse on my part, I couldn't let them get to me. Her news had galvanised me into action and I ran home as fast as the milling people and traffic would let me.

A couple of blocks from my apartment I slowed down to a walk. That old familiar prickling sensation in my ears was starting up again. This was getting very tedious: clearly I was somebody's flavour of the week. I took the next street more cautiously, scanning parked vehicles and shadowed doorways for any sign of lowlife. I reached the outside door to the apartments and opened it carefully. So far, so good.

Silently, I climbed the stairs, drawing my knife.

On the gallery, I felt my blood chill and automatically dropped to a defensive stance. Someone was sitting on the floor outside my apartment. In the dim light of the corridor, I could just make out the slumped shape: pale hands lightly clasped on bent knees; a pale face turned in my direction.

"Who are you, and what do you want?" I demanded.

"Is this any way to greet an old friend, Silke?" The voice was smooth, sexy and unpleasantly familiar. For a second I had the strange sensation I was travelling back in time. A young man got to his feet, smiling broadly and holding out his hands to show he was unarmed, except for an envelope. He was darkly handsome, in the way of his mixed Romish and Ellenoi ancestry, but with black hair rather than green. He was dressed casually in crumpled clothes that looked as if they were second-hand, but in fact probably cost a mint. Tall and oozing charm, he didn't fool me for a moment.

"What are you doing here, Dervan?" I relaxed my stance a little, but didn't put my knife away.

Dervan raised a brow at the unsheathed knife. "Are you going to gut me with that thing, or say hello nicely?"

"Why would I want to do either?"

"Well, at least let me give you this." He held out the envelope, smiling. "A courier just brought it and I signed for it for you. Wasn't that helpful of me?"

I scowled and snatched the envelope from him.

"It's been a while, Silke. I wanted to come and see you again . . . and catch up with news. We had something once. Remember?"

I rolled my eyes at him, but put my knife away and tucked the envelope inside my jacket. "Don't kid yourself. That was then. I'm no longer the vulnerable street kid you took advantage of."

"Oh, please. You were never *that* vulnerable, Silke. We had some good times." He made an offensively slow appraisal of my figure. "You're looking good, Silke. Filled out nicely."

I sighed. "Just why are you here, Dervan?"

Dervan lowered his hands. "Aren't you going to invite me in? We can't talk here in a public corridor now, can we?"

I had to think quickly. I didn't want to invite Dervan into my home, since I really didn't trust him.

"There's a diner near here," I said. "We can go there and you can buy me a late lunch. You look as if you can afford it." After two lots of sweet cakes, I wasn't sure I could manage much, but I couldn't let the opportunity of a free meal pass me by.

Dervan sighed with exasperation. "Fair enough. After you."

"Oh, no. You first. I watch my back these days."

I heard him give a light, derisory chuckle.

Jake's Place still had a few late diners – shift workers, mostly, on their way home from the dockyards. Nobody looked up as Dervan and I made our way to a table near the window, but Jake sauntered over and gave the table a cursory wipe with a damp towel.

"What'll it be? The krillcakes and hagfish are off, but I could do you a nice fish stew, omelette or a sandwich platter."

Dervan opted for just a glass of wine, and I ordered a platter.

"Coming up." Jake went back to the bar to get the order.

"So, why are you here?" I asked again.

Dervan rested his chin on his hand, his elbow on the table, and looked at me through sleepy eyes. "I told you. I wanted to look you up again. I've missed you, Silke." He reached across the table and put his hand over mine, stroking it with his fingers. My ears zinged.

I took my hand away before the magic he was subtly putting out could take effect. "Nice try, Dervan. But it's bad manners to try magic on a fellow fey, and it's guaranteed to make me suspicious. So, what are you up to now? Something illegal I daresay."

Jake arrived with our order. He put everything down on the table in front of us and Dervan tossed him some coins, which Jake swept up in a large hand.

"Enjoy your meal," said Jake automatically, and left us to it.

"Why don't you tell me what *you're* doing these days?" said Dervan, sipping his wine.

I took a bite of sandwich and shrugged. "Not much to tell. Surviving."

"I heard you were a private investigator." He said it with lifted eyebrows and a patronising drawl.

"I find a few lost pets and stuff," I said, dismissively. "It pays the bills."

Dervan was giving nothing away himself, and I resented it.

He watched me, a half-smile still on his face. "Finding lost puppy dogs doesn't exactly challenge someone of your . . . *talents*, Silke."

I met his stare. "And what talents might those be?" I took another bite and casually wiped some crumbs from the side of my mouth with a finger. *Darn*. He was stirring some of the old feelings inside me.

I heard him laugh softly. "Oh, I can remember you . . . raising a fire or two."

"I don't do that stuff now," I said, not taking my eyes off him. He and I had run a few scams together in our time. I'd magically raise a fire somewhere, leaving him free to break into the building to "rescue" valuables while the owners were preoccupied with firefighting. I took most of the risk, since fire-magic always left a "signature" behind which could lead the Enforcers to the perpetrator. I was always very careful, however, to change my spell formula regularly, and since I wasn't a registered fire-mage, they never managed to catch me.

"That's a pity, Silke. Because I'm looking for someone to work a little magic for me."

I sighed and tossed my sandwich down on to the plate. "All this double-speak, Dervan. It's so tiresome. Just say what you came for and then go back to whatever hole you came from. If you just want a date, the answer's no. If you're after confidential client information, it's still no. If you want me to do a job for you – it's definitely no."

"You don't leave a guy many options. Whatever happened to romance?"

I snorted and saw a flicker of annoyance in the dark eyes watching me. Then Dervan recovered himself, ran a hand through his long, thick black curls, and gave a false laugh. "Looks like I've lost my touch since I've been away. Who's taken my place, Silke?"

"Just as arrogant and self-opinionated as ever," I observed. "It's none of your business." I stood up, scraping my chair back noisily. "Thanks for the lunch, Dervan. Can't say it's been a pleasure seeing you again." I swept out of the diner, seething with rage, not bothering to see if he was following me.

Back at my apartment, I let myself in and locked the door behind me, resting for a moment with my back against the door, my eyes closed. Dervan had deeply unsettled me. He had been my mentor in more ways than one in my street days, and he still managed to wind me up emotionally. With the vulnerability of youth, I'd found him beautiful and exciting. That was before I understood what an evil *schlunk* he could be. I didn't relish the thought that I might not have seen the last of him, or that he could still stir me up. I realised with some chagrin that I should have kept

55

him talking longer: he was up to something devious and I should have sussed it out instead of storming off in a snit. Well, it couldn't be helped. No way was I going back out to apologise to that creep.

I checked the crystal for messages, but there were none. The envelope crackled inside my pocket and I fished it out: as I thought, it was the invitation to the Sunfire Rooms, courtesy of my client. I tossed it on to my bed and began stripping off clothes while heading for the shower.

For now, it was time to get myself ready, put on a journalist persona and check out the mysterious Mr Stone.

FIVE

The entrance to the Sunfire Rooms was an elegant statement in glass and marble. I looked around, getting my
bearings, and saw eight different images of myself reflected
in the long mirrors round the walls. It was extremely
disconcerting, so I moved quickly into the main reception
room: another dazzling display of a huge central chandelier,
a painted ceiling and rich carpeting woven with an abstract
pattern of flaming suns. The whole room was a warm,
sunset tapestry of creams, reds and dusky pink.

Open double doors at the far end gave a promise of even
more opulence in the dining room, where large, round
tables seating ten guests each were arranged in front of a
podium where presumably the guest of honour would be
making a speech later in the evening. Silver cutlery and
fancy table candelabra sparkled and glimmered.

Trying to search a roomful of noisy individuals while
looking comfortably at home was not easy. These were

definitely not my kind of people, and I'd have been far more comfortable at a dockland bar brawl, but I reckon I managed to look the part enough to blend in. I wandered among the hundreds of guests exchanging polite small talk, drinking and nibbling on canapés, and picked up a fruit juice for myself from a tray as it went past on the arm of a waiter. Finding my mystery man in this lot was going to prove impossible. It was too glamorous a do for guests to wear anything as vulgar as name-badges.

I was just steeling myself to ask someone to point me in the direction of Marcus Stone, when the room abruptly fell silent. Heads turned to the door and I recognised Prince Vyktor arriving with his entourage. Dressed splendidly and wearing his royal (honorary) decorations, Vyktor looked much older than his fifteen years, but I couldn't help noticing, with a smile, that his personal bodyguards had been carefully chosen to be the same height as the prince, or a little shorter, so that they didn't dwarf him. Vyktor still had some growing to do. Certainly, I was able to recognise the family resemblance between him and Veelya. They both had the same aristocratic features, thin blonde hair, and pale skin.

While all eyes were on the prince, I slipped through a doorway into a side room. It had occurred to me that since Marcus Stone had agreed to be interviewed, he would have probably made himself available, away from the crowd. I was right. I wasn't prepared for what I saw, however.

The room had a large bay window area. Seated in a wheelchair, gazing out of the large glass doors into the garden, was an elderly man wearing an evening suit. There was a copy of *Death Merchant* by Marcus Stone lying on the table next to him.

"Mr Stone?" I asked.

The man turned his head to look at me, then propelled his wheelchair so that it faced me. Whatever else Marcus Stone was, I could see at a glance that he was not a well man. In addition to his inability to walk, his face looked cadaverous in a way that only comes from long illness and sustained pain. Or drugs.

"Ah. Ms Flambard?" he asked. His low, husky voice sounded weary and sardonic.

"It's . . . ah . . . good of you to see me, Mr Stone," I began. I sat at the table and took out my notebook. Then suddenly wondered how I was going to carry this whole thing off and get any useful information. If, indeed, there was any to get. "Perhaps we could start with you telling me just how you got the idea for *Death Merchant*." I waited, pen poised.

He stared at me with unfriendly eyes. "Perhaps you could start, Ms Flambard, with telling me how you got my personal crystal code."

"I beg your pardon?"

"Marta says she doesn't know you," he said.

"At the agency?" I replied, brightly. "No, she wouldn't. I'm new on the scene and we haven't met yet."

"Isn't it usual for journalists to get permission for an interview from the agent, *before* intruding on the personal privacy of the interviewee?" he asked. I was liking his tone less and less. This was not going to go well, I could see that much. But since this guy was sick and in a wheelchair, I couldn't see how he could be involved in harassing Princess Veelya. There was nothing supernatural about him, either, that I could detect.

Maybe Stone was just an ordinary guy who got his shirts cleaned at the KleenKwick Laundry, and happened to write a best-selling novel. I judged it would be expedient to make a quick retreat.

I stood up. "You're right, Mr Stone. I apologise. I'll get in touch with your agent and we'll conduct this interview at a better time to suit you."

"Not so fast, young lady!" he spat at me and grabbed my wrist with an almost skeletal hand. "You haven't told me how you got my crystal code. It's not in any database."

"Please let go of my hand, Mr Stone. I wouldn't want to have to break your arm." I spoke with what I thought was icy calm.

"Dad?"

I turned sharply to see a young man standing about a metre away, staring at us. He looked familiar.

"What's going on?"

Then I realised. It was the man from table five at the Ambassador Club!

It was my turn to stare. "You!" I said. "What are you doing here?"

He glared at me suspiciously. "What business do you have with my father?" he demanded. "You're making him upset."

"He shouldn't lay a hand on me, then," I snapped. "It brings out the worst in me."

"I don't trust her, Lucius!" said Marcus, peevishly. "She won't tell me how she found out where I lived."

"She's a private detective, Dad."

"What?"

I stared at the son and my head whirled. How did he know that? As far as he knew, I was just a waitress at the Ambassador Club.

He laughed at the expression on my face, then turned to his father. "It's OK, Dad. I'll deal with this. You go on into the dining room with the others and I'll join you in a minute. Save me a seat."

I narrowed my eyes at the son while the old man propelled himself out of the room. "Maybe *you're* the Stone I'm looking for!" I said. "What were you doing at the Ambassador Club the other night?" I demanded.

"Having a drink," he said. "Why were *you* pretending to be a waitress?"

"If you know that much," I snarled, "you must know the answer as well."

"Oh, yeah," he said, as if the thought had only just occurred to him. "*Protecting* your client."

I didn't care much for his derisory tone. OK, so the restaurant had been fireballed. But at least we'd got Veelya out unharmed.

We were slowly circling each other without realising it. Sizing each other up. I noticed he was wearing a snappier outfit than the one he'd worn to the restaurant: a military tunic and trousers in soft grey leather. It fitted his tall, lean frame well and the high collar of the tunic showed off his haircut. His hair still looked invitingly dishevelled. And the glasses still gave him an air of intelligence without being nerdish.

I found I had brought up my hands defensively. This guy really made my ears zing.

I saw him glance swiftly at the carafe of water on a table nearby. Was he planning to throw it at me?

"The Ambassador is an expensive place to choose for a drink of water," I said, flexing my fingers. "Funny how the place went up in smoke just after you left."

"Funny how a fire-mage was on the spot when it happened," he retaliated, watching me intently with those sexy eyes. *Get a grip.*

"Funny how *your* crystal number was in the hands of

someone who probably wants the princess dead!" I replied. "Were you sent to do a quick recce? Make sure of the target?"

For a moment he looked completely baffled. He stood still for a moment, and shut his eyes. I couldn't believe it. I made a quick jab towards him, but his left arm shot out blocking my right.

"Hey!" I said. "You did that without looking!" Light dawned. *Duh. How dim can you get?* "You're a telepath!"

His eyes shot open, glinting with what looked like surprise and amusement. "You really did think I was involved in that restaurant hit!"

That did it for me. I was furious. Not only was this creep a telepath, but he'd snuck into my head to find out what I'd been thinking. "Keep out of my head!" I snarled.

He opened his mouth to reply, but at that moment, we were both suddenly distracted by an enormous magical pressure gathering in the direction of the reception hall. Both of us gasped and I covered my painful ears. As the young Stone made a grab for the carafe of water, I was already running towards the door.

The pressure of the energy build-up was causing other people to cover their ears. Some were already collapsed on the floor, bleeding from their noses and ears. Others were screaming in fear and pain. The stench of magic was making the air unbreathable.

"The chandelier!" I yelled. "*Clear out!*"

Stone looked up, along with several other people, as I pointed. The central chandelier was shaking, expanding, its many crystal lamps enlarging and bursting into wild, blue-green flames that licked at the ceiling and curled round the thick chain holding up the great weight. As we all watched, mesmerised, it became a massive inferno. Burning glass dropped like molten wax on to the floor beneath. The whole thing looked ready to explode. I wondered if I'd be able to contain that much firepower myself. I'd give it my best shot, but judged I just wasn't really up to it. Even so, I prepared to gather my magepower.

I was forestalled by Stone, who pushed me roughly to one side and tossed the contents of the carafe at the huge mass. I almost laughed at the absurdity of it. But then, as I watched, he spread his arms wide and shut his eyes, focusing his own power. I could feel my hair springing like wire, and clapped my hands over my ears. They felt as though they might drop off at any moment.

Stone's face began to drip with sweat as he concentrated. Suddenly, I heard something more terrible than the cracking glass and distorting metal of the chandelier: it was the roar of the raging torrent and the thunder of the waterfall. Without realising it, I was hugging myself tightly and gasping like a landed fish. This was definitely not my element, and I had an overwhelming urge to run for my life.

Fire, I could manage. Water was death.

There were more screams from the terrified patrons still trying to escape from the room, as water burst over the flaming chandelier in a great hissing and steaming torrent. Fortunately no one was standing near enough to get scalded, but it didn't do the glitzy carpet much good. Don't ask me where it all came from: this was no domestic burst pipe! It doused the flames and sent acrid, choking smoke curling into all the corners of the ceiling. Then I felt Stone calling on something else: something cold and icy calm that sent goosebumps up my arms.

Miraculously, snow fell. Icicles formed. There were gasps of surprise and delight from the crowd pressed against the walls of the hall. *Awesome*.

"Everybody stand clear!" Stone yelled. "The chain's breaking!"

With a great, shocking *crack!* the chain of the chandelier snapped. What was left of the molten mass came crashing down to the floor, where it smashed into a million pieces of crushed ice.

We all looked at it in stunned silence.

The immediate danger over, I took off before the crowd could come to their senses and get in my way. The smell of the magic was still strong and it wasn't difficult to track. With any luck it would lead me to the mage responsible for it, though I wasn't too hopeful. I couldn't imagine he would stick around. I was thinking "he" because I already had a shrewd idea as to who was involved here. There was a style and signature to this magic that I knew all too well.

Beyond the dining room, double doors opened out on to a large patio and a flight of steps led down into the formal gardens, laid out with shrubberies, ornamental trees and a central pool with a fountain. Swinging lanterns provided occasional lighting, but my night vision was good enough without them. I hurtled down the steps and raced along the paths after my quarry. I almost tumbled headlong into the river in my rush.

I leant forward with my hands on my knees, dragging air into my lungs, shutting my eyes to concentrate. But I knew he had escaped. There was a bench nearby; I slumped on to it and held my head in my hands while my heart rate and breathing calmed down.

"Are you OK?"

I looked up, wearily, to see the young Stone standing in front of me.

"He got away," I said, dully. "At a guess, I'd say he took off in a boat. I can't follow a spell over water."

Stone stepped to the edge of the river and stared down it in both directions. "They went that way." He pointed downriver. "Not that that helps us much. Do you know who it was?"

"Yes. Well, I'm pretty sure I do."

He took off his glasses and wiped them on a handkerchief, waiting for me to say more. But I wasn't playing. This was *my* concern, not his.

"Who's Sattine?" he asked, putting his glasses back on again.

There is something deeply offensive and shocking about having your most private thoughts read, particularly by a stranger you've never met before. I felt a sudden rage that threatened to spill out of me and set something alight. "Never mind!" I hissed at him. "Just keep out of my head! I shan't tell you again, Stone."

"I don't go *into* your head," he said. "You were broadcasting it. You obviously have strong feelings about him."

"Well – stop listening, then!" I snapped, then felt myself redden as I realised that was rather a stupid thing to say. Good job it was dark and he couldn't see me well enough to notice. "You don't need to know. I'll deal with it."

"I might be able to help."

"Thanks, but as I said, I'll deal with it."

He was standing in the light of one of the lanterns. Only then did I notice the sooty sweat stains on his face, shirt and in his hair and remember how I'd left him. "Was the fire put out?"

"Yes."

I got to my feet. "I'd better check it out."

"No need. I *dealt* with it." He put a sarcastic emphasis on his words.

I narrowed my eyes at him. "What *are* you, Stone? And *who* are you? I only know you're Marcus Stone's son. Do you write novels, too? Or are conjuring tricks more your speciality?" I made "tricks" sound like a cheap circus thrill, which was rather ungracious of me. Jealousy, I guess.

Stone shrugged and sat down next to me on the bench. He took a small card from a pocket inside his jacket and handed it to me. It only gave his name – Lucius Stone – and contact details. Nothing about his occupation.

"That's me," he said. "I'm just an empath with some telepathic ability that I inherited from my mother. I have . . . an affinity with water. Ice, actually. So I guess there are mage genes in the pool somewhere. Probably a distant female relative on my mother's side." I could see he was uncomfortable about himself. But I was intrigued. The irony of it suddenly hit me and I laughed.

"That's rich!" I said. "Ice and Fire. Complete opposites." I was impressed with his professionalism. "I forgot to bring mine with me," I lied. I'd just never got round to having any made. Anyway, I'm not sure I hold with leaving stuff about myself all over the place. You never know who's going to use it.

Lucius was quiet for a moment. Then he smiled. He had a very nice smile, I noticed. "Ice and Fire. Yes, I see what you mean." He thought about it some more. "Maybe . . . it was meant. We might complement each other. Maybe we should work together on this case. Especially since both our clients are . . . closely connected."

"Are you in my head again?" I snapped.

He shook his head. "I already know you're working for Princess Veelya. I've been hired by her brother."

I laughed. "Well, yes, they are certainly closely connected. But no deal. I work alone." It seemed ridiculous to refuse to work with him, but I had my personal pride at stake here. Besides, I didn't want this well-intentioned nerd showing me up in any way.

"So do I," he said. "Usually. But I sense this time I'm up against someone a bit out of my league. I have some talent, but I'm not a mage. I have to leave spells to others."

I thought about it. I had to admit that there was much about this case that was out of my league as well. Especially if Sattine was involved.

"If it helps any," Lucius went on casually, "I don't believe the princess is trying to kill Vyktor."

I stared at him. "Vyktor thinks *Veelya* is trying to kill him?" I asked, astonished. Lucius nodded. I shook my head and laughed softly. "Has he been receiving threatening notes, too?" I asked.

"Too? You mean, Veelya's had them?"

I nodded. "And bad-taste practical jokes. I may as well

tell you Veelya hired me to find out who was responsible. Vyktor is her number one suspect. She thinks he's after the throne for himself. You were my only lead, Mr Stone. Or at least, your crystal code." I flashed him a smile of my own. "Veelya thought you were a hired assassin."

Lucius laughed. "And you got hold of the wrong Stone. Bet you were a bit fazed to find my father in a wheelchair."

"You can say that again."

"You were *my* chief suspect. Your cloak caught on the door of the Ambassador Club, and I used the threads to track you to your apartment. That's where I discovered you were a fire-mage." My mouth must have fallen open. "You have a wardspell on your door," he explained gently, then waited while I digested this. I couldn't believe that he'd followed me without my knowing it, and it stung. "Are you just known as Silke, or do you have another name?" he asked.

I could see a smug gleam in his eye as he played his trump card. OK, so he was a better detective than I was. It was an irritating thought, but I had to live with it. Like I had to live with his magic talents as well. This was not a good day.

"Smart guy, huh?" I said. "Yeah, I'm just known as Silke. What else did you find out?"

"Oh, not a lot. But I know you had a meeting with the princess this morning at the Salon, and that someone tried to fry you in the marketplace. That, I'll admit, did give me a fright. I was about to direct the fountain on to you, but you managed the fire yourself. Very impressive, by the way. And after that, you went to visit the herbal shop in Lepp Street. I guess you were after information, since the area's notorious for its underground connections."

I must have looked shocked. I certainly felt it. How did this guy know so much? And if *he* knew my entire movements, who else did? I found myself speechless for once. Had I really been so careless?

"Don't feel too bad," he said. "It's relatively easy for me to follow people. I can stay quite a way behind you and just follow your aura. You'd never have seen me two streets away."

It was a neat ability. And one I could have done with myself. I worked hard at not registering my dismay and frustration. I remembered that I *had* felt something behind me, so I'd just have to trust my instincts better in future.

"If you don't want to work with me, could we at least swap some notes?" Lucius asked. "In the interests of our clients, I mean." That smile again. I felt myself weakening. "We both know they aren't trying to kill each other, despite what they might think. And we also know that a very powerful fire-mage is involved." He raised an eyebrow at me. It stood to reason that since I was a fire-mage myself, albeit an amateur, I would probably know about the involvement of one more practised. Clearly he'd ruled me out of the list of suspects.

"Yeah, I suppose," I said, grudgingly. I didn't add that I thought the mage was using help inside the palace.

"I think, myself, that he's getting help from inside the palace," Stone said. I shot him a look, but he didn't meet my gaze. Had he snatched that idea from my head? "Anyway, maybe you *can* help me with this . . ." He dug something out of his pocket and gave it to me. It was a small wooden box. "Vyktor found this in his dressing room this morning. It gave him a scare, but otherwise doesn't seem to have caused any damage."

I took it carefully, turning it round in my hands.

"Nice box," I said.

Lucius said nothing.

It was small and light, made of dark polished wood inlaid with silver and other metals. The lid showed a beautifully executed dragon, breathing tendrils of fine copper fire from its nostrils, and weaving sinuously in and out of a name engraved in gothic capitals. VYKTOR. Expensive. I sniffed at it. *Hmmm.* As well as a sooty smell, there was the residue of magic. I took no chances, but cast a warding spell over the box to protect myself from any nasty surprises. Then I opened it.

"Ugh!" I had to turn my head away and gagged at the stench. "The spell's decayed, I'm afraid."

"What can you tell me about it?"

Inside the box was a carved wooden figure, rather like a

chess piece, wearing a stylised crown. It was scorched and blackened, as if it had been in a fire. I flipped out my knife and moved the figure with the point. Underneath was a card printed in gold. It just said *Sunfire Rooms – tonight.*

"Not much, now," I said. "It's a curse box. The box itself isn't too important – just a bit of conceit on the part of the sender. The dragon is the symbol of a fire-mage, as you probably know." Stone nodded. "Some like to portray themselves as a firebird, or a flame lizard. They're all creatures aligned to fire. The name on the top just tells us that this message was very personal, but then they usually are."

"There was a compulsion spell on it," said Lucius.

I nodded. Poor old Vyktor would have been irresistibly drawn to the box and unable to stop himself opening it. "That's common," I said. "Although, with a box as fancy as this, I wouldn't have thought it was necessary. People usually can't resist opening pretty boxes with their name on them. Did Vyktor get burned?"

"No," said Lucius, grimly. "I did. Vyktor brought the box to me. I got no telepathic vibes from it at all, which was unusual. Not even the manufacturer. Usually I can get a picture of whoever has handled an artifact, especially if strong emotions are involved. I iced up the box before I opened it, but when I picked up the figurine it still burned my fingers."

I raised an eyebrow at his naiveté.

He shrugged his shoulders. "It was my first experience of one of these things. I had thought the ice would have insulated me from any spell. I shall know better next time."

"A curse box is a strong magic," I told him. "There's not much you can do to neutralise them. The dolly, as it's called, is the message: if it burns, then you can expect a fire of some kind. If it blisters, or causes nausea, you can expect poison. If there was a thread tied round its neck, you can look forward to strangulation. And so on. As you can imagine, there are endless possibilities. I once saw one wedged inside the mouths of a three-headed slarsk."

Lucius shivered. "What happened?"

"You don't want to know."

"Are they ever booby-trapped? You know, rigged to explode when they're opened, or something?"

"What would be the point? You'd destroy the message, and might even destroy someone you wanted to keep alive."

"So, how can someone like me find out what the sender of one of these things has in mind, if it's not immediately obvious? Presumably if you don't pick up the dolly you never know what's threatened."

I handed back the box. "No. You need a mage. Someone like *me* who can see the spell and tell you what it is. This one, of course, was a firespell." What I kept to myself was the knowledge of where this box originated. This kind of finesse was exactly Sattine's style. It was his fancy dragon design, too. Of course, someone could have copied it to incriminate him, but I doubted it. It was so like Sattine to want to advertise his genius.

"Yeah. I realised *that* when I burned my fingers!" Lucius admitted.

"With a bit of concentration, you could probably work out other spells. It just takes a bit of practice. And logic."

"Fine. Thanks. So this, then, was to warn Vyktor about what was going to happen tonight?"

"Looks like it. Arrogant piece of work."

"Hmm. And from someone who can afford such arrogance," Stone mused. He looked straight at me. "Not your average, jobbing fire-mage?"

I may have had the grace to blush and look away.

Lucius put the box back in his pocket. "I doubt Vyktor would have stayed away, in any case. You know how stubborn these royals are."

I rolled my eyes. *Tell me about it.*

"I'd better go and make sure Dad's all right," he said, pushing his glasses up his nose and standing up. "I daresay they've cancelled the dinner now."

"Suits me. I wasn't going to stay, anyway." Besides, I had no wish to get involved with the inevitable Enforcer questions.

We began walking back to the party.

"Could we meet up somewhere tomorrow?" Lucius asked me before stepping through the double glass doors. "Have a chat over kashla, perhaps?"

"I suppose," I said, thinking quickly of my plans for the next day. "I'm down at the harbour tomorrow. Veelya's launching some boat, I think. You could join me there just after ten if you like, and we'll talk then."

Lucius smiled. "It's a yacht. And I was going to attend anyway. You've got my contact details if you change your mind. Oh, that reminds me." He rummaged in his pocket and brought out a writer and another of his cards. "Could you give me your code?"

I gave him my crystal number and he scribbled it on the back of his card.

"OK. I'll see you tomorrow morning, then, at the harbour. Any problems, give me a call."

"Oh, you do use conventional methods of communicating, then?" I asked, dryly.

"It's less effort," he grinned. He nodded, by way of saying goodbye, and disappeared into the crowd to search for his father.

I turned in the opposite direction, left the building and snagged a cab to take me back home.

SIX

There was already quite a crowd gathering along the approach roads to Ysgard Harbour when I arrived early next morning. They were waiting for the princess's small cavalcade to drive past. Little groups of schoolchildren were lining up here and there, with their flags and baskets of flower petals. Streamers and bunting decorated the streets, draped from the windows of buildings or across lampposts and trees. One or two householders leaned out of their upper windows, watching the street and shouting across at each other. It all seemed rather over the top for just launching a boat, but then again the people of Ysgard love any excuse to have a holiday.

I was surprised to catch sight of Lucius Stone down by the waterfront. I hadn't expected him to be here so early. He was dressed, as I was, completely in black – looking very sexy, actually, with shades over his eyes – and sat perched on a large mooring stanchion looking out at the great white boat (sorry, *yacht*) lying in the middle of the river.

I first had to check the security arrangements with the palace guards milling round the temporary podium set up for the launch. I picked out a senior officer I recognised, introduced myself, and pointed out a couple of strategic areas that I felt they should cover. Once we had agreed protocols, I left them to it and went back to find Stone. He was still sitting with his back to me, gazing out at the river. Without turning his head he said, "Good morning, Silke."

I felt a shiver of annoyance and must have been scowling nicely as he turned round.

He gave a soft laugh. "I sensed you coming. I'm sorry. I don't mean to wind you up."

"Huh." I nodded down the promenade. "Let's go to that café."

Wisely keeping quiet, he left his stanchion and followed me across the street. The enterprising café proprietor had draped all his pavement tables with cloths of gold and red – the royal colours – and decorated each centrepiece with little flags and red and yellow flowers. Very patriotic.

We sat at a red table with a good view of the harbour area, and when the waiter appeared, ordered the breakfast specials. Nothing like good, hot food and drink to set a person up for the day.

So far there were just security people, harbour officials and a huddle of media types wandering around, waiting for action.

"Seems pretty quiet so far," said Lucius. "Do you think we should be anticipating another firespell?"

"I'd be surprised," I said. "He's used them twice now, so if he tries anything at all, I would imagine it'd be something different. Sorcerers like to show off their expertise, in my experience, so it's likely to be something flamboyant. You just need to keep your eyes and nose alert for anything strange. Bad smells, for instance."

"Bad smells. Fine," said Lucius, looking doubtful. I could see why: the harbour already smelled pretty strong with oil fumes, rank fish, human debris and the river itself, which looked none too clean from here. "Then what?"

I pulled a face. "Duck, I guess. If it's going to happen, it will happen pretty quickly."

The waiter arrived with our order. It looked and smelled delicious and put all other thoughts out of our heads as we tucked in with gusto. After a while, Lucius said, "You neutralised that spell aimed at you the other day without any problems that I could see."

"That was different. I saw the mage preparing to send it in my direction and could focus a counter spell." I purposely didn't elaborate further: no harm in letting him think I was more powerful than I am.

I stirred two heaped spoons of sweetener into my kashla and saw Lucius wince as he watched.

"Something wrong?" I asked.

Lucius just shook his head and smiled. He knew better than to antagonise me again.

"I'm Ellanoi," I told him. "We need plenty of sugar. Our metabolism is different from you humans."

"Uh-huh." He gave me a look that showed he thought it was as good an excuse as any.

"So, we're here to swap information, aren't we? Are you going to start?"

He swallowed a mouthful of food. "I haven't got much in the way of tangible evidence, but I brought these." He fished in his pocket and brought out two notes printed on white paper. One read HERE LIES VYKTOR, R.I.P., the other TAKE A GOOD LOOK – IT MAY BE YOUR LAST. "Vyktor received these before he hired me. The first was found on his pillow when he woke up one morning. The other was stuck to the mirror in his private dressing room."

"Why did he hire *you*?" I asked as I picked up the notes. "You don't *look* like a hard-boiled private eye."

"He'd been given my name by a friend, who happened to be a client of mine at one time. I'd helped this guy pinpoint someone in his company who was embezzling funds. I'm not exactly a private eye: I . . . find things for people, for want of a better description."

"A psychic investigator," I supplied.

"Whatever." He nodded. "Vyktor thought it was Veelya trying to kill him and wanted me to check her out. I went to the Ambassador Club to try and see if I could get any strong vibes from her."

"And did you?"

"No. She was too focused on you and her companion. Anyway, that wasn't really a good place to try it. I needed to get nearer, and that security grille they have there blocked most of their thoughts."

I could understand that.

"Did you get any 'readings' from the notes themselves?" I asked.

"No. All I got was Vyktor's agitation." He seemed to want to explain further. "As an empath I'm particularly tuned into emotion. Vyktor's fear sort of wiped out anything else."

As it was "show and tell" time, I opened my belt pack and brought out my collection of notes sent to Veelya, spreading them flat on the table.

"These are Veelya's notes," I told him. They seemed to have come from the same source as Vyktor's: paper and print style appeared identical.

Lucius picked them up one at a time, looking them over carefully.

"Feel anything with these?" I asked.

He shook his head. "You've had them for too long. I can only sense you."

"They look the same, don't they? You'd think they'd have chosen different paper or something."

"Whoever's responsible for them doesn't have much imagination. They look so . . . amateurish. But maybe that's what they wanted – to make the notes look like the kind of thing two teenagers would have sent each other."

"I agree," I said. I picked up one of the notes. "This last one arrived that evening at the club. I sensed the spell coming and just managed to get them out of the way in time. Afterwards, I looked up an . . . acquaintance of mine, who used to take on that kind of job, to ask him if he knew anything about it. Unfortunately someone got to him first."

"The guy in the Goat's Beard? Sarvik?"

I stared at him. "Have you spent *all* your time following me around, Stone? I can't say it makes me feel very comfortable knowing you've been watching me."

He shrugged dismissively. "You were easier to track than the princess. At least *I* don't want you dead. If you'd been following me, I'm afraid you wouldn't have learnt very much. Vyktor's magic box and his two notes are the only solid clues I've had to go on. So far no one's tried to set fire to me or kill off anyone I know. Apart from last night, that is." He took a sip of his drink. "My take on this is that someone inside the palace is deliberately setting the two royal kids against each other, for their own ends. Or, they could be working for someone on the outside. Either way, it seems to be political rather than any personal vendetta. Otherwise, why wait till now? Who stands to gain if the royal couple is taken out? Some obscure royal relative, the next in line to the throne? Bit too obvious. Besides, it would have been easier to kill them both as infants. Or . . . maybe someone ambitious, high up in the pecking order, wants to do away with the monarchy altogether."

"Well, that gives us scope," I said. "Except that the last note was delivered at the restaurant. It changes the pattern."

We were silent for a while, thinking things over. Then Lucius said, "You know, all this doesn't put *you* in a very good light, does it?"

"You mean the firespells?"

"Well, those, and also the last note. You being a fire-mage, and working with the princess, you must be a likely candidate for planting the note and directing the spell at the restaurant."

"Oh, yes?" I shot him a hostile glance, daring him to suggest I might be working some kind of scam. "And what's *my* motive?"

Lucius met my glance and shrugged. "Money?"

I think I might have opened and shut my mouth a few times, but couldn't think of anything to say. He was right. It did look bad. Fortunately, he had another hypothesis.

"It's also a possibility that someone might be trying to *frame* you. Or at least trying to get rid of you. Do you have any enemies, Silke?"

Does a flower attract bees? I stared round the harbour, hardly seeing the gathering Enforcers and security people, the press vans and media crews setting up their equipment, and the gleaming new yacht waiting for its royal baptism. I reflected briefly on the many enemies I'd made during my street years. Back then, it had been a case of survive or die, and there wasn't a lot of loyalty to spare for anyone except yourself. There must be lowlife aplenty who would like to have a part in my downfall, but I couldn't think of any that would have the gumption to try it. Then a name popped into my head.

Sattine.

Stone took off the shades. It was quite a shock to see that his eyes were actually an icy, penetrating blue. They bored into mine. An eyebrow lifted.

I stared back defiantly, wiping the name from my mind. "Well, my priority for now has to be for my client," I said quickly. "I have to get inside the palace – see if I can find any evidence of inside collusion."

"How are you going to do that? There has to be a thousand people working there. Where are you going to start? They're not going to jump up and say, 'I'm plotting against the monarchy!'"

I shrugged, ignoring his sarcasm. "You can learn a great deal just by listening to servants. I could get a job in the kitchens or someplace where I could pick up the gossip."

"Disguise yourself as a waitress, you mean?" said Lucius with a smirk.

"Don't knock it!" I shot back. "It works!"

"Maybe, but if I come with you, I could eavesdrop for you."

"I told you. I work alone!"

"And I told you, we could work together on this and help each other out."

"You mean, you could get all my information for free!" I countered, irritably. I picked up my cup and drained it, dropping it back into the saucer with a loud clatter that turned a few heads nearby. "Why don't you talk Vyktor into forming a truce with his sister while we find out who's trying to kill them? Save us having to work against each other at least. And ask about any new employees at the palace who've been behaving furtively."

Lucius sighed. "No need to patronise me, Silke. OK, I can do that. But we've already agreed our clients are in the same danger, and it seems to be increasing with the king getting weaker by the day. All I'm saying is that by working together, we can help them more effectively."

I knew he was right, but my ingrained stubborn streak just wasn't going to give way on this. I didn't know this guy at all – only that he could do weird things with frozen water. I had no idea how he'd be in a sticky situation, or whether he was able to look after himself if things got dangerous. Could I trust him at my back?

In the event, the question became academic.

I tossed my share of the bill on to the table and stood up.

"I have to go and meet Veelya," I said. "Just don't get in my way, Stone."

I stalked off, without looking back. I couldn't say why I was so waspish with him, and it made me feel edgy. After all, he had behaved OK: not pushy or arrogant. A little dark thought crept into my brain that perhaps I was behaving childishly. *What, me?* Could it be the young man pushed a few of my buttons that I wasn't prepared to have activated? I gave a little sigh. It had been a while since I'd dated anyone: my experiences so far hadn't been great, so in general I gave guys a miss. I was focused on making my new business work and had no time for distractions – or that's what I told myself.

As I joined the swelling crowd round the podium, my ears began their familiar tingling and my hand automatically went to the hilt of my knife. I'd picked up another shadow. Well, I'd never spot them in this lot. I'd just have to wait for them to make a move. Even so, I turned in my tracks as if avoiding collision with someone in the crowd, and quickly scanned the people around me. Suddenly I caught sight of Stone pushing his way through the press and trying to catch my attention. I couldn't hear him, but I could see that he was shouting something. The swelling crowd pushed us further and further apart.

Just then, I heard the sound of cheering in the distance. The cavalcade was arriving. But as the cheering grew louder, another sound began to resonate from the direction of the river. It turned my blood cold. Nearby there were cries of dismay turning to horror. I snapped round to see what was happening, and almost gagged as the most appalling stench washed over me. It was the stink of evil magic, overlaid with centuries-old stagnant river silt. Enough to turn the hardiest stomach.

I pushed my way roughly to the waterfront and stared out at the river. It was surging and boiling, tossing the moored boats around like they were toys. The air pressure was changing, too: my ears popped. Then something very large and dark began to surface from the water with squelching, sucking sounds. A huge, scaly head emerged on a long neck, dripping with riverbed ooze and weed, and two enormous, red eyes swung in my direction.

For a moment my heart stopped. *Don't look! Don't look!* My instinct was to run, but the red eyes held me and I felt terrible hunger, anger, hate and elation. Whatever this creature was, it was ancient, malicious, and free after a great many years of incarceration. As I felt the weight of its gaze,

I remembered Lucius. What was it doing to him? A telepath wouldn't want to get inside the mind of this little number – but maybe he wouldn't have a choice.

The river was now steaming and roiling; turning green-brown with the sludge dredged up by the creature as it laboriously drew itself from the mud. People were backing away and screaming in earnest, but morbid fascination prevented them from moving too far.

Security guards lined up on the harbour wall and began firing their weapons at the monster in the water. The huge head turned angrily towards them and the mouth screamed and roared in defiance, causing a fresh swell of screaming from the crowds.

"NO!" I heard someone yell. "STOP! CEASE FIRING!"

The guards took no notice. They were probably too scared to stop, but their ammunition was having no effect on the thick, armoured skin of the creature. Its shoulders were free now, and the crowd gasped as enormous wings lifted slowly and wetly out of the water, trailing slime. Laboriously they worked, dragging the heavy body free, and showering the harbour area with stinking brown river water. I didn't have to be a fire-mage to know what kind of creature it was.

It was a dragon.

I'd never seen one this close before, and I was willing to bet that no one else in the crowd had, either. It was truly awesome. I didn't know much about dragons, but guessed that any minute now it would start throwing flames around, especially if the guards kept annoying it. What *I* did next came entirely from instinct. I turned to the guards and fired my own stunner into the air. It made enough of a noise to catch their attention.

"CEASE . . . FIRING!" I screamed at them. They looked at me with shocked, uncertain eyes, but lowered their weapons a little. "GET BACK!" I waved my arms, indicating that they should move back from the harbour edge. "GET THESE PEOPLE BACK!"

"Look out!" One of the guards pointed behind me. I swung round, to see the dragon rearing up, about to scorch me.

I raised my arms. "*An-athewata!*" I commanded. "*Go back!*" I had no idea where the word had come from, but I knew it was the right one.

The dragon tossed its head and stretched out its wings, screeching dragon curses at me. But it did back off a little.

"*An-athewata!*"

Defiantly the dragon belched an enormous gobbet of fire in my direction.

My mouth was dry, my legs shaky and I couldn't think for terror. All I could do was fling up my arms to protect my face.

The flame engulfed me.

Strangely, it felt cool and magical. This was no ordinary fire. The creature it came from was millions of years old, and there was an ancient, primeval quality to the element that I had never experienced before. For an instant, I dropped my guard and let it caress me. Old fire to new fire. I felt the strength and power of it seeping into my very bones. I shut my eyes, allowing heady strength and magic seduce me. The harbour, the people and all the noise and smells were shut out entirely as I basked in it.

The mage who commanded such fire would be powerful indeed.

"Silke!"

A voice intruded in my thoughts. *Stone.* I shook my head and realised at that moment just how far the dragon's breath had ensorcelled me. This was no dumb lizard. Dragons were tricky, intelligent and amoral, and I had better remember that. They knew just how to make use of weaknesses.

I snapped back into focus, in time to see the dragon turn its head and rear back to disgorge another belch, but this time at the crowd.

"AN-ATHEWATA!" I screamed again.

I felt, rather than saw, Lucius fling up an ice barrier conjured from the river itself to protect the crowd as the dragon discharged its flame. There was a great hiss and clouds of steam rose up as the flame and ice connected. The dragon bellowed in pain and tossed its head to one side as dozens of flashlights went off: foolish, intrepid media photographers catching the pictures of a lifetime. The dragon angrily swept a line of them with its lethal breath and they went down like ninepins, writhing and screaming, trying to beat out the flames on their clothes and hair.

The dragon had backed off a little, churning the water and smashing nearby boats into matchwood, but it still screeched angrily and belched flames in every direction. It occurred to me that if it were to take off in flight, it could cause enormous damage and terror across the land. I doubted I could kill it. Ordinary weapons were notoriously useless against dragons. Somehow I had to persuade it to go back into its underwater lair, but I had no idea how to do that. My brain seemed to have seized up.

There was a bright glint of gold from further down the riverfront, near the jetty. The dragon snapped its great head in that direction and gave a great throat rumble. It sounded eager. Pleased. With laborious mud-sucking steps, flapping its great wings, it began to make its way downriver towards the shiny, golden thing.

I jumped up on to a stanchion to get a better look and my heart sank even further. The golden glitter was Veelya's carriage and the dragon was headed straight for it. Their love of gold and precious, glittery things was legendary. How to give Veelya's security team time to take her to safety? I knew I was dithering and each second I wasted, the dragon was getting nearer to reducing Veelya (not to mention the good citizens of Ysgard) to cinders. Veelya's unmistakable glass-shattering scream, which soared above the crowd, galvanised me.

"*Dragon!*" I yelled.

The creature tossed its head, but did not stop.

"*Dragon! I command you!*" I put as much authority into my voice as I could, but it was not easy. I was quaking with nerves and my voice was cracked.

Foreleg raised, the dragon slowly turned towards me and fixed me with its glare. The bat-like wings lazily swept the air. There were no words, but I received a very clear message: *Don't mess with me, little mageling.*

Oh, if only I knew more about this stuff! A great wave of despair washed through me. How could I possibly match skills with this ancient monster?

"*You're a mage!*" said a voice in my head. "*Be one!*" Suddenly I was very angry. Some creep had summoned this beast regardless of the consequences. How dare they! Be a mage, huh? OK, watch this.

I raised my arms and let my magepower surged upwards into my fingers. Sparks of blue fire shot from the tips. "*Dragon!*" I said again. "*See, I am a fire-mage. As a creature of fire, you will do as I say. An-athewata! Go back, dragon. This is not your time. Go back! An-athewata!*"

The dragon roared, tossed its head and thrashed the water with its wings. The noise was unbelievable. Then it started to move towards the harbour front, trampling on boats and snapping mooring lines as it came. With a sudden lunge, it brought up its forelegs on to the quayside and roared at the squealing crowd, sweeping its head in a menacing arc towards them. I heard a small cry and saw to my horror a child toddling towards the dragon's massive clawed feet that were making huge white gouges in the harbour stonework. Any moment now the dragon would notice it. Sweat poured down my face.

"Dragon! Listen to me!" I commanded. But I was sure my voice sounded raw and unconvincing against the panic of the crowd.

Be a mage! How could I be something I'd never really tried before? This was a far cry from the simple fire-raising I used to do. We were all going to be killed because I didn't know the foggiest about controlling primeval creatures. Well, it's not something that had ever come up before. The only primeval creatures I dealt with were gutter scum like Yorgish.

Yorgish. I suddenly remembered his knife. I was still carrying it. Maybe the weapon would be effective against the dragon. I pulled it out and immediately it shone with an eerie green light. It resonated with so much magic that I had a hard time keeping it in my hand. Gripping the handle firmly, I held the knife up.

"*See this, dragon?*" I waved the knife at it. "*It will be your death. Go back, or I shall kill you!*"

The dragon shied away and bellowed. The light from the knife seemed to cause it pain. There were gasps from the crowd, and one brave soul darted forward and grabbed the inquisitive child while the dragon was distracted.

I walked forward, holding the knife up like a torch.

"*An-athewata! Go back, dragon. Leave this place.*"

The dragon backed off with thrashing tail and wings sending water and debris flying round it. Then just as I was beginning to think I was winning, the dragon launched itself out of the river. Wings pumping, it rose up and up. I had only one card left to play: with all my strength I threw the knife towards the beast's soft underbelly and saw it sink home.

The dragon gave a deafening squeal of rage and pain and began to fall.

Now, at last, the crowd scattered. Wings flailing, the creature struggled to stay airborne, while evil-smelling wetness was spraying over the harbour from the knife wound in its belly. No one wanted to get that stuff on them: who knows what it might do?

Finally, with a great splash, the dragon sank beneath the turbulent surface of the river and disappeared in a rush of bubbles.

I dropped my arms and felt light-headed with exhaustion.

Now that the danger of being fried or scalded was past, the crowd started to grow ugly. They wanted to blame someone for the monster that had terrified the life out of them, and they'd already picked out their target. I leaned against a mooring stanchion, recovering from the incredible lassitude that followed such an expenditure of power, vaguely aware that the voices around me were angry and belligerent. I looked round and saw a contingent of black-clad Enforcers pushing their way towards me, shoving people aside roughly with the butts of their weapons. They didn't seem too friendly, or concerned about the damage they might be causing. They weren't the only ones. Hysterical bystanders were also pushing and pointing in my direction, shouting out demands that I should be chained up, or burned or thrown into the river with the monster I had conjured.

With a very real feeling of panic, I stared round, looking for a way out. But with the river at my back, I was out of options. I certainly couldn't swim. The safest bet as far as I could see was to give myself up to the Enforcers.

I remained passive when two of them grabbed my arms and fastened a security chain on my wrists and ankles. They frog-marched me through the crowd, while others formed a ring around us, and somehow managed to get me unharmed into an armoured carrier without windows. I was tossed unceremoniously into the dark interior and the doors slammed shut, leaving the angry mob yelling and pounding their fists against the reinforced steel. I heard the sirens start up and lost my balance as the carrier shot away.

Only then did I realise that I was not alone in the transporter. There was a body lying in the dark with me, and I had just fallen over it.

SEVEN

"*Ooof!*"

Evidently the body was still alive. I scrambled up and felt along the walls of the vehicle for something to hold on to. At the rate we were moving, there was a good chance I'd be tossed around like a ball in a slot machine. My hand hit a webbing restraint and I grabbed hold.

The body on the floor gave a groan. "Silke?" The voice was barely more than a whisper, but enough for me to recognise.

"*Stone?*"

I heard him moving on the floor. I stretched out my hands in the darkness, flinched as I touched his hair, and quickly moved down to his shoulder. "You OK, Stone?"

"No."

I waited. Then, "Are you hurt?"

"They stunned me."

Eeuw. He must have a giant-sized headache. "What happened?"

Stone shifted again, and I heard the soft clink of chains like the ones I wore.

The transpo had stopped rocking quite so much, so I guessed we were on a straight pathway. Must be clear of the city. If we had been going to Central Enforcement HQ, we'd have been there by now. I figured I could wait a bit before telling Stone that particular news.

He cleared his throat and I could tell he was working some saliva into his mouth. His words came slowly, as if he were drugged. "Um . . . well . . . when you left me at the café I noticed a guy following you . . . with hostile intentions. So, I followed him. I tried to warn you, but you couldn't hear me. And then the fun started with the dragon. I tried to stop the guards firing at it. We could have handled it if they hadn't made it so angry. I had to flatten one of them, and I think I might have broken the nose of another. And then I felt the dragon was about to blast everyone, so I threw up an ice shield. The next moment, there were Enforcers everywhere, and I got zapped." I heard the crick of his neck muscles as he moved his head in a circle, trying to ease his discomfort. "How about you?"

"Not much to tell," I said. I wasn't particularly proud of my performance back there. "I managed to get the dragon to back where it came from. Then the crowd got nasty and so I let the Enforcers take me. What can you tell me about the guy who followed me in the crowd?"

Stone took some time to answer. "Um, tall. My height, I guess. Slim. Black hair. Didn't see his face. Moved well: like a gymnast . . . or combat trained."

Hmmm. I thought it could have been Dervan: he'd fit that description, and he had looked me up yesterday.

"What made the dragon appear?" asked Stone. His voice sounded strained still.

"It was summoned."

"Well, yes," Stone replied with some irritation. "Dragons don't turn up to watch a yacht launch every day of the week." He gave a dry cough. "Maybe I should have asked *who* made the dragon appear?"

I shrugged, but he wouldn't have seen me. "It was more than likely summoned by the mage that's done all the other tricks so far." That was all I was prepared to say for the moment.

"Could *you* summon a dragon?" he asked.

"No. Well, I don't think so. It's not something I've actually tried."

"But you knew enough to send it back."

"Well, not exactly. But it went – that's all that matters."

There was a silence between us for a while and we listened to the transpo rattling along its way.

"Any idea where we're going?" said Stone eventually.

"Do you want brutal truth, or comforting lies?"

He gave a little laugh. "If I'm honest, neither. I suppose you could entertain me with the lies first, and then knock me flat with the truth."

I squatted down on to the floor, my back against the side, legs stretched out. Stone sat somewhere to my right. "Well, if we're lucky, this is a palace security transpo, and they're taking us to the HQ in Pelagra to debrief us on what happened at the harbour," I began.

"But you don't think it is," Stone supplied.

"Nope." How to put it palatably? "I don't think these people are Enforcers at all. I think they may be working for our rogue mage. And I suspect they are taking us . . . out of the way."

"Out of the way," Stone repeated. "You mean, someone thinks we're interfering too much, so they're neutralising us."

"Yes."

"And you know who it is, don't you?"

"I have a good idea."

"Are you going to share it?"

"Not yet. I may be wrong," I said. "And don't you go poking around in my brain, either."

Stone sighed. "Please. Give me credit for some finesse." There was a pause. "Besides, I can't think straight with my head about to explode."

100

I felt for him. I'd had experience of stunners myself. They were deeply unpleasant and could take several hours to wear off, depending on how strong the charge had been.

"Here, can you come a bit nearer? I can probably get rid of some of the pain for you."

There was no reply for a moment. Stone was probably assessing whether he wanted to trust his head in my hands or not. Then I heard him shuffling awkwardly towards me. He lost his balance a few times, so I reached out for him and just brushed his fingers before he snatched his hand away as if it were burnt.

"*No*. Not the hands. Not if you don't want me reading you like this morning's news-sheet."

I stared in his direction, barely able to make out the shape of him in the dark. Was he really that good an empath? "OK," I said. "Sit in front of me, and rest your back against my knees."

He scrambled over my legs and I guided him by the shoulders into position. Heat is an excellent healer of pain, so I concentrated on carefully drawing some of my magefire into my fingers. Then I placed them gently at key points at the base of Stone's skull. It was a skill Esther had taught me years ago. I could feel the heat from my fingers penetrating muscle and bone, relaxing the tension and soothing the damaged nerves.

"Mmmmmm, bliss!" he sighed, leaning back against my bent knees. "That is soooo . . . good."

I grinned, feeling him arch his neck and flex his shoulder muscles with pleasure.

I moved my fingers down his neck, kneading out the knots of pain and sending magefire heat into the soft tissue.

"Oh, my," Stone sighed again.

"Enough?" I asked after several minutes. "How does your head feel now?"

"Never enough. Not in a lifetime," he said. "My head feels wonderful. How about healing the rest of me?"

"I don't think there's much wrong with the rest of you," I replied curtly, removing my hands. "At least, that I can put right." The physical contact was beginning to give *me* warm feelings deep in my gut. Time to stop, I think. "We need to plan, Stone."

He slid away from me and leaned back against the opposite side of the vehicle, so we were facing each other in the total dark. I could feel his trousered leg alongside my own and the proximity was somehow comforting.

"Well, if you're not going to tell me who you think is involved and where we are being taken, I don't see that we have much we can discuss," he said. There was a hint of irritation back in his voice.

I suppose I would have felt miffed, too, if he'd left me

ignorant. I was about to say more when the vehicle gave a lurch and slowed down.

"Looks like we might have arrived," I said quickly. "Have you got any weapons, Stone?"

"Apart from my hands and my brain? No."

"Well, for now let's play it that we don't know each other. It might not help for them to think we're working together."

"Oh, are we?"

I ignored that. My own stunner had been lifted when they grabbed me at the harbour, but I still had my small, flat knife strapped to my ankle. Pity the dragon had disappeared with the Taurug knife. I slipped it out of its sheath and tucked it into a special pocket in the back of my shirt, between my shoulders. Not that easy with my hands chained together. It wasn't a place commonly frisked for weapons, so I could only hope no one would try it this time.

I'd barely put my hands back down when the doors were flung open and strong daylight made us both blink and turn our heads away. Black figures climbed in and reached for us, and we were dragged roughly out of the transporter. They wore uniforms very like those of Enforcers, but there were no logos or numbers on the pockets or epaulettes, and no bands of ribbon on the sleeves to denote rank. Their heads were encased in hard helmets with black visors. Belts round their waists carried the usual array of Enforcer weapons and a few others I didn't recognise.

"Where are we?" I asked. There was always the possibility they would give me a polite answer. OK, only a faint one.

I was ignored. Rough hands frisked us both for weapons. They didn't find my knife. More chains were attached to the ones we both wore, and Stone and I were pulled along awkwardly behind our captors like cattle being led to market.

We were in a large courtyard, walled on all sides, with massive, reinforced double gates behind us, firmly shut. Ahead was another set of doors leading to a huge, round tower with unassailable walls that showed no signs of windows for the first fifteen metres. I'd no idea where we were and racked my brains for memories of local towers and keeps. But I was a townie, and so far in my life had had little occasion to venture beyond Ysgard. Put me down, blind-folded, in a Ysgard street, and it would be a different story.

I glanced behind us at the transporter, but it was just plain black: no emblems, or insignia to identify it. My suspicion was confirmed. These were not Enforcers, but a bunch of heavies who were trying hard to pass as Enforcers.

"Hey!" I demanded, like any outraged innocent citizen. "What gives with you guys? Are we being charged with anything? I want my lawyer."

The two men in front of us exchanged a glance (well,

their helmets turned to each other) and we heard grunts exchanged that might have been hysterical laughter for all I knew. Then, without warning, one of them swung round and hit me across the face without a word, knocking me sideways. I gasped with the shock and pain of it. He jerked me forward with the chain and I was dragged along the ground for a few metres before I managed to tug it back and get to my feet.

Stone stumbled along beside me, but gave no hint that he was at all interested in what happened to me. Nice. You can carry play-acting too far in my opinion. If it *was* play-acting.

The doors of the tower opened and we went inside. The entrance hall was wide, with huge grey flagstones on the floor and a strip of woven carpeting leading from the door to wide stairs on the left that curved away up the wall to the next floor. Sconces with flickering flame lamps were fixed all round the room and up the staircase, so the place was filled with warm firelight and smoky fumes. I breathed in deeply, but even my enhanced senses could detect nothing useful. With only a moment's pause on the threshold, we were jerked forward and ascended the stairs.

Up and up we climbed, with no break in the pace they set. Past one landing, then another, and another, with rooms leading off each. Their closed doors, however, gave us no clue what was inside them. Finally we reached what must surely have been the last floor, as we seemed to run out of stairs. Our escorts showed no sign of fatigue, but I admit I was breathing heavily and Stone looked ashen. He hadn't yet recovered fully from his recent stun.

There was only one door on this floor. It was big, and heavily moulded in bronze. We hadn't even knocked when it was flung open by unseen hands. Our escorts went inside and Stone and I, naturally, had to follow.

A tall, elegant figure stood to one side, by a window, his face defined by sunlight. He wore a long, decorated robe of what looked like fine wool interwoven with gold thread that sparkled as it caught the light. As we entered, he turned and looked straight at me.

I stood straighter and met his dark, violet gaze without flinching. "Sattine," I said in a tone as disinterested as I could make it. "Fancy seeing you here."

The exquisitely handsome Ellanoi raised an eyebrow and gave a lazy smile. Long green hair framed his pale, oval face of smooth, unlined skin. He didn't look any different from when I'd last seen him. Sattine crossed the floor towards us, his hands outstretched as if he planned to embrace me.

"Silke!" he said. "It's good to see you."

I lifted up my hands with their chains attached. "Yeah. You made that clear."

"My apologies. But they needed to make your arrest look authentic for the crowd," he said. He nodded to the two "heavies" and they went out of the room, shutting the door behind them. He flicked his fingers at my chains and they fell off. Neat trick.

"There," he said. "Better now?"

"What about him?" I asked, nodding my head in Stone's direction. He had kept himself in the background, carefully not drawing attention to himself. Of course, he may have felt too wretched to do anything else.

Sattine glanced at him. "Ah yes. The Ice Warrior. Who is he?"

I rolled my eyes. "Don't ask me. You should have quizzed your crew about him. They picked him up."

Sattine gave Stone a considering appraisal and walked around him. Stone stood perfectly still, keeping his gaze averted.

"Human, more or less," muttered Sattine. He breathed in deep and pursed his lips. "With some power. Ghall told me you created an impressive ice wall to meet my dragon's breath." He put a hand under Stone's chin and lifted his face up to study it. Sattine was somewhat taller than Stone, so Lucius had to look up to meet his gaze. "Oh, yes! There's very definitely power here!" Sattine showed his teeth in an unpleasant smile. "But what? Are you a threat, I ask myself, or just a do-gooder in the wrong place at the wrong time?"

"Why don't you just ask him?" I said, irritably. "I daresay he's got a tongue in his head."

"My men don't pick up just any old flotsam," said Sattine. "So, my fine young man. What should we call you?"

Stone looked at Sattine calmly. "How about Harold?"

I turned away to hide a smile.

Sattine's brows shot up. "Harold?"

"I always fancied the name," said Stone, his face bland.

There was a moment of silence. Then, before I could give any warning, Sattine lifted his hand and a spark of magefire shot towards Stone. The chains round his wrists suddenly turned white hot. There was a smell of burning flesh. Stone screamed and fell to the floor. Shattered chainlinks clattered harmlessly beside him.

"What have you done?" I yelled, appalled, as I ran over to Stone. He was unconscious: his wrists were blistered and bleeding. I glared at Sattine, who watched me with an unreadable expression on his face. "There was no need for that!" I spat at him. "What harm had he done you?"

"For his sake, I hope nothing," Sattine replied coolly. "But he needed to learn respect. The scars will remind him."

"Respect for what? A fire-mage who can't control his temper?" I asked. "Just what are you after, Sattine? Why are we here?"

"Don't get hysterical, Silke. Come and sit down. I had no intention of involving you in my plans, but unfortunately you took up with those ridiculous twins of old Vyktor's and began to meddle. I admit I made the mistake of getting one or two of my more inept associates to . . . render you harmless, shall we say. But they made a sad botch of their tasks. Anyway, now I've seen for myself what you can do, I'm rather pleased they failed. You are much more use to me alive and well. So, you're here now, and you'd better get used to it. You won't be able to meddle much within these walls." He looked around the room. "It's not a bad place, all things considered. But I can't allow you to interfere, Silke: I've waited too long, and planned too carefully for this." His lips pressed into a tight line and those cold, mage eyes bore into mine. I had great trouble not flinching.

With more calm than I felt, I took a seat on an antique sofa. The position gave me a view of Stone, so I would see if he began to stir.

"I thought you'd retired to the Southern Isles for good," I said. "What happened to change your mind? Got tired of all your little playmates?"

He gave a small laugh and shook his head. It was probably not a good idea to bait him, but I really wanted to goad him into giving me some idea of what he was up to.

"Did you imagine I was lying in indolent luxury out there, surrounded by lovely creatures to do my every bidding?" Sattine smirked as he leaned lazily against the big stone fireplace that dominated the room and idly fingered a gold dragon medallion suspended on a chain around his neck. There were logs burning in the grate, but they didn't heat the unpleasant chill of the room. "There's not much to interest an Ellanoi with my skills on an island barely the size of Ysgard, with no indigenous population to terrorise." He gave me an ironic look and I had to concentrate hard on not showing just how tense I was feeling. Sattine was the most powerful, ruthless mage I knew, full of all kinds of tricks to bend the will and confuse the mind. I didn't underestimate him for a moment.

"I do have a very fine home on Farfeld Island, I have to admit. It would be nice to think of idling away each day in indulgent pleasure, but I think after a time I'd get very bored. It's a pity you never came to see me." He pushed away from the fireplace and moved over to one of the chairs opposite me. Smoothing his robe carefully, he sat down and rested his hands on the arms of the chair. The dragon medallion glittered in the firelight and caught my attention. With some difficulty, I looked away. It was undoubtedly magical. My ears were already tingling and I wanted to rub at them.

"It was not my idea to leave Elginagen," he continued. "Good old Vykrem the Bloody saw to that when he realised what a great mage I was. It was unofficial banishment: he threatened some rather unpleasant things if I hung around, and at that time it suited me to leave. But I've used the years profitably since then. I have grown strong, Silke.

Stronger than you could imagine. And I have recruited some very useful people to help me." He looked straight at me then, to see my reaction.

"Like Yorgish, I suppose!" I sneered.

"Yes, well. I underestimated you, my dear." His violet eyes held mine. "You might want to think about working with me."

"Is this an offer?"

"I won't deny that your mageskills added to mine would be formidable. You may not be as powerful as I am, but that's only because your education has been neglected. I realised some time ago that I should have taken you to Farfeld with me. You've shown some quite impressive abilities lately, Silke."

So, his spies *had* kept track of me. "Thanks, I think," I said. "But I like being independent. Besides, I have an old-fashioned belief that if someone pays me to work for them, I owe it to them to deliver the goods. If you are planning on wiping out the Royal Family, Sattine, you'll have to go through me first."

He burst out laughing. "Oh, how sweet! Where did this sentimentality suddenly come from, Silke?" The grin vanished and his voice suddenly became hard. "The last I saw of you, my dear, you were a filthy little street rat, living off the proceeds of your nasty little arson scams. What a waste of talent!"

I leaped to my feet in fury and slammed a bolt of magefire at him. The room rocked with the force of it, but the blast never reached him. He had merely put up his hand and stopped it with a gesture. The door suddenly flew open and one of his henchmen ran into the room, a heavy cleaver-knife in his hand.

"It's all right, Ghall," said Sattine.

Ghall lowered his cleaver reluctantly, and backed slowly out of the room again, glaring at me.

I slumped back on the sofa and clawed my hands through my hair, cursing myself for my lack of restraint.

"That was quite a show of temper, Silke. I see that hasn't improved with the years. You always were something of a wild cat." Sattine left his chair and went over to a table where there was a decanter with some glasses beside it. "Would you like some wine?" He poured a glass for himself and glanced over at me for my answer.

I shook my head, too full of anger and frustration to speak.

"Well, you can't say I haven't tried. If you won't change your mind and work with me, then I'm afraid you'll have to stay here until my plans are accomplished. It won't be too bad. I'll leave this young man for you to play with. Unless you'd rather I got rid of him?" I looked at Stone, still motionless on the floor, and shook my head again. "No? I thought not." He tossed back his wine and put the glass down on the table. "Afterwards, I shall have to think about what to do with you. Now, do excuse me – I have an appointment at the palace."

He went over to the door and beckoned to the heavy mob stationed outside the room.

"Take our guests to their *suite*, Ghall," he said. "Make sure they are comfortable, won't you? I daresay they'd like some refreshments." I didn't imagine for a minute Ghall would bring us silver service.

Ghall came into the room and said nothing, but strode over and grasped my arm. He lifted me off the sofa like I was just one of the cushions. A Ghall clone came in and picked Stone up off the floor, tossing him over a shoulder. Now that they had removed their helmets, I could see that they were both Taurugs. Ugh. Sattine was really scraping the employment barrel.

"Until we meet again, then, Silke." Sattine swept out of the room and down the stairs in a rustle of cloth. "Enjoy your stay!" I thought I could hear him laughing. I wriggled in Ghall's grasp.

"There's no need for this," I snapped, but to no avail. He pulled me down a couple of levels and pushed me into a room. The other guard tossed Stone down on the floor beside me, then they both left, slamming the door shut behind them. I heard a heavy key turn in the lock.

I bent down to check Stone. He looked extremely pale

and felt very cold to the touch, but his pulse was slow and steady. I looked around. There were two beds in the room, made up with grey linen and a thin blanket. I pulled the blanket off one and threw it over Stone, then I grabbed the pillow and put it under his head. I turned him onto his side, so he would be more comfortable, and checked his wrists. They looked nasty, and needed salve, but I didn't have any. The best I could do would be to bind them, to keep the wounds clean.

The rest of the furniture comprised a table and two chairs. There was a freestanding mirror pushed to the back, and a pewter basin, which doubled as a washstand.

There was another, smaller door. I went over to see where it led. Just a basic privy: a hole in the floor. But there was a hand basin with a single water tap, and linen towel. Clearly we weren't in five-star accommodation, but it was a step up from a cell in a damp dungeon. I snatched up the towel and felt in the collar of my shirt for my knife. Still there, thank goodness. I took it out and used it to rip the towel into strips, which I carefully bound round each of Stone's wrists and tied them off. They'd still hurt abominably, but they were less likely to get infected. Unfortunately, magefire wouldn't heal burns, but only make them worse.

I made another inspection of the room. It had a barred window, giving us some light, but only a small pane that opened to let in a breeze, barely large enough for a rat to climb through. Looking out, I could see the landscape stretching away into the distance, and knew we were too high up to be able to escape that way even if we *could* squeeze through the bars.

Just then I heard footsteps approach the door. It was unlocked and kicked open. Two Taurug guards stood in the doorway. One shoved a tray across the floor, while the other looked on with a stunner aimed at us. They fell back and slammed the door shut again. The key turned.

Curiosity took me over to the tray. It held tin bowls, two wooden beakers, a jug of wine, a small loaf of bread, a handful of dried fruits and a crockery jar with a lid on it. No cutlery. I lifted up the lid and sniffed at the contents of the jar: a beige mush with lumps in it. Surprisingly good fare for prisoners, all things considered. Maybe Sattine didn't want us dead just yet. I wasn't sure if I was hungry enough to risk the stew: Taurugs ate some funny stuff, and I couldn't be sure they didn't have a hand (literally) in the making of it.

I tore a piece off the loaf and picked up some of the fruits, glancing over at Stone to see if the smell of food had aroused him at all. Apparently not. Chewing thoughtfully, I paced the carpeted stone floor. It felt very solid. The walls were stone. We had no flame lamps or candles. Once the sun went down, we'd be in the dark unless I could contrive some magefire light. It took a lot of energy to maintain, though, and until I had a plan I wanted to conserve all I had. Finally, I sat on one of the beds and looked down at the figure lying at my feet.

"Well, Stone. I hope you've got some good ideas, as I'm fresh out of them."

EIGHT

Stone began to stir. I bent down to help him up.

"Here, sit on the bed," I told him, and guided him over to it.

His face was beaded with sweat and he looked feverish.

"How're you feeling? You look pretty awful."

He gave me a hard look and declined to answer. Instead he stared round the room and, noticing the basin, said, "Can you get me a bowl of water?" It came out almost as a gasp.

I took the bowl from the washstand, poured brownish water into it from the tap in the privy, and brought it over to him.

"If you're thirsty we have . . ."

He shook his head. Then he held his wrists over the bowl. His hands shook; I guess the pain from the burns must have been ferocious. "Please . . . soak my wrists."

I did as he asked, scooping up water and pouring it over

the stained bandages until they were well soaked. Stone gasped and closed his eyes, concentrating, and I felt my ears begin to prickle. *Magic!* Stone was drawing on power again. I stared, fascinated, as sparkling layers of ice crystals formed round the wet towelling strips on his wrists. Ice! Of course. That would ease the burns. It would help his feverishness, too.

"Great thinking, Stone," I said. "At least he didn't fry your brains."

After several minutes he said, "You can take the bowl away now."

"Yes, sir!" I saluted smartly.

He gave a pained smile. "Thank you." Then he clenched his fists a few times, and the stiffened cloth began to crack and break, like ice on a pond. Stone began to peel it away.

"Hey! Don't do that!" I said. "You need to keep the wounds clean!"

"It's OK, Silke. I know what I'm doing. Did you bind them up?"

"Yeah."

"Thanks. You can give me a hand to undo them if you like."

What the heck. I gingerly began to work at the bandage on his right wrist while he fiddled with the other one. Then they both came off completely, like broken eggshells, and I whistled in admiration. The burns were still visible, but they had faded and reduced, as if they had happened weeks ago. Gone was the bloody, blistered flesh: Stone's ice pack had magically healed it.

"Wow. That's impressive," I admitted.

"I don't know that it rates as high as subduing a dragon," he commented as he flexed his fingers again, working the blood back down into his hands.

I shrugged. "Each to his own. Do they still hurt?"

Stone shook his head. "Not much. It's more like a memory of pain."

"I'm sorry."

He looked up, surprised. "What for?"

"Well . . . " I flung my hands out at nothing in particular. "All this. And for what Sattine did."

"Not your fault," he said. "Goes with the job, I expect. Besides, you did try to warn me off."

Feeling a little awkward, and wondering if I would be that generous if the tables were turned, I passed off the moment by picking up the food tray and putting it on the bed beside him. "Here. We have food. I've already taken what I want. The stew's still fairly warm, I think, but I haven't tried it. Wine's drinkable, which is more than I can say about the tap water."

It occurred to me then that Stone wasn't wearing his spectacles. "Don't you need your glasses?" I asked.

Stone picked over the food. "My eyes are unusually

light sensitive, so I wear special glasses that adjust to the light input, to protect them. They come in handy as a disguise, too. Make me look like Mr Ordinary." He dipped his bread in the stew and declared it edible, but I still declined it. Instead, I filled the beakers for us both from the wine jug.

"I'm not sure I'd go that far," I said. It would be difficult for Stone to look *ordinary*, exactly, but maybe that was my feminine side talking.

"Why don't you tell me about Sattine?" he said, taking a sip from his beaker. "It was obvious you two weren't strangers. And you're both Ellanoi, aren't you?"

I got up and started to pace the room. I wasn't sure where to start, or how much to tell him. All my life I had kept stuff to myself: it was the only way to survive. Even though we'd shared the last twelve hours, Stone was still a relatively unknown quantity to me. I wasn't prepared, yet, to share my entire life history with him. I stopped at the window and looked out once more. The sun was well down now and it wouldn't be long before our room grew too dark for us to see each other.

"There's not a lot to tell that you don't already know," I said at last. "He's a very skilled, very dangerous fire-mage. He was banished years ago by the king at that time, who felt he was too dangerous to keep around. There was probably more to it than that, but Sattine didn't choose to tell me. I was too young to know what was going on. I know he's *behind* the threats to the royal kids, but I don't know why. He says he's recruited a number of skilled followers over the years, no doubt several from inside the royal household. And I think an old associate of mine might be in his pocket, too. The guy you saw following me at the harbour. At one time I thought someone might have hired Sattine to terrorise the royals, but I think this is all his own grand plan, which I can't begin to fathom."

Stone was thoughtful. "He doesn't look a *lot* older than you. Ten years at most, I'd have said. But you talk as if he was banished a lifetime ago."

"We're Ellanoi, don't forget," I said. "You can't apply human years to us. Sattine would be two hundred or more by your reckoning."

"Two hundred?" Stone was astonished. "I had no idea. How old does that make you?"

"You're asking a girl to reveal her age?"

He grinned. "Sorry. But tell me how you know each other."

"He's my brother."

There was total silence for several heartbeats. All kinds of emotions played across Stone's face: he clearly didn't know how to respond.

"Ah," he said finally. "And you don't get on, is that it?"

"You could say that. When our parents died he took off

without so much as a by your leave, and left me to fend for myself. We've had no contact at all until now."

Stone looked at me. "I'm sorry. How did your parents die?" He must have caught something in my look, as he added, "It's OK if you don't want to talk about it."

"I don't," I replied. I wanted to move this conversation on. "We need to think about getting out of this place, Stone. Veelya and Vyktor are in great danger from Sattine. We must warn them and get them away from the palace."

"Fine. Do you know where we are? You have a plan?" Stone stood up, then, and stood with me at the window. He peered through the glass. "I hope it doesn't involve jumping out of the window."

"We were in that transporter about half an hour," I said, ignoring his flip comment. "If Sattine is working with someone inside the palace, it can't be that far away. My guess is that we're not more than twenty miles . . . somewhere north east."

"And that's based on what? The position of the sun?" Stone asked.

"Yeah."

"But you don't know how fast the transporter was travelling."

"No."

"Well, I wasn't entirely comatose when I was in that room with Sattine. I did pick up some stuff from him."

I felt a quick surge of excitement. I'd forgotten Stone was telepathic.

"He didn't seem to be aware of you tapping into his consciousness."

"I didn't have to," said Stone. "He's very self-assured and arrogant: he doesn't bother to shield himself too carefully. I got several images from him, but I don't know what they mean."

"Shoot. They might mean something to me." I listened carefully as I busied myself examining the door lock, to see how much of a challenge it would be.

"When we first went into the room, he was standing by the window. When he saw you, I sensed surprise . . . and approval. There was something he hadn't anticipated. Have you changed much since he last saw you?"

I thought about it while I picked at the lock with the tip of my knife. I wished I had my picks with me. "I guess so. I was a grubby little pre-adolescent tyke in those days, running with the street gangs." I remembered the spiteful words he used only too well.

"Well, I think you impressed him. There's something about you that makes him nervous. Your talent, maybe."

I snorted. "That I can't believe."

Stone went on. "I saw a man and a woman. He looked like an Ellanoi. She was frail . . . very beautiful."

"Sounds like our parents, Magrit and Tabathane."

"The memory seemed to cause him some . . . regret, I think."

"I should hope so. He killed them."

"Killed them? Why?"

I sighed. "We weren't going to talk about this, remember?" Then I shrugged and continued. "It was all put down to an accident. I don't know what happened exactly, but Sattine burned the house down with a firespell while my parents were asleep. I woke up and ran out to safety." It was a very bald account of an event that had changed my whole life and caused me to hate Sattine with a vengeance. I tried to keep my thoughts bland, so Stone didn't pick up on them.

He said nothing for a minute or two then, "Were your parents fire-mages?"

"No. My father was Ellanoi, but without mageskills. It skipped a generation, I think. My mother was human." I didn't like the route he was taking. "Tell me more about Sattine's thoughts."

"Black stone."

"Black stone?" I turned away from my fruitless lock picking. What was black stone? Two words or one? *Blackstone.* Could it be the tower we were in? "Is it the name of this place, do you think?"

"Could be. Have you heard of Blackstone Keep?" he asked.

I shook my head. "Should I have? Don't forget I've spent all my life in Ysgard."

"It's an ancient fortification built on an elemental power conduit to defend Elginagen from hostile forces coming across the Eastern Sea. I read about it once."

"Did you read about how to get out of it?"

"No," he smiled. "But I don't think that's what Sattine was thinking about. I had a great sense of . . . desire. Greed. Lust almost."

"*Lust?*"

"It was a power thing. Sattine wants to get hold of something very valuable . . . or powerful. Black stone has something to do with it."

I sat on the floor, leaning against the door, thinking. "If Sattine wants to get rid of the royals," I mused, "then they must be in the way of his plan. I can't imagine he wants to take over as ruler of this tinpot little country, so there has to be something else he's after."

"Something the royals have," supplied Stone. "Something that will enhance his power."

"Yes."

"Or maybe getting rid of the royals is his bargain with whoever is helping him in the palace."

We both reflected silently on all the implications. But then snapped back to the here and now as we heard heavy footsteps approaching the door. I leapt to my feet and pressed myself to the wall, my knife already in my hand, ready to take on all comers. Stone stood up, too, but went and calmly placed his palms flat against the door itself.

"*Stone,*" I hissed. "*Get out of the way!*"

Stubbornly he ignored me, resting his face against the door as well.

"Changing guard," he mouthed at me. There were more footsteps, the creaking of armoured leather, and muffled talking. I couldn't hear much: the door must have been too thick, but Stone seemed to be hearing something. After a moment or two he lowered his hands and stood away from the door, beckoning me to follow him to the window.

"One guard," he said quietly. "He's made himself comfortable in a chair outside the door. Sounded like he put his feet up on something, so he's not expecting trouble. He won't be relieved for at least a couple of hours, I would guess. So if we're going to do something, we ought to do it now."

"Oh, right!" I said with heavy sarcasm. "I'll just initiate Plan A, shall I?"

"If you would."

"Did you hear all that," I asked, "or use your Sight?"

"Bit of both. I'm surprised your Ellanoi ears didn't pick up more."

Yeah. Come to think of it, why hadn't they? Something was having a dampening effect on me, now I thought about it.

As if I was covered in a heavy blanket. "This place is getting to me a bit," I said. "Makes me feel . . . wooden, somehow. Flat." Out of interest, I tried to call some magefire in my hands again. It came, but very sluggishly. I could feel heat, but little energy.

"Strange. It was OK in Sattine's room."

Stone considered it. "It must be the elemental conduit!" he said. "Earth! It would naturally have a gradual dulling effect on Fire. The longer you stay here, the weaker your magefire will become. That could mean this place *is* Blackstone Keep, as we thought!" He sounded excited.

"Why isn't it affecting you?" I asked.

"My element is Water. Water and Earth harmonise with each other."

Stupid girl. Why didn't you think of that? "If that's true, then this place must affect Sattine," I said. "Or if it doesn't, why doesn't it?"

"Perhaps he's found a way of harnessing Earth power, too."

I wasn't happy with this thought. "If he's able to harness Earth power, then that's bad news, Stone. Earth and Fire. If he's able to tap into Water and Air as well, there wouldn't be anything he couldn't do! He'd be the strongest Ellanoi since . . . grief, we haven't had such a powerful mage since the Dawn."

Stone glanced down at my hands, grabbing tightly at his

arms. I suddenly realised what I'd done and released him hastily. Wordlessly, he smoothed the fabric of his sleeves. I rolled my eyes.

"Perhaps that's what he's aiming for. Maybe this thing he wants will give him that capability," said Stone. "If that's the case, it makes it all the more imperative that we get out of here. The longer you stay, the less you'll be able to do. So let me handle this."

My hands went belligerently to my hips. "Want to test out my survival skills, wise guy? I don't think they're affected. I could still cut your throat before you could send up a prayer."

He threw up his hands in resignation. "Sorry. Sorry. I didn't mean . . . *oh*—"

He swore. "OK. I'll try some ice on the door. As soon as we're through, you can take on the guard. Will that suit?"

"Fine. Just keep out of my way."

"No problem."

We seemed to be back where we were twelve hours ago, bickering over pack supremacy. I was sorry in a way, but he had lit my fuse and I was feeling uncomfortable about my magepowers being reduced in this plaguey building.

Stone picked up the washbowl and filled it with water at the tap in the privy. He went to stand in front of the door with the bowl and settled himself, breathing deeply.

I stood waiting to one side, slightly behind him, my knife in my hand.

My ears began to prickle. My hair felt as if it was rising, as he called on the magic of his craft. I heard that crashing, booming sound in my ears, but dared not turn round. I had to hope he wasn't calling a tidal wave into the room.

Suddenly, Stone flung the water at the door. The bowl fell with a clatter. He raised his arms, hands stretched. He said nothing, but his eyes were shut and his face frowned with concentration. The water running down the length of the door froze. Ice blossomed like flowers in hoarfrost as I watched, spreading over the heavy, ancient wood. My head throbbed with the tension in the room. Then I heard booted feet hitting the floor, and a chair scrape.

There was a shouted enquiry from the corridor outside.

And then the door shattered outwards into a billion frozen, petrified slivers.

The guard screamed once and then fell silent, my knife stuck in his throat. It was overkill, however: he already had half the door embedded in whatever part of him was not covered by armour. I was put in mind of a porcupine.

"Come on!" I pulled Stone from the room, clambering over what remained of the door. He was looking rather shocked. Maybe he hadn't used his power this destructively before, or maybe he never knew he had it in him. I took a moment to yank my knife from the guard, and wipe it on his trousers. Then I frisked him of his stunner and a cleaver-knife, which I held out to Stone. "Here!" He took the knife reluctantly, like someone in a dream.

There was only one way to go: downwards. It was a nightmare, since the staircase was the only access route. It meant, of course, that we would be running straight into anyone coming up to see what the commotion was about. But we managed to get down two levels before anyone showed themselves. A door opened and a guard stepped out, adjusting his trousers. I dropped back into a shadowed alcove, while Stone walked on purposefully. On the darkened landing, with only a few wall lamps for illumination, he could be mistaken at first for another guard.

"Yar dormashk?" inquired the guard. He had a voice like a chainsaw.

Stone grunted a reply, then plunged his cleaver-knife into the guard's chest, putting all his weight behind it. The guard made a low sound and then crumpled remarkably quietly. I slipped out of my alcove. "Quick!" I whispered. I had to tug at Stone again: he'd gone into zombie mode once more, staring at the dead body and the spreading pool of blood at his feet.

I shook him. *"Stone! Come on!"*

He snapped out of his trance and came with me. We continued down the stairs as quickly and silently as we could, until we finally reached the entrance hall. I ran up to the main doors. They looked even bigger than I remembered, and a heavy bar rested across them.

"Give me a hand," I hissed.

Together we threw our combined weight at the bar. I didn't think it would budge, but gradually I felt it lift. We raised it out of the slots in which it rested and slid it back sufficiently to clear one door. We both stopped then, breathing hard, and listened for any sound of discovery. Amazingly, no one appeared. I jerked my head at Stone and squeezed through a crack in the door. He followed close behind.

We pulled the door closed behind us and I looked round the vast courtyard. It was later than I thought. The darkness was absolute now, but there were security braziers round the walls, which made it easier for us to get our bearings.

Stone tugged at my sleeve. "Over here!" he said in my ear. He sounded excited. I followed and saw ahead of us a small flyer, the kind used by those who could afford them to make trips into the metropolis, or to cruise their estates. Sattine's spare runabout no doubt.

It was a nice toy but useless to me. "I can't fly," I said softly, shrugging my shoulders.

"I can."

My stomach did a kind of flip. I wanted to say, *"Fine. You take the flyer and I'll follow on foot."* But Stone was already guiding me up to the wretched thing. He grabbed my leg and tossed me up to the passenger hatch door. I fumbled it open and tumbled awkwardly inside. There was a small noise and then Stone's grinning face appeared opposite me, as he dropped into the pilot's seat. He was like a kid with a birthday present.

"You have no idea if it's flight worthy!" I said.

"Well, I'll soon find out. This is a beauty!" he said, and began flipping switches and pressing buttons. I nearly screeched when the motors started up. The sound was huge in the silence of the courtyard.

"Strapping you in!" he shouted over the noise and vibration. The throttle increased and I felt the nose of the flyer turn slowly. At the same time rigid straps suddenly shot across me, taking me completely by surprise. They clicked into place, rendering me immobile and plastered to the back of my seat. Claustrophobia gripped me and I screeched, grabbing at the straps with impotent fingers. It was probably time I confessed that I had never been in a flyer before.

At that moment, the courtyard lit up with flares and we heard shouts.

"Stone!" I yelled. "We won't make it! Get me out of here!" I stared out of the window, watching half a dozen guards running towards us, some of them still strapping on weapons. Sattine must have left a small contingent behind to take care of the place. I checked the stunner I had stolen and switched it on to operational: low stun. Low stuns would conserve the amount of charge it held.

The engines roared, and the flyer continued to turn until we faced the complete length of the courtyard and the massive entrance gates were straight ahead. Was the fool going to smash through them? I stared, terrified, not knowing which was worse: the guards firing at us, or the imminent possibility of being mashed into a pulp.

Stone cut the brakes and the flyer catapulted forward, leaving my stomach somewhere back in the keep. Just as I thought we would collide with the gates, the nose of the craft lifted sharply at an acute angle and we shot upwards at some impossible speed. I was pressed back in my seat, barely able to breathe. I think I might have been screaming.

When I opened my eyes again, the flyer had levelled out. Stone did a circuit of the keep, which was lit up below us like carnival night, and then headed due south. He looked across at me with a boyish grin on his face, his hands loosely and confidently on the controls.

"Not bad, eh?"

I did not trust myself to reply, but pretended to be interested in what was outside the window. I felt drained of blood. *Never* would I let on just how close I'd come to wetting myself. Or worse.

NINE

Getting back to Ysgard was relatively simple, as Stone was a surprisingly confident pilot and knew how to communicate with Air Traffic Coordination at Ysgard Port. We left the craft in the private parking zone and walked nonchalantly away from it. Sattine's regular pilot would have to explain to the port authorities how it came to be there, and argue about the hangar fee. Bureaucracy. Don't you just love it?

It was a great relief to be back on solid earth once more. Despite Air and Fire being companionable elements, I did not want to find myself airborne ever again.

While Stone went off to find some fast food for us both at one of the port vendors, I went to a public comm booth and put through a call to Veelya. I got the night security officer. I gave my name and explained it was urgent I spoke to the princess.

"Her Royal Highness is unable to take calls at

present," she said. The bat knew me from past conversations and made no secret of her disapproval of me.

"Where is she?" I demanded.

"That's no concern of yours. She has an important engagement this evening, and cannot be disturbed. I will tell her you called. You may make an appointment to see her if you wish."

"Look, the princess is in grave danger!" I told her. "I *must* warn her. At least let me talk to one of her PBs!"

"I will do no such thing. She is quite safe in the confines of the palace, I can assure you. We do know our job, you know."

"And so do I!" I yelled, and slammed the unit down in fury.

Stone had been standing outside, chomping on a hot savoury roll and fries. They smelled divine, reminding me that we'd hardly eaten in the last twelve hours. He shoved a second paper-wrapped roll at me, and without asking for an explanation said, "I'll try Vyktor."

My mouth salivating, I took the food eagerly from him and changed places. He did slightly better than I did: the upper-class accent he was able to switch on probably did the trick. I heard Stone murmuring solicitudes into the unit before he disconnected. He made a quick call to his father to reassure him, and then stepped out of the booth.

"I got Vyktor's valet," he said. "Apparently the king went

into a decline in the last few hours. Veelya and Vyktor are with him now."

"We'll just have to go to them," I said, wiping the last of the crumbs from my mouth. "Thanks for the food. I owe you."

He merely shrugged. "Any time."

I stopped the first cab that came along and told the driver to drop us in Tork Street, which ran behind the palace. It was nearing midnight now, and in this part of Ysgard there was little traffic and few people on the streets. The area round the palace, for security reasons, held no shops, restaurants or theatres, and the tourists would be long gone to their hostelries and inns. There were, however, security guards patrolling the perimeters of the palace grounds – some of them with fierce dargbeasts.

Stone paid off the cabbie once we arrived. I tried to persuade him to stay in the cab and go home: sneaking around the palace, not to mention breaking and entering, was something I'd rather have done alone. But he was determined to stay. So, I led the way and trusted that when push came to shove, Stone would not be a hindrance.

As it happened, I might just have cramped *his* style.

Tork Street itself was a one-sided, continuous terrace of small town houses with front doors opening on to the street and a vista of nothing but the blank wall surrounding the palace grounds. They had small shuttered windows and an occasional narrow walkway between them, leading to back yards. At this time of night there were few lights to be seen through windows: only the dull glowlamps that illuminated the street enough for the night watch to patrol. There was a resonant perfume of cooked cabbage leaves and rotting waste.

I slipped silently down the side of the street with the houses, in case I had to dodge into an alley at any time. I was aware of Stone close behind me and surprised that he was managing to keep so quiet too. In fact, I glanced round at one point just to make sure that he was keeping up. I saw his white teeth grin at me in the gloom.

Suddenly his hand gripped my shoulder and I was propelled into a dark alleyway before I could even squeak a protest.

His mouth came to my ear. "Patrol!" he whispered.

I strained my senses and at last began to make out the faint crunch of boots falling methodically on the cobbles of the street, then the creak of leather and the quiet *shush shush* of fabric on fabric. They were all small sounds, but they told me a great deal: the guard was pacing in a routine way, so he – or she – hadn't spotted us. And there was no dargbeast. Those ugly animals wheezed and slobbered the whole time, giving little grunts and coughs as they lumbered along. Their long talons clicked on the pavement and their tails swished eerily as they dragged behind them.

We both froze in our alley and watched the dark patrolling figure walk past us, unseeing. We waited until we were both quite sure the danger was past, then continued up the street to a small door in the palace perimeter wall. It was the entrance used by the palace workforce: everyone from the gardeners to the chambermaids. Those legions of minions who kept the palace functioning, but were more or less invisible to all but the senior housekeeper who employed them.

I used a little power on the bolt and we both slipped through, closing the door behind us. For a moment we stood flat against the wall, waiting to see if there was any new danger. The path to the kitchens was clear: but it was bathed in moonlight and there was no cover for us. We'd just have to leg it and hope no one was watching. I looked at Stone and he nodded. I took off.

There was a soft light illuminating the first of the kitchens. As I peered through the glass window in the door, I could see that the room was empty of staff, but that didn't mean that there was no one around. The palace was one of those places that never sleep: there would be staff on hand right through the night.

I tried the door handle and was surprised when it turned. Some careless lackey had forgotten to lock it. Or else they felt that with the outside door bolted, they were safe from intrusion. Certainly, there were no gardens on this side of the buildings to hide anyone. I looked at Stone again and raised a brow. He just shrugged, so I pushed the door open further and we went cautiously inside.

"We need to find the royal apartments," I whispered to Stone.

He nodded. "Let me go first. I can 'hear' people."

I understood what he meant and reluctantly stood aside to let him lead the way. At least I'd be able to cover our backs.

Miraculously, we got as far as the third floor without anyone seeing us. Admittedly, the corridors were not brightly lit, and there would only have been a skeleton staff on duty anyway. But then our luck changed. I heard a door open behind us as we headed for the next flight of stairs, and a small, yappy dog came flying at me. I recognised it as one of Veelya's pets. My knife was already in my hand, and I could have silenced it in a second, but I didn't think Veelya would thank me.

"Quiet!" I hissed at it, but the stupid dog kept up a racket loud enough to wake the dead.

I heard a sleepy female voice call out, "Jinks! Quiet! Come here, Jinks!"

Then Stone pushed me to one side and squatted in front of the dog. He held out his hand and murmured something that might have been dog language for all I knew. The dog stopped its barking and went up to his hand to sniff it, its little stubby tail twitching like a demented metronome. Satisfied, it turned round and raced back to the room.

"Jinks! Good dog!"

The voice went quiet and since Jinks didn't appear again, and his barks hadn't alerted a cohort of security guards, Stone and I carried on up the stairs. As we had progressed from the lower levels, so the style of decoration of the palace increased in magnificence. The staircase we were on was carpeted in thick, deep red pile woven with a pattern made out of the royal coat of arms. The walls were papered in gold velvet flock and hung with portraits of sombre-looking royal ancestors.

There was no time to gawp at the gallery, however. Halfway up the stairs, my ears began to tingle. I put out my hand to stop Stone, but he must have already been aware of something. We both stayed still, listening. There were soft voices coming from one of the nearby rooms. One door was slightly ajar, with light streaming out on to the darkened landing. Slowly, we moved up a stair at a time and then along the landing.

Stone stood as close as he dared to the open doorway, his back to the wall and eyes closed. I guessed he was "listening" to the people inside the room and I kept watch. I could just distinguish a female voice and two or three different males. One, at least, had magical talent that was affecting my ears.

I felt a tug on my sleeve and Stone was pulling me away

from the door. I went back down the long landing with him, into a dark recess. We seemed to be doing this a lot lately.

"Five people," he whispered. "Veelya, Vyktor. Their father, I think. Someone else – maybe a doctor. And one other."

Someone with magic. "Sattine?" I asked.

He shook his head.

"Someone's working magic," I said. "Could be an illusion spell, or a covering mask."

"We need to get Veelya or her brother out here so we can warn them."

"Any ideas?"

He smiled. "Yeah. You could dress up as a maid and go in there."

"Very funny. Can't you bring them out with a bit of mind-bending?"

"*Mind-bending?*" Stone winced and shook his head in exasperation. "You really have a crude idea about what I can—"

"*Sssh!*"

We flattened ourselves into our alcove – no mean feat, since it already had the bust of a royal relative in it – as an elderly, stiff-necked butler character came mincing down the corridor holding a small silver tray containing a bottle of brandy and two glasses. He didn't see the blow from my stiffened fingers that knocked him out cold, or the deft way Stone caught the tray before it fell from nerveless fingers. We quickly stripped off his jacket and trousers and without a word Stone exchanged them for his dark pants and black bomber. The trousers were a little short in the leg, and loose at the waist, but they'd serve. As luck would have it, one of the doors in the corridor opened on to a cleaner's cupboard, and we stuffed the unconscious butler inside. Stone slicked back his hair, picked up the tray and straightened the bottle and glasses.

"Won't be long," he said with a wink, and strode confidently to the room with the voices.

Waiting was agony, but there was absolutely nothing I could do. Nevertheless, I was surprised and relieved when at last Stone emerged from the room, followed by Vyktor. Vyktor's face was pale. His eyes widened when he saw me, but he just jerked his head towards one of the other rooms, opened the door and ushered us both inside.

"*What do you think you're doing?*" he began, all outraged bluster.

"Vyktor, be quiet. Listen to me," said Stone. "This is Silke. She's employed by your sister but we're working together. We discovered today that there is a powerful mage trying to kill you both. It's very important that you and Veelya get away from the palace, to somewhere safe where he can't find you."

"Don't be absurd, Lucius," said Vyktor. "My father's dying in there. We can't possibly leave him now."

"I'm aware of that," said Stone. "But I'm afraid you must look at the wider picture. You are both the last of the monarchy. If you two are killed, Elginagen will probably be taken over by a tyrant – an extremely dangerous mage. Do you think your father would want that? You must take Veelya and get away from here. Leave Silke and myself to find out what's going on and help put a stop to it."

Vyktor looked torn with indecision.

"Vyktor," I said, "who's in that room with you and Veelya?"

"Um, well, my father. But he's in bed. He's very weak. And Baracleth – my father's physician. He's known the family for years."

So who was the other person Stone had "heard"?

"No one else?"

"Oh, well, Lord Joslin had been with us, but he left the room a few minutes ago."

"Joslin?"

"Yes. He's a kind of chief of staff. If anything happens to the king, Joslin has to know about it."

"If your father dies, Vyktor, do you and Veelya automatically take over?" I asked.

"No. We're too young. Joslin would take over as

regent until we're eighteen." He gave a half smile. "Or until we marry someone who is already a reigning monarch."

"Is that imminent?"

Vyktor pulled a face. "You're joking. Have you met any reigning monarchs lately? Most of the ones in the civilised world are octogenarians."

Stone and I exchanged glances. Here was a motive.

"Do you think you could get Veelya out for us?" I asked.

Vyktor gave a shrug. "If I must, I suppose so. Can't we leave her out of this?"

"No."

He sniffed, then left the room and went back down the corridor.

"We need to get them away, Stone," I whispered.

"I know, but if we knock them out, how are we going to carry them out of the palace?"

I chewed my fingernails and paced, trying to find an answer. By the time Vyktor and his sister joined us, I had only succeeded in making my fingers sore.

"Silke!" exclaimed Veelya when she saw me. "What are you doing here?"

Not this again.

"Never mind, Veelya," I said. "Can we go somewhere more private? Where we can talk through things without being interrupted? I should warn you that there is an irate butler in the cupboard down the corridor, who is going to wake up soon and raise the alarm."

"Really?" said Veelya, her eyes alight. "Hoo! I bet that's Charles! I'd better go get him, and smooth his ruffled feathers."

"I don't think . . ." I started to say, but Veelya was already scooting out of the room, followed by her brother. I turned to look at Stone, but he just shook his head. I think we both felt very tired all of a sudden. It had been an extremely long day.

The pair returned, dragging the groggy Charles between them: Veelya clearly amused to see the dignified retainer sporting Stone's clothes.

"I may as well have those back," said Stone, taking off his borrowed jacket.

We divested poor Charles of his jacket and trousers again. Back in his familiar outfit, the butler seemed to be more himself and less inclined to heart failure. Veelya couldn't seem to take her eyes off Stone as he put his pants back on, but I glared at her and she blushed and turned away.

After accepting the explanation of his betters, and our apologies, Charles stood up, straightened his jacket and his dignity, and said, "If that will be all, your Highness?"

"Yes, Charles. Thanks. And not a word, mind, to anyone," said Vyktor, rather imperiously.

"Of course, your Highness." Charles backed out of the room and closed the door silently behind him.

"Veelya," I began, "we have to get you and Vyktor out of here. There's a fire-mage called Sattine who's trying to kill you both."

Veelya's eyes widened in surprise. "Sattine? But he's a good friend of Lord Joslin's. He made some marvellous fireworks for the Jubilee celebrations last year, didn't he, Vyk?"

"It's a pretty safe bet that the two of them are in this together," Stone told them. "Joslin helps Sattine get rid of you both, then Sattine helps Joslin take over as regent."

"But if we were dead, he wouldn't be regent," said Vyktor.

Stone sighed. "Well, *emperor* then. Whatever you like. He might even call himself King of the Thousand Isles if he chose. What does it matter? The important thing is that we have to keep you both safe until we can get help to put a stop to their plans."

"Was Sattine responsible for those notes and things?" asked Vyktor, without looking at his sister.

"Yes," I said. "We're pretty sure he was. At least, one of his people would have been acting on his orders."

Brother and sister looked at each other, then glanced away quickly.

"What does Sattine get out of all this?" asked Veelya.

"We think he's after something that your family has. Something that's going to give him a great deal of power. Joslin might rule the country, but Sattine is going to have control of much, much more. Joslin will just be his puppet."

"Can you think of anything that might have a great deal of magical power?" asked Stone.

Vyktor and Veelya frowned as they concentrated. It was hard to think at this time of night, and thinking had never been one of their strong points.

"There's the Treasury, I suppose," ventured Veelya. "If he were after money, jewels, that kind of thing."

"This has to be something *very* special. Think. Do you have any family legends about some fabulous jewel, or stone?" I asked. "Does the black stone mean anything?"

They looked at each other some more.

"Do you suppose they mean the *Darkstone?*" asked Vyktor.

Veelya shrugged. "Could be."

"What's the Darkstone?" Stone and I asked together.

"It's kept in the family vault with the crown jewels," said Vyktor. "It's a large, black stone that sits in the centre of the Imperial Crown that was made for the first king of Elginagen. He defeated some great sorcerer, so the story goes. He cut out the sorcerer's heart and tossed it into a volcano. The volcano erupted then, and spewed out the heart at the king's feet. It had become the Darkstone."

"The Imperial Crown is only brought out for coronations," supplied Veelya. "No one gets to see it much. It's incredibly valuable."

"So where's the family vault?" Stone asked.

Another exchange of looks. "Only a *very few* people know that," said Veelya carefully.

Stone and I waited for more.

"It's a closely-guarded secret," added Vyktor.

"So?" I said.

"So, if Vee and I were to tell you, we would be violating the most sacred trust of the Royal House of Elginagen," he said, solemnly.

I slapped my head with exasperation. "Spare us the loyal heroics! We're talking *life and death* here, Vyktor."

He looked down at his feet, awkwardly.

"Vyktor, it's OK," said Stone, quietly. "You don't have to break a solemn vow. Just tell me, is there some special password, or code, that's necessary to open the vault?"

Vyktor was silent for a few moments. "Yes. Sort of."

"I see. Well, that's it then," said Stone. "We'll have to forget about it. Now, where can the two of you go that will be safe? We ought to be making a move – someone's going to come looking for you both before long."

I stared at Stone and couldn't believe he was giving up so easily. These two kids had the safety of the realm in their grasp and they were throwing it away for the sake of some old-fashioned sense of family duty. I wanted to yell and scream. Stone touched my arm, as if to reassure me, so I kept my mouth shut. To distract myself, I looked around the room. It was decorated in pleasant shades of dusty pink and pale green. Most of the walls were lined with a great many bookshelves. A small, inlaid writing table stood against one wall with a straight-backed chair in front of it, padded with a pink needlepoint seat and back rest. There were other chairs dotted around, but on the whole the room looked functional rather than somewhere, say, to have an afternoon nap.

"What's this room used for?" I asked.

"It was my mother's writing room," said Veelya. "She used to come here for an hour or two each morning and write her letters. And escape from my father, I think."

"Escape?"

"Yes. See that bookcase over there?" Veelya pointed to a floor-to-ceiling set of bookshelves stuffed with leather-bound volumes, all shades of yellowy-beige. "It opens up to another small room and a staircase out of the palace."

"*Veelya!*" I nearly shouted at her. "Why didn't you say so before? We could have all been long gone!"

"We haven't said that we're going yet!" Vyktor pointed out. "I personally think Veelya and I should stay. Now that we know what's going on, we know what to look out for."

"Silke and I can't keep you safe while you're in here and we're out there," said Stone. "This place is as much a prison as a fortress."

"Maybe," said Vyktor. "But we *know* it. We know all its hidey-holes and escape routes. Vee and I have grown up here, remember."

"But you don't know who your friends are," I said. "The very people who are closest to you might be your enemies. Think about the threatening notes, Vyktor. The curse box. And the dragon attack at the docks today. You and Veelya just aren't able to cope if magic is used against you. And believe me, Sattine is the best when it comes to magic."

There was a long silence as the two teenagers thought about what they should do.

But they had run out of time. We heard raised voices coming from the corridor. Someone was asking loudly if anyone had seen the prince and princess.

Veelya looked at her brother. "I think we'd better go with them, Vyk," she said.

He nodded. "OK."

"Should we go and get a few things to take—?" Veelya began.

"No!" Stone and I replied together.

Stone jerked his head at the room. "Where's this staircase?"

Veelya ran across the room and pulled out one of the

books on a shelf. As we watched, the whole section of bookcase rolled silently out exposing a dark room beyond.

We didn't need any urging. The four of us piled through the narrow doorway and the shelves rolled back into place behind us. It was very dark.

"Is there a glowlight anywhere?" I whispered.

" 'Fraid not," said Veelya. "This route isn't used much."

There was no avoiding it: I cupped a hand and drew some magefire into it. The light was just enough to show me where the staircase lay, and to enable me to make my way down it without tumbling headfirst, but there was always the danger that someone sensitive would detect the use of magic. I just had to hope the palace walls were thick enough to conceal us. The others followed me cautiously, each with one hand on the person in front. Stone brought up the rear.

Down and down we went, until I could go no further: I seemed to be up against a brick wall. Veelya pushed past me. I held my hand up so she could see and she pulled at a lever in the wall. Slowly the portion of wall moved outwards and revealed a passageway which I guessed was somewhere in the labyrinth of the kitchens. We stepped out into the passage and watched the wall slide back into place. There was nothing to distinguish it except a small portrait of a young woman sitting under a tree, her hand resting on the head of a fine-looking hunting dog.

"My grandmother," Veelya explained. "She had the staircase built."

"Sensible woman," I said. "Now where?"

"This way," said Vyktor, and he strode off down the passageway. We followed in his wake, but I was not at all happy. My ears throbbed and my gut was churning. This was all too easy. There was magic about and something was going to go wrong, I could tell. I didn't like situations out of my own control.

We stopped at an ancient leadwood door.

"This leads into the pantry," Vyktor whispered with a grin, and I could just imagine generations of royal children sneaking through here at dead of night for clandestine feasts.

He put his hand on the door latch to open it, when suddenly Stone grabbed his hand and stopped him. "*Wait!* There's someone on the other side," he whispered.

We all froze. But before we could back away, the latch rattled and the door suddenly swung open. Light streamed in from the room beyond and lit us all up like frightened rabbits, mesmerised by a snake. Momentarily blinded, I was only aware of the overpowering scents around us of assorted foodstuffs.

"Well, well!" said a voice that put a chill in my heart and my hand on my knife. "Your Royal Highnesses! I get the prize for finding you!"

"Good heavens!" said Veelya. "Vander! What are you doing here?"

"Looking for you, of course!" said the young man they called Vander, pleasantly. "There's been quite a hue and cry. Why don't you come through into the kitchen, and you can introduce me to your friend."

Friend? I looked round quickly. Stone had vanished.

Veelya looked round, too, and I managed to warn her with a look. "Oh, yes. This is my friend, Silke," she said. "Vyktor and I have been showing her some of the secret passages in the palace. Silke, this is Vander, the nephew of the Illithgarten Ambassador. Remember? I told you they'd be here today."

I stared coldly at Dervan who had stood back from the pantry door and was leaning indolently against it, his eyes glittering with amusement and a smug smile on his handsome face.

"I'm afraid you're mistaken, Princess," I told her. "This is not an ambassador's nephew, and his name's not Vander. He's a one-time street lord called Dervan. And if I'm not mistaken, he works for Sattine."

TEN

Dervan laughed easily. "Your friend has a very vivid imagination, Highness," he said. "A street lord? My, how very exciting! And who is this Sattine? But come, it's very late, you know. Too late for playing games. I think we'll all be better for a good night's sleep, don't you? We can all answer questions in the morning." He snapped his fingers and four security guards came into the kitchen to join us. It was getting very crowded.

"Escort their Royal Highnesses safely back to their rooms, sergeant. And we'll have to find a guest room for their friend."

Did I imagine it, or was there a particular emphasis on the word "guest"?

"You're taking a lot upon yourself for a mere ambassador's nephew, aren't you?" I said. "Who put *you* in charge of the prince and princess?"

"Yes, you are coming over a bit familiar, Vander,"

154

remarked Vyktor. He stared meaningfully at the guards. "Since when have palace security answered to you?"

Dervan smiled, unruffled. "Since Lord Joslin engaged my help to find you, Highness," he answered smoothly. "The sergeant and I were drafted to search down here. Weren't we, Chard?"

I saw the sergeant wince a little at the familiarity. He cleared his throat. "Er, yuss, er . . . sir!" he stammered.

"Well, then," said Dervan, as if that settled the matter. "Now, shall we go upstairs? I believe Lord Joslin wants to see you both before you retire. You gave him quite a fright, you know."

I bet.

"If you don't mind, your Highness," I said, addressing Veelya, "I'll be off now. It was good of you to see me, but it's best I get back. I don't sleep well in a strange bed."

"That's quite all right, Silke," she replied, playing the game. "Perhaps we can meet up at the usual place in the morning?"

"Fine." I moved to leave the kitchen by an outside door, but Dervan blocked my way out in an astonishingly quick move.

"Nice try, honey," he said so quietly that only I heard him, "but you're too good to lose now." He raised his voice. "Nonsense. We can't possibly allow you to roam the streets of Ysgard at this time of night. It wouldn't be safe. I insist you accept our hospitality. Besides, the palace is locked up for the night. It would upset the security system to unlock it now. Come, lady."

He smiled charmingly, but he had my arm twisted cruelly behind me in a way the others couldn't see, and the pain was excruciating.

"I wouldn't dream of upsetting your security system," I said between clenched teeth. I walked stiffly back to the others and he released my arm. For a brief moment I thought about taking him on, but the guards were watching me, and they all had stunners in their belts. I had to console myself with the knowledge that at least Stone was still a free agent.

For the second time that night – and what a long one it was turning out to be – I climbed up the flights of stairs to the royal apartments. We were a silent group. Security guards don't indulge in idle conversation anyway, but I was tired to the point of exhaustion, and the royal kids were doing their we-don't-talk-to-minions act. The higher we climbed, the less I cared what happened. I just wanted to sleep.

"In here, please." Dervan had stopped by a double door and pushed one half of it open. Veelya, Vyktor and I went in to an opulent room kitted out with some beautifully elegant furniture, old paintings, and drapes and swags made of rich brocade material. It was a vision of golds, blues and greens that almost hurt the eyes, and I couldn't begin to imagine how much it was all worth. Of course, Veelya and her brother had seen it all before. They only had eyes for the man sitting at a finely-carved leadwood desk, scribbling away on parchment. Some people just never seem to want to go to bed. Work, work, work.

"Joslin? What's going on?" asked Vyktor, nicely pompous.

The man stopped writing and looked up, as if he hadn't noticed our arrival, and then got to his feet. "Your Highness! There you are. I might ask you the same question. One minute you and the princess were with the good doctor and myself, and then you were gone with no explanation. We were very worried. Anything might have happened to you both."

He looked hard at me, as if he were suggesting that this was all my fault. Well, in a way I suppose it was. I stared back. My ears were prickling, and it wasn't just Dervan. This guy was definitely not what he seemed, but I couldn't yet tell what he was hiding. I wished, not for the first time, that I had Stone's skills.

"And this is . . . ?" he asked no one in particular.

"Silke," I supplied. "I'm a friend of Princess Veelya's."

He raised his brows and glanced at the princess for confirmation. "Have we met before?"

I looked harder at him. He seemed to be challenging me to remember something, but whatever it was, I was too weary to worry about it. He could have seen me at the Ambassador Club, I suppose.

"No, I don't think so," I replied.

Veelya looked at the timepiece on her bracelet: there was a small clock-face nestling amongst all the precious jewels in the wide gold band. "Joslin, we've all had rather a long day. I'm sorry if we caused you concern, but as you can see we are quite safe now, so if that's all you wanted us for, we'll say goodnight and go to our rooms. I trust my father is comfortable?"

Joslin looked as if he'd like to have said more, but it was too soon in the game for him to start throwing his weight around where Veelya and Vyktor were concerned. They were, after all, still the heirs to the throne; while he was just a rather highly-placed hireling with privileges.

"Yes, he is, I'm glad to say. I understand your wish to retire, Highness, but I would just like to point out before you go that just at the moment things are very difficult indeed with the king so ill. It is imperative that you both remain near to him . . . in case." He gave a polite cough. "It would not do for either of you to be . . . um . . . missing, shall we say, should anything happen. Might I suggest you sleep in the anteroom next to the king? I'll get the staff to bring you blankets."

"We understand, Lord Joslin," said Vyktor, "and commend your concern."

It seemed to me to be a good time to back out of the door, but of course, we still had Dervan to contend with. I turned my head to see him leaning nonchalantly against it, with that gloating expression that I was dying to smash with a fist.

"Have we a room for . . . um . . . our guest, Vander?" Joslin inquired.

"Oh yes, my Lord," he replied. He turned and pulled open the door again, inviting me through with a wave of his hand.

I turned back to Joslin. "This creep works for you, does he?" I tossed my head in Dervan's direction.

Joslin bristled visibly. I daresay no one had ever used that tone with him before. "You're very impertinent, young lady. I don't see that it's any concern of yours, but yes, he does. His uncle is the most devoted, loyal amb—"

"Yes, yes, I know," I cut him short. "The Ambassador of Illithgarten. So people keep telling me. I wonder what ever happened to the *real* nephew?"

Leaving that thought hanging in the air, I turned and went out of the room. As the door closed, I swung round and slammed my foot into Dervan's guts, but he forestalled me. He caught my foot before it made contact and twisted it painfully.

"Uh-uh," he said, shaking his head. "Forget it, Silke." He deftly tossed me over on to the floor, smacked me in the back with his knee – knocking all the breath out of me – and brought both my hands round, snapping them into silver wrist restraints. While I was still dragging air into my lungs, he hauled me by my belt back on to my feet. He was stronger than I remembered. "This way, sweetheart."

His hand firmly on my belt, he marched me along the corridor and down another set of stairs. I was beginning to feel I never wanted to see another staircase in my life. Two of the guards fell in behind us, their boots making a rhythmic tattoo on the stone floors.

We followed a rabbit warren of back stairs and corridors, each becoming progressively gloomier. Somehow I doubted these were the VIP guest quarters they were taking me to, but Dervan never hesitated in his route.

"Pretty much at home here, aren't you, Dervan?" I said.

"Oh, I've been coming here for *years*," he replied. "Those two royal brats never noticed me if I wasn't dressed up and accompanying old Talben at some function or other. They only know me as Vander." He laughed. "The tasty little Veelya even has a crush on me! You're never going to persuade that one that I'm anything but wonderful!"

"Talben's the ambassador, I take it."

"You got it. We have the real nephew in a safe place, don't worry."

"We?"

"Now, Silke," he purred in my ear. "Enough of that."

He yanked me back against himself and reached round me to unlock a door, taking time to nuzzle his face against my neck. "Mmmm. You taste good, Silke."

I kicked back sharply and felt my boot heel connect forcefully with his shin – hard enough to crack the bone.

He yelled in pain, then slammed me up against the wall and gave me two vicious backhanders across my face that jerked my head and split my lip open. He screamed a string of expletives at me, then threw me into the room with such force that I fell headfirst on to the floor, wrenching my arms and whacking my forehead on the stones. That hurt. It also stunned me for a while, and I had no strength to do anything but lie there: bruised, aching and exhausted, and mentally kicking myself for having stupidly made him mad when I could have played along and maybe got him to tell me more. I was aware of the door slamming shut, but nothing else.

ELEVEN

I don't know how long I lay there, or whether I slept or was just unconscious for a while. I was cold, stiff and had the mother of all headaches. There were no windows in this "guest" room, except a small grille in the door, so there was no natural light to shine on me and wake me up. There certainly wasn't a maid with a fresh cup of kashla and plate of hot, buttered breakfast cakes.

But there were noises. With my ear literally to the ground, I could hear tiny scratches, squeaks, the occasional flapping noise and then the soft dragging sound of something moving very carefully. Towards me. I opened an eye and peered into the blackness.

Nothing in front of me that I could see.

Shuuuuush . . . click, click . . . shuuuush . . . shuuuush.

I carefully rolled on to my other shoulder. There! Two small globes of light, about two metres away from me. *Eyes?* But to what kind of creature did they belong? I swallowed, but my mouth was dry. My wrists were cramped underneath me in their restraints: I needed my hands free if I was going to raise any magefire. I hauled myself awkwardly on to my knees, and then on to my feet, never taking my eyes off those pale lights. There was another scuffling sound, and another set of eyes moved up alongside the first. I stared until my eyes smarted. Then I heard a small sound to my right, higher up. I snapped my head round and gave a little shriek, as I looked into two multi-faceted globes on a level with my own. Could these things fly? Climb up walls? Suspend themselves from the ceiling?

I really didn't want to know. As I struggled to wrench my hands from the bracelets, something heavy, with sharp points, landed on my back. I screamed, and twisted my body into some bizarre dance to dislodge whatever it was that had fallen on me. The things on the floor seized their opportunity and scuttled in. One of them fastened itself to my leg, another clung to my sleeve. I was terrified, and imagined hundreds of the things waiting to attack. Not knowing what they were only added to my horror: for all I knew they could have venomous bites, or lay parasitic eggs. I had visions of being eaten alive down in this hole and no one being any the wiser.

I staggered over to a wall and threw myself against it, trying to crush whatever was on my back. I felt a disgusting damp stickiness soak through my jacket. Then I twisted round and tried to smash the creature on my sleeve, but only knocked it off. I kicked at the one on my leg with my other foot. Something flapped in my face and I ducked away, but there was a sharp pain in my cheek as another of the creatures flew at me. Screaming and sobbing, I slammed my face into the wall and the thing dropped away.

And then the door opened.

"Get me out of here! Help! Please, get me out of here!" I sobbed hysterically, my face and body jammed up against the wall so nothing could fly at me again.

"Be quiet!" Someone grabbed me with strong hands, pulling at me. I heard curses, and small bodies slapped against walls and floor as they were kicked and slapped out of the way. Then I was shoved roughly through the doorway and the door was shut behind us. I could still hear sickening thuds as the creatures threw themselves at the heavy wood.

I sank to the floor of the corridor, sobbing and shaking with terror.

"It's OK, Silke. It's OK." Cool hands were wiping at the blood and tears on my face. I winced as they touched the cuts and bruises.

"Stone?" I couldn't stop my teeth chattering, so the word came out all trembly.

"That's me!" He spoke very softly, like you might do to a rabid dog you didn't want to upset. "I tracked you down but had to wait till everyone had gone to bed."

I never thought I'd be so glad to see anyone in my life. I threw myself against him, pushing my face into his chest, and he wrapped his arms awkwardly about me, patting my back while I howled and shook.

"Hey, you're all right, Silke. You're all right. They're gone," he whispered. "But we can't stay here. You must come away, Silke. Come on. Before someone hears us. Up you get!"

He helped me to my feet and I sniffed and rubbed my face awkwardly on my sleeve, like some pathetic, wet-nosed kid. I was so ashamed, I wasn't sure I'd ever be able to look at him again. My lank, untidy hair flopped over my face, but I was glad of it: I couldn't bear anyone to see that I'd been *crying*, or to know that I'd been scared witless by crawlies.

But, of course, Stone knew all that. He led the way silently down the dark labyrinth that made up the cellars of Ysgard Palace, and I followed meekly, trying hard to get a grip on myself and rid myself of the feel of those *things* on my skin, even if I couldn't dismiss the areas of pain where their claws and teeth had penetrated.

At the first opportunity, I asked Stone what time it was. Sleep and light deprivation were having a weird effect on my brain and I needed to get reality back into perspective.

"About half three," he whispered. "We have to get out of here before the day shift arrive."

I'd forgotten that. Chambermaids and kitchen staff

probably began work at something like four-thirty in the morning.

"What about the kids?" I whispered back. He'd know I meant Veelya and Vyktor.

He shook his head. "They'll be OK while the king's alive. You and I can't do anything while we're trapped in here."

Suddenly I recognised where we were. There was the portrait of Veelya's grandmother on the wall! So the pantry door should be somewhere nearby, if I could only get my brain to work. At least I'd stopped trembling.

"Here." Stone plucked my sleeve again and drew me to the door. He waited for a minute or two with his head pressed against it, then slowly turned the handle and lifted the latch. It was impossible to do it silently. We just had to hope there was no one near enough to hear it. "Come on!"

Those intoxicating pantry smells surrounded us again, but I was much too strung out to feel hungry. We inched past hams and sausages dangling from a ceiling beam; shelves piled high with jars of preserves; bags of dried pulses; cheeses and bread bins. When we came through the first time I never noticed it all. We skirted baskets of onions and sacks of flour and tuberous vegetables, until we finally reached the door to the kitchens. Stone opened it carefully and peered out. He waved at me to follow.

This room was much the same as when I'd been in it earlier, except someone had put piles of crockery and cutlery on the table in readiness for breakfast. There was no one around, but we could both hear the clatter of pans and the sound of a grate being vigorously emptied of ash in one of the other kitchens beyond.

Stone jerked his head towards the outside door. We went across and he tried the handle, then shook his head. Locked. I looked around for a likely hiding place for a spare key. Stone looked too. Then I noticed the narrow stone shelf built into the wall over the door itself. I nudged Stone and he looked up, following my gaze. He reached up and ran careful fingers along the shelf, dislodging some dust and plaster as he did so. Then his fingers closed on to something and he grinned down at me, flourishing a key in my face.

We were outside in seconds. I stopped for a moment just to breathe fresh air, but the sky was already streaked with grey dawn, and we had no time to waste. We'd come out from a different door to the one we'd gone in, so we needed to get our bearings. At this point we almost came to blows – or would have done if I'd had my hands free – because Stone wanted to go one way and I wanted to go the other. Instead we hissed and snarled at each other until finally Stone threw up his hands in a way that said, "OK, have it your way" and gestured to me to lead on.

Relying on my Ellanoi senses, which admittedly hadn't been too wonderful lately, I picked a route carefully round the building, pausing behind trash bins and anything else that gave us cover. Twice we heard voices and the sounds of people going about their usual morning routines, but there was no tramp of guards' boots, grunts from dargbeasts, or shouts of panic or alarm. And then I saw the door in the wall that we'd come through, what felt like weeks ago. But it was open, and one of the kitchen staff was standing right in our path, talking to a woman delivering milk churns. Stone and I just had to stay flat behind a stack of wooden delivery boxes, listening to them exchange bantering insults and speculations about the weather.

As we crouched there, I became aware of a pungent smell coming from the box by me. There was a label stuck to the side. I twisted a little to read it and discovered that it was the delivery company's advice note for a consignment of twenty measures of pressed silith root. *For the attention of Lord Joslin. Perishable. Store away from light, etc etc.* My mind did a quick replay of my visit to Esther and her chance remark about the price and scarcity of silith root. It looked as if Joslin might be buying it all. Why? But just then I heard the two at the door taking their farewells, and seconds later, the sound of a milk churn being rolled towards the kitchen door, metres from where we were hiding.

As soon as it was safe, Stone helped me up and we walked briskly past the kitchens and out of the door that still stood ajar. No one challenged us. Once through, we ran down

Tork Street as fast as we could, with Stone gripping my arm so that I didn't lose my balance. It's not easy running with your wrists tied behind you.

Now that the immediate danger was past, I was aware of only two things: I wanted to get the restraints off me, and I was starting to feel very ill. I ached all over, and my face was throbbing from the different cuts and bruises it had been dealt lately.

What I said was, "I really, really hope those bloodsucking crawlies jump all over Dervan when he opens that cell door!"

TWELVE

Even at four in the morning there were cabs to be had in Ysgard; we flagged one down only three streets away from the palace. If the cabbie noticed my wrist restraints, he didn't bat an eyelid. Wise man. We decided it would be best to go to Stone's place rather than mine. Dervan knew my apartment, so it would be the first place he'd look for me. On the trip across town, I filled Stone in about Dervan and how he had been passing himself off as a diplomat's nephew. There were some things, of course, I kept to myself: like Dervan and I having a history.

We tiptoed through Stone's front door so as not to wake his father, who slept on the ground floor because of his disability, and Stone took me through to the spacious kitchen. He immediately pulled out a toolbox from a cupboard and found some heavy-duty wire cutters. They made short work of the restraints.

"Nice place," I said, rubbing my wrists and feeling

relieved that we *weren't* at my apartment. I'd make pretty sure that Stone never saw it, either.

"Thanks. It's Dad's really, but because of his life expectancy he's already signed it over to me." He was already busy pouring drinks for us both. I didn't care what I had, as long as it was wet and cold, but one swallow told me it was chilled blackfruit juice. *Mmmm*.

"Well, I can understand that," I said after knocking back half the glass. "But what's to stop *you* getting taken out before your three-score years and ten, or whatever it is you humans consider a normal life?" I slumped wearily into a chair at the kitchen table and leaned it back against the wall, shutting my eyes to rest them.

Stone took a long swig of his own drink. "We might not be able to match Ellanoi standards, but I should be most put out if I didn't reach *five* score years and ten at least."

I grunted. "What's wrong with your dad, anyway?"

"Oh, one of these slow, debilitating diseases of the nervous system that they can't cure," he replied. I could relate to that. I had one of those myself right now.

"Before you fall asleep," he said, "I think we'd better do something with those cuts and bruises. Stay there – I'll get the first-aid box."

He was gone a while and I dozed, but when he came back he was towing a sleepy-eyed, tall Narthian man behind him, and carrying what looked like a medical bag.

I sat up sharply.

"We're in luck!" said Stone. "This is Trace. I found him bunking in one of the spare bedrooms. He's Dad's nurse. Apparently Dad hasn't been too good, so Trace stayed here while I was out. I've asked him to look at you."

I blinked. "Gee. Thanks, Stone." I wasn't at all sure about this. I never have anything to do with doctors, medics, or sickshops. Apart from being deeply suspicious of them, they usually cost an arm and a leg (literally). "But I'm not sure we should drag Trace out of bed, should we, just to look at a couple of bruises?" I was on my feet and backing away from them without realising it.

But Trace was immediately all professional, which probably said a lot about my appearance. Gone was the sleepy-eyed look as soon as he saw me. He took the bag from Stone and put it on the table, then firmly pressed me back down into my chair, brooking no argument. "You've got more than a few bruises here," he said. "What happened?" He busied himself pulling stuff out of his kitbag. When the hypo appeared, I began to feel faint.

"Hey. You're not going to stick me with that thing!"

"Silke," sighed Stone, taking a seat opposite me at the table. "He knows what he's doing. Let the guy do his job, will you?"

"I am *not* – repeat not – having any hypos. So there."

"Fine. No hypos. So are you going to tell me what made

all this mess of your face?" Trace tipped some antiseptic liquid on to a pad and started to wipe it over my skin. It stung like seven hells, but with two guys watching me it was more than my life was worth to complain.

"Ahh . . . well, the cut lip was a backhander. Um . . . the forehead was an intimate meeting with a stone floor."

"What about your cheek?"

I glanced at Stone. "Dunno. Some hideous crawler that flew at me."

Trace looked to Stone for an explanation, but Stone just rubbed his jaw with a hand as if thinking about what to say. Meanwhile, Trace stuck something in my ear and took a temperature reading. He looked at the result and shook his head.

"I don't know what they were," Stone admitted. "They were in this . . . er . . . cellar. Small things. Like flying rats with a lot of legs and bug eyes. Never seen them before, sorry. Never want to again, either."

Trace shook his head. "Well, I don't like these wounds. They're showing signs of infection already. The creatures may have been poisonous."

"What?" I sat up straighter. "Can't you fix it? Don't you have an anti . . . anti . . . whatsit?"

"Antidote?" Trace supplied. "Not unless I know what it was that bit you. I could give you a fast-acting antibiotic, which might slow down the infection."

"Yeah, right. That'll do," I said, desperate. I was having visions of dying an agonising death, or maybe even morphing into some hideous monster.

Trace looked smug. "It'll mean a hypo."

"Aw, no."

"Silke! Don't be a baby," said Stone, mildly.

"Did you get bitten anywhere else?" Trace asked. He was still working on my face, daubing on salve and sticky strips to catch the edges of the wounds together. I must have looked a picture.

"Not sure. One landed on my back. Another grabbed my arm and another my leg."

"Let me see."

I stared. "What?"

"Young woman, I can't treat a wound I can't see, now can I?"

I saw Stone covering up a smile. I glared at him and he got the message. He picked up his glass and stood up. "I'll just go and wait in the other room," he said, all diplomacy.

Reluctantly, and painfully, I shucked off my jacket and then took my shoes off so I could work off my snug trousers. I was wearing a sleeveless knit top under the jacket, and pants under the trousers, so felt fairly modest. As the jacket fell to the floor, I could see all the grisly stains on the back of it. No way was that going back on until I'd cleaned it.

I looked at Trace. "Enough?"

He said nothing but just gestured with his long fingers that the top would have to go as well. I sighed. He shook his head as if there was no understanding the prudishness of some people, but his hands were gentle as he turned me round to look at my back.

I felt the swab sweeping over my shoulder blade, and knew by the stabs of pain and tender flesh that there were open wounds there, too. I had to hand it to Trace: he was thorough. He examined my arms and legs, treated my wrist sores and checked nearly every inch of me for further damage. He looked into my eyes for signs of concussion, then in my mouth. Satisfied, he told me to get dressed again. While I did that, he filled his hypo. I shut my eyes and braced myself for the worst.

Trace gave a small laugh when he saw my face screwed up with anticipation.

"Relax!" he said. "I haven't killed anyone yet."

Grudgingly, I had to admit I barely felt the small sting in my arm.

"All done," he said, packing away his kit. He turned to the door and called Stone into the kitchen.

"OK, Silke?" said Stone, looking at me.

"Yeah. I suppose so," I growled.

"Now listen, both of you," said Trace, frowning from Stone to me. "I don't know what's caused these lesions, but

I do know that the cocktail I've given you will not prevent poisoning, or any allergic reaction. My advice is that you see a specialist as soon as you can. Drink lots of fluids. And get plenty of rest. The more you move around, the quicker the toxins will circulate in your system. Now, if you don't mind, I'm going back to bed."

We listened solemnly to his directives, but deep down I thought he was just being a typical alarmist medic. The thought crossed my mind that I would go and see Esther if the opportunity arose, but Stone and I had far more important things to do first, like finding the Darkstone before Sattine got hold of it.

Trace turned back just before he disappeared out of the door. "By the way, it's only fair to tell you that you'll feel pretty drowsy before long." He gave me a triumphant grin and I scowled back at him. *The rat.*

"I've made a bed up for you, Silke," said Stone. "This way."

I was going to protest, but then I felt the sedative Trace had slipped me begin to kick in. I shut myself in the room Stone gave me and just managed to throw off my clothes, roll into the bed and pull up the covers, before I crashed out cold.

Then the dreams came. I was in fire. I was standing on a black rock surrounded by molten lava that spat and bubbled and roared and I basked in the sulphurous heat. I was the fire. It flowed from me. I lifted my hands and stretched up to the black heavens and I felt myself shout out the power of fire within me. I shouted again and heard the beating of vast wings. Hundreds of them. Dragons! I was calling dragons! But as they came nearer I saw that they weren't dragons at all. They were black, with black membranous wings, long red talons on their feet and hands. Cruel teeth. Bat-like ears and long tails ending in stringy hair. Their black bodies were thin and naked, encrusted with pus-filled sores and scabs. They hissed and spat like the lava, their foul breath making me gag.

"We come!" they whispered into my fevered head. "Who calls us? You are not the same one. But you look like him."

I screamed.

I woke up suddenly, completely disoriented. My head was buzzing with the horrible images of my dream and I was afraid they would never go away.

I was in a strange bed, in a strange, darkened room. My mouth was so dry my tongue was glued to the roof of it. There was a small glowlight on a stand by my bed and I could just make out a figure sitting in a chair, facing me. I was aware of an elusive, green-woody smell. For the life of me I could not remember where I was or what I had been doing. I tried to sit up, but a pain shot through my head and I had to lie back against the pillow again.

I heard the person in the chair stand up and come across to the bed, rattling and jingling for some reason.

"You feeling better, dearie?"

I stared into the gloom. "*Esther?*" I rasped. "What are you doing here?"

Esther picked up a cup and put a hand under my head. "Here, child. Have a sip of this."

I sipped at the drink, but pulled away with a shudder. It was bitter and smelled aromatic.

"Now, drink it all, pet," coaxed Esther. "You've been very poorly, but old Esther has kept you with us. My word, you did give that young man of yours a fright. Came banging on my door at crack of dawn he did. Dragged me right across town in that fancy transpo of his. Hoo hoo! You've never seen old Esther look so nobby!"

I was very confused. "Where are we? What time is it?"

"Well, dearie, you're in Mr Stone's house. As for time, it must be about mid afternoon I suppose."

"I've slept all day?"

Esther shook with laughter.

"Bless me, no," she said. "You've been out for *three days*, child! You had such a temperature: anyone without magefire in their blood would have popped their socks. But it was the poison that was causing all the trouble. Fortunately, Esther had seen it before and knew just what would sort it out. And that nice young Narthian has

been very attentive, dearie. Despite all his medical learnin'
he didn't mind old Esther bringing in her own healin'.
Give him his due, what he don't know about looking after
sick folk don't bear worrying about. You couldn't have
been in better hands with the two of us, though I says it
myself."

Three days! I couldn't believe it. "I must get up, Esther!
It's very important . . ." I struggled to sit up again, despite
the throbbing pain.

"Now, don't talk nonsense! If you think you can stand
the light, I'll open the shutters a little way." Esther went
over to the windows and let in a crack of afternoon light.
Immediately my eyes smarted and I had to turn my face
away.

"There, you see?" she said. "The eyes are always affected.
And I daresay you've got a few troll hammers going in your
skull, too. Aren't I right? So you just stay where you are for
a bit and I'll go and get you some nice soup."

I lay back, realising I was far too weak to go anywhere,
and shut my hurting eyes. *Three days!* I'd never been this ill
in my whole life.

"Hi. How are you feeling?" A guy's voice.

I opened my eyes again. "Stone?"

He came closer to the bed. "Yeah. That's the one. Good
to have you back again!"

I smiled. "I guess I've been a bit of a pain. Sorry."

"Don't worry about it. You can thank Trace and your friend Esther for pulling you back from the brink."

"She said you went to fetch her. What made you go there?" Despite feeling sleepy still, I was hungry for information. Stone looked as if he didn't want to get into a long explanation at this time, but my expression must have moved him.

"Trace didn't have the know-how to counteract the poison in your system. You started burning up, and then your skin broke out in purple blotches. We put you in ice, but it wasn't enough. I remembered that place you went to in Lepp Street, and so I went round there and told Esther what your symptoms were. She seemed to know exactly what you needed, so we grabbed stuff and I brought her back with me. She and Trace have been working shifts with you the last three days. I have to take Esther back to her shop for a few hours each day, and bring her back here in the evening."

"What about you?" I asked. "Have you heard any news from the palace? Are the kids all right?"

At that moment, Esther bustled in carrying a tray with a bowl on it.

"Now then, master Lucius. That's enough of that. You'll get our patient all agitated and it'll undo all our good work. They'll be plenty of time to talk when she gets stronger. Here we are, my lovely. A nice bowl of hot soup. My own

180

recipe. It'll soon get you back on your feet. And there's someone else to see you, isn't there, my pet?"

I saw Stone smile and move away. Something grey and furry jumped on to the bed and padded delicately up to me.

"Hey! Juniper!" I said, grinning foolishly. The old cat pushed his head into my hand, then circled a few times and made himself comfortable at my side. I could feel his purrs vibrating into the mattress.

"Juniper used to sleep on my bed when I was a kid," I told Stone.

He nodded. "Esther says animals can help invalids get better quicker, so we're trying it out. If it works, I might get one for my dad!" He went over to sit in the chair while Esther perched on the edge of the bed to give me my soup.

I so wanted to hear about everything, but with my last mouthful of soup a great weariness swept over me. I snuggled back down as Esther closed the window shutters again, and went back to sleep.

"Alley-oi, Silke?" People were calling me. "Where are you, Silke? Answer us. We need you." In my dream, I was drawn inexorably to their whispery voices.

"Here I am!" I said.

"Where? We cannot see you!" And then I recognised them. It was the demons!

"No!" I cried. "I don't want you. I never called you. Go back! Leave me alone!"

"We cannot leave you, Silke. You belong to us. You have drunk of the ghoulswine. It will bind us to you for ever. Tell us where you are, Silke. Tell us where you are."

"Never! Never!"

Cold claws snatched at my wrists and held on to my hands. I tried to shake them off . . .

I awoke to find I was feebly trying to pull my wrist away from long cool fingers that held firmly on to it. I looked up to see Trace standing there, patiently checking my pulse.

"Trace!"

Trace just nodded. "You were having a bad dream. Shot your pulse up a bit. But you're making good progress. Your Ellanoi powers of recuperation, I suppose. Would you like the washroom? A warm bath would do you good, and I could change your bedclothes."

"Well, yeah. OK, then." I carefully shifted myself up on the pillow, but Trace held up a hand.

"Wait there while I get it ready for you."

No problem. I lay back and idly stroked Juniper, who was still fast asleep at my side. He purred and rolled over a little, so I could scratch his belly. I reached over to the small table beside the bed and helped myself to a glass of what looked like water. The dream had faded into nothingness and I was definitely feeling much better. I could have a bath, get dressed and seek out Stone for some long talking. Maybe have something to eat. Good plan. Then it occurred to me that I didn't have a stitch on.

I was just looking around for some clothes, when Trace came back.

"Ready?" he said.

"Uh . . ."

He swept back the bedclothes and scooped me up as if I weighed nothing at all, then strode across the hallway with me and into the bathroom, depositing me gently into a bath of warm water. I was too stunned and embarrassed to speak.

"I'll leave you to have a good soak," he said. "Here are some towels and some of Lucius's clothes to put on. We don't have much else for you to wear, I'm afraid. He'll have to go and get some stuff for you. Back in a while."

He went out, closing the door. I shook my head. Maybe it was because I had been ill: I was feeling very vulnerable and stupid.

I got down to the serious business of washing away the sourness of the last four days. I found foaming stuff to lather all over myself, and some other stuff for my hair. I scrubbed and lathered and scrubbed, till I felt clean again and my hair squeaked when I rubbed it. Then I got carefully out of the bath and dried myself. It was then I caught sight of my reflection in the mirror – and my mouth fell open in shock.

Some emaciated, hollow-cheeked waif stood before me, with untidy strings of wet weed stuck to her head and shoulders, her face blotched with purple-yellow bruises and dark red scabs over cuts. Pale lavender eyes, much too large, were ringed with yellow, under swollen red eyelids. And all over my face and torso were blotches of purple-tinged skin, like I had somehow been tie-dyed.

It was while I was staring, frozen, at this horrible spectacle, that Trace came back into the bathroom. He must have seen the look on my face.

"Don't worry about it," he said. "You'll be good as new in a few days. Here, let me help."

Dumbly, I let him help me step into a pair of casual grey pants with a tie belt. I held up my arms while he pulled a short-sleeved white knitted shirt over my head. They were both too big, but I was too depressed to care. Trace picked me up again and took me back to my room. The professionally turned-down bed looked tidy and clean. There was no sign of Juniper, but he'd probably gone out for a stroll. He hated disturbance. The window shutters were open, and daylight made the room bright and welcoming. Under normal circumstances I would have enjoyed it.

"Sit in the chair a minute and I'll dry your hair," said Trace, standing me on a soft rug. I took a few shaky steps and then sat in the chair he pulled forward. Trace rubbed at my hair with a dry towel, massaging my scalp at the same time. It felt very strange, but oddly comforting. I couldn't remember even Esther drying my hair for me.

I felt a comb pushed into my hand. "You'd better comb it. I might pull."

I smiled and began to draw the comb through my long green locks that reached almost to my waist. *Weeds*, I thought. *Rank weeds. I'd like to cut them all off.*

"Could you cut it off for me, Trace?"

There was a silence. "You want your hair cut off?" Trace asked slowly, as if he thought he hadn't heard me right.

"Please."

"Are you sure? Maybe you'd better wait for Lucius, or Esther, to—"

"No, Trace. You do it. They'll probably try to make me change my mind."

"You're feeling low. Don't do anything you'll regret . . ."

"It's OK, Trace. Please do it. Now."

He went away to get some scissors and came back with a large towel as well, which he spread on the floor. I got up out of the chair and he repositioned it over the towel, then I sat down again. I felt him parting my hair at the back and lifting up a hank.

"How short?" he asked.

"Three thumbs."

I heard a sigh of relief. "You just want it shortened by three thumbs?"

"No. I only want it three thumbs long. My thumbs, not yours!" His were twice the length of mine.

Silence again. Then I felt the scissors making slow, careful cuts. With my head bent, I watched long strands of newly-washed, glittering green hair tumble to the floor and litter the towel spread under my chair. The familiar weight of it was falling away: my head felt cool and light. It was like saying goodbye to some part of me that was no longer important. I felt new.

"There." Trace brushed the last cut strand from my shoulder and blew away a few stray snippets so they didn't fall down my neck. "Go and sit on the bed and I'll clear this away."

I watched him shake the hair to the centre of the towel, then roll it up neatly. In minutes the room was back to looking spotless and neat.

"I expect Esther would be glad of the hair," I said.

Trace regarded me, an odd look in his eyes. "Maybe, but she's not having it."

Whatever else Trace felt about Esther, he certainly didn't trust her enough to leave something as valuable as my hair in her hands. If she were a disreputable witch (which she wasn't, as far as I was concerned), it would give her a great deal of power over me. I didn't bother to point out to him that she'd had no end of opportunities to simply cut some off if she'd wanted to.

I ran my fingers through my new hairstyle and felt a mad urge to giggle. When Trace came back and handed me a large pair of thick socks to wear instead of shoes, the hysteria bubbled up inside me. The socks were designed for someone with feet three times the size of mine and they flopped around like dead flippers. I rolled on the bed howling with helpless laughter, gasping and snorting, tears pouring down my face.

Trace took a firm hold of my shoulders and sat me upright with a little shake.

"Take some deep breaths, Silke, and calm down."

I hiccupped and laughed and cried some more. It was all so *funny*. And Trace's long Narthian face was so *serious*. That was funny, too.

"Want me to get my hypo?" he said.

That did it. I took a gulp of air and let it out in a quick huff. Trace handed me a handkerchief and I blew my nose and wiped my eyes.

"No," I said, with careful dignity. "That won't be necessary." I shot him a crafty look. "But I'd really like a plate of hot, buttered breakfast cakes with slices of crisp, smoked vorpel meat and two fried darvil eggs sunny-side up. Oh, and lots of fresh kashla with two spoons of sweetener."

THIRTEEN

When Lucius came home later that day, having taken Esther back to her shop, he found me sitting on his sofa wrapped in a wool rug (Trace's idea) with Juniper asleep on my lap. His dad was reminiscing about the glory days when his books had made him a household name. Trace was folded into an armchair, reading some dry medical journal.

It hadn't taken me long to appreciate that Marcus now lived in a little world of his own, cushioned by drugs. He had his lucid moments (he had been *very* lucid at the Sunfire Rooms) but more often than not he acted like a character lost in one of his own books, even forgetting that he was an invalid. How he managed to attend such public gatherings as that posh book launch, I couldn't imagine. He had no notion of having seen me before, or indeed why I was in his home, but just took me for granted. It spared me some awkward explaining. Trace told me that Marcus spent most of his day working on his next novel, but that it was mostly gobbledegook. Still, you never know – that might be the next literary craze. There was no accounting for taste.

I saw now what Esther had meant when she said Trace was good at looking after sick people. Watching him with Marcus was a humbling experience. No way could I ever be so patient and forbearing. It went beyond professional duty.

The door opened and Stone walked in. "Hi, Dad. Trace," he said, then stared hard at me, pretending to show no sign of recognition. "Hello. Have we met?"

I grinned. "It's my new image," I replied, carelessly dragging my short hair into spikes. "The black and blue look, offset by startled green. Everybody will be sporting it by next season."

"I might pass on that one," he said with a smile. "Short hair suits you, Silke. I'm glad you're feeling better. Are you up for some fast food, or still sticking to Esther's soup?"

There was a snort from Trace.

"What do *you* think?" I said, gently tossing off the cat and my rug and following him out to the kitchen on legs still a bit wobbly. My floppy socks were quite a safety hazard, too, so all things considered, I had to move carefully.

There were a number of takeaway packages on the table, giving off exquisite aromas.

"Does your dad have his meals with you, too?" I asked, as Stone busied himself with plates and cutlery. I sat at the

189

table, feeling strong enough to eat, but not to stand up. I undid a few of the packets and sniffed the contents, barely able to keep from drooling.

"Not now. Trace looks after him. His rooms are better equipped for someone in a wheelchair." I sensed he didn't really like talking about his father. I never knew mine, so I didn't have to watch him die. My thoughts drifted to Veelya and her brother and wondered how they were coping. They were both pretty disparaging about their family, but that may just have been a front to cover up their real feelings.

Stone divided up the contents of the takeaways, poured us drinks and took a seat opposite me. We ate for a few minutes in silence, then I said, "We need to talk about the case, Stone. And we need a plan."

"I know. Esther figured you were over the worst, by the way, and didn't need her any more. She was worried about losing her customers."

"That's OK. The thought of Trace's hypo will keep me from any relapse."

He gave a tired smile. "The palace has issued a press statement to say that all royal engagements have been cancelled until further notice."

"OK. That means the family is now under house arrest, I suppose."

Stone nodded. He ate silently for a while and I had a

feeling that there was something he was turning over in his mind, perhaps wondering how he was going to broach it.

"Silke, I know you and Esther go back a long way together . . ."

"Uh-huh."

He shifted uncomfortably.

"Say what's on your mind, Stone."

"She knows stuff, but wasn't letting on. I don't mean anything about being a witch, or the deals she does with some of her clients. I mean, she knew about the creatures that bit you, and she knew about the poison."

I stared at him. "What do you mean?"

He shrugged. "It's just what I picked up from her. She was edgy and nervous and trying to hide it. It was very easy for me to read her, Silke. There were images of those . . . creatures . . . in her mind. And Sattine. She's very afraid of him. I think he has some hold over her."

"So, in other words, you think Esther is involved in all this somehow?"

He nodded, watching me to see how I'd respond. "But I think it's probably an involuntary involvement. Sattine could be blackmailing her, or just threatening to . . . put her out of action."

I thought it over. What would Sattine need from Esther? With her specialist knowledge, she'd make a very expert consultant for anyone wanting to work organic magic to their advantage. She was also an opportunist: she'd always been quick to recognise a potentially profitable situation and wasn't too bothered if it was legal or not. But she was not a sophisticated soul. It wouldn't take much for Esther to get completely out of her depth. Working for Sattine might very well count as just that. Yes, I could imagine Esther embroiled in a very unpleasant relationship with my scheming brother.

"When I was there," I said carefully, "she mentioned what I thought was just a throwaway piece of information. She told me silith root was becoming very hard to get hold of, and very expensive. I didn't think anything of it at the time, but then when we were sneaking out of the palace I noticed those wooden cases outside the kitchens. They held a consignment of silith root for Lord Joslin."

"What's silith root used for?" asked Stone.

"No idea."

His brow shot up.

I shrugged. "Just because I shared my early life with a witch, I didn't necessarily pick up all there is to know about herblore. I wasn't much interested in that stuff."

"Well, I daresay we can ask her, or find out some other way."

"How about the Darkstone? Isn't it more important that we find that?" I asked.

He shook his head. "I know where the Darkstone is. But there's a bigger picture here that we need to discover. Sattine's plan is undoubtedly a complex one. I can't believe it's just about becoming a super-mage."

"Just back up a bit there," I said. "Did I hear you right? Did you say you *know* where the Darkstone is?"

"Yes."

He was being insufferably close with his information. "Well?"

"It was easy," he said eventually. "Remember when I asked Vyktor about the royal vault? He obligingly visualised it for me in his head."

Light dawned. "And then you asked him if there was an access code to the vault . . ."

"And he thought about that, too. So I just lifted them from him."

"So where is it?"

"It's in Blackstone Keep, of course. The very name is a clue. That place was tailor-made for defence. What better place to secure the crown jewels?"

"Well, well," I mused. "And do you suppose Sattine knows this?"

"I'd be surprised, as he would have taken it by now. The keep is a good base for him. I imagine he negotiated with Joslin to allow him to move in while he put his master plan into operation. Want some dessert, or kashla?"

I switched back mentally to eating mode. "What's the dessert?"

Stone flung open the double doors of the coldstore and peered among the shelves. He took a bowl of something out, stared at it, then tossed it into the waste disposal. He picked up another dish and sniffed at it. That went the same way. I was beginning to lose my appetite.

"Iced cream," he said, finally.

"That'll do. Thanks." As far as I knew, iced cream couldn't give you food poisoning, but they do say ignorance is bliss.

He took out a large tub of something pink and yellow, pulled off the lid and scooped a couple of spoonfuls into two dishes. Then he poured sauce from a bottle over both and set a dish in front of me. It was surprisingly good.

The kashla jug went on the thermal ring, ready for when we wanted it.

I was beginning to feel almost a whole person again, even if I did look like a walking disaster. One thing about being Ellanoi: we heal fast. I just needed some good, hard exercise and a few days of nourishing food and I'd be back to normal. The thought spurred me to get to my feet and pour us both some kashla.

"Thanks," said Stone as I put a cup in front of him. He gave a little smile as he watched me go through the routine with the sweetener. "By the way, if you ever want to work

194

out, Trace can show you where we keep the exercise machines. Don't overdo it, though."

I narrowed my eyes at him, but his face remained blandly innocent, so I gave him the benefit of the doubt: deciding that he *wasn't* reading my thoughts.

"I might do that," I said, taking a sip of my drink.

Stone leaned back in his chair and stretched out his long legs. "I didn't finish telling you about what I picked up from Esther. I need to digress a little."

"OK."

"The symptoms that you developed, Silke: the blue blotches on your skin, fever, delirium, loss of weight—"

"Excuse me?" I frowned. "Delirium?"

"It's OK," he grinned. "Your secrets are safe with me."

"What kind of stuff did I come out with?" I asked, feeling very alarmed.

"Nothing incriminating, Silke. I'm only joking. Most of it was in Ellanoi, anyway. But you did have a few nightmares."

I nodded. That was an understatement. "Go on, then."

"Well, remember when I went into the king's room, pretending to be the butler?" I nodded again. "The king showed signs of having the same symptoms. I remember thinking that his skin looked discoloured. He was feverish and thin, and kept up a constant muttering. I didn't think much of it at the time, after all everyone knows he has a wasting illness. But what if he's being slowly poisoned, Silke? What if someone has been giving him small amounts of the venom from those creatures in the cellars? Maybe even hoping he'd reveal the information they wanted while he was delirious?"

"It's possible, I suppose. But wouldn't his physician recognise what was wrong?"

"Not necessarily. Baracleth has been the family's physician for years, and he's pretty ancient and out of touch. He's probably been treating the king for a non-specific wasting illness like Dad's, giving him traditional medications to help relieve the symptoms. But what the king needs is what Esther gave you: a specific antidote developed for that venom."

"Do you think that maybe silith root has something to do with it?"

He shrugged. "Could be. We need to question Esther. My bones tell me, Silke, that she has the answers."

I thought about it all as I drank my hot, sweet kashla. And I thought about what Sattine and his little helpers might have been getting up to in the last few days while I had been out of action. It made me shiver. The quicker I got back to work, the better. I also needed to figure out how to get into my apartment without Sattine's goons noticing. My message crystal was probably backed up with stuff. Dozens of prospective clients all wanting my expert services. I doubted it, but I hoped not: I had enough on my plate.

"Tomorrow, Stone," I said. "We'll take Juniper back home and ask some questions."

FOURTEEN

We left very early next morning, cutting across the city before the commuter traffic built up. Stone did indeed have a fancy transpo, thanks to his daddy's royalties. It was specially equipped with an auto-lift and an extended rear compartment to accommodate Marcus's chair, and if the situation was an urgent one, it could be turned into flyer-mode and launch itself into the sky. That explained why he was a flyer-pilot. He'd need two sets of licences to drive such a vehicle.

I was past feeling jealous. I sat back into the soft leather seat, holding Juniper on my lap, and just hoped Stone wouldn't want to leave ground level on this trip. It felt good to be back in my own clothes again – even if they did hang a bit loose now – and to be in action once more. The morning was crisp and sunny and I had a great urge to beat up a few Taurugs or run until I dropped. I had my window down and was luxuriating in the familiar smells of my world, when suddenly I caught a whiff of the river and my senses went into overdrive. I thought of the docks, the noisy, smelly harbour, my home stamping ground, the Goat's Beard tavern and a kaleidoscope of other familiar things.

And I had an overwhelming need to see my cosy apartment. My mind was swamped with homesickness.

"How about we take a detour down by the docks, Stone?" I said. "No one will recognise this transpo, will they? And I can see if anyone's on stakeout at my apartment."

Stone frowned and didn't say anything at first. "I don't know. This isn't exactly an inconspicuous vehicle to be driving through dock territory. It's bound to turn a few heads. Are you sure it's worth the risk? We can always go down there later, dressed for the part."

He was probably right, but it took a great effort of will to agree with him. I shrugged. "OK. Later, then."

The city was just coming to life. Shopkeepers were opening their doors.

Deliveries were being made. It was all bizarrely normal. What did I expect?

We cruised down the narrower streets of the Old Town. But as Stone turned the transpo into Lepp Street, I gasped. Where Esther's shop had stood was now a smouldering ruin.

I dropped Juniper into the back compartment, and even before the transpo had rolled to a stop I was out of the door and running towards the scene of disaster. The tubs of special-offer herbs that sat outside the door were now turned over, scorched and spilled. There was Fire Department tape tied across the front, with its warning messages that the property was unsafe, trespassers would be prosecuted, and such like. I stepped over it. Then I heard, rather than saw, Stone come up behind me. He caught my arm.

"Wait, Silke. Let me go first and check it out."

I shook him off, angrily. "No. I must do this. It was once my home, remember. The place reeks of magic. It was no ordinary fire, Stone. Stay behind me and let me know if you sense anything . . . wrong. Or if you find anything."

I stepped carefully over the ash and rubble that were all that remained of the doorway and shop. Mort's perch was tipped over, leaning against the black and blistered shelving that once held all those magical jars and bottles, but I saw no sign of Mort – I dreaded the sight of charred feathers or tiny bones. I hoped he had escaped the conflagration.

Rare and precious ingredients for every known spell and remedy, lovingly stored, preserved and filed in a system that only Esther had fully understood, were all reduced to so much stinking debris; broken, tipped and spilled in wanton destruction. Small curls of smoke still trickled upwards here and there. My heart ached with a sense of loss and a burning rage. Part of my life had gone up in smoke here, too. Then I remembered all Esther's companions.

"Stone," I whispered. "She had so many animals. Do you think . . . ?"

He shook his head. "I can't *sense* any life here, Silke, but I've not tried listening for animals before. Maybe Esther managed to get out and take them with her."

"We need to look in the back room," I told him. I couldn't share his optimism and I had to be sure that there was nothing here that needed help, though my common sense should have told me that the Fire Department would have made sure of that. I was oblivious to the tears streaking down my face.

There were so many fallen timbers and smashed bottles that picking a way through was hazardous and far from easy. My shoes were already caked with unpleasant tarry stuff. We had to lift obstacles out of the way, and it was while I was bent over, trying to lift the corner of what was once a cabinet, that I noticed the sealed jar on the floor. The jar itself was not surprising, except in so far as it had survived the flames, but the object inside riveted my attention. I picked it up gingerly and brushed soot from the sides with tingling fingers. Two white, globe-like eyes stared out at me and I almost dropped the jar in shock.

"What? What is it?" asked Stone.

"Look! I think it's one of those . . . *things*. I recognise the eyes."

Stone took the jar from me and turned it round,

examining the contents. "It's OK," he reassured me. "It's quite dead. It's been preserved. I'm sure you're right, though. It could be one of those creatures that bit you. I wonder why the jar didn't explode in the heat?"

"It's warded," I said. "Can't you feel it?"

Stone concentrated, his hands moving lightly over the jar. "No," he said, shaking his head. "It's too subtle for me."

I was surprised. He had detected the ward on my apartment door, so why did this one elude him? Me, I was practically tingling all over. My ears, my hair, my fingers – even my skin – were buzzed with adrenaline and the prickling of magic. My nose was so clogged with the smell of the firespell that had been wrought on this place, and the residue of scorched herbs and aromatic powders, that I felt I would never be able to breathe fresh air again.

Stone pushed the jar into his jacket pocket. "I'll hang on to it, and show it to Trace when we get back."

I reached the second doorway. The bead curtain was no longer there, of course, but still I hesitated before going further. A quick look round showed me that it was going to be even more difficult to search this room. Esther's bulky furniture lay in charcoal ruins: so much broken timber, springs and fabric rags. The narrow staircase that led up to the second floor was completely gutted: we'd never be able to get up to the two small bedrooms without scaffolding of some kind, or a ladder up to a window. I stood at the bottom and stared up at the inaccessible, blackened landing, reaching out with my senses to try and tell if there was anything alive up there.

It was a very faint sound, but I heard it.

"Something's up there, Stone," I whispered.

He came and stood beside me, looking upwards. We both listened hard. "It must be small," he said. "I can barely sense it."

I had a horrible thought. "Supposing it's one of those *things*!" I said.

"Not likely," he said. "I think they come from the dark. Underground. They weren't creatures of light."

Sometimes you just had to jump right in. "Hello?" I called. "Anyone there? It's me, Silke."

My voice sounded strange in that smoky silence. There was a fluttering sound and something small and black came tumbling down the stairwell, straight towards me. I screamed and flung up my hands to protect my face.

For a moment I was too panicked to make sense of what was happening. There were harsh screeches. I felt feathers and claws beating against my head and hands, and was aware of Stone cursing and falling backwards over something behind me. I might even have sent him flying as I struck out in self-defence.

"Mornin' darlin'. Mornin' darlin'. Mornin' darlin'!"

I looked up to see a familiar little figure hopping from

foot to foot on a skeletal chairback, balancing with outstretched fluttering wings.

"Mort!"

Stone was groaning and thrashing about on the floor. I pulled bits of rubble off him and linked my arm under his to pull him to his feet. He brushed himself down, but the damage was done. He was covered in sooty filth from head to toe and looked furious.

"Ding dong! Do call again!" chirped Mort.

Stone scowled. I tried not to laugh.

"It's Esther's pet mimic bird, Mort. He's been here for years. I'm so glad he's OK." I held out my hand to Mort. "Hey, Mort. Come to Silke."

Mort shook his feathers, then launched himself at me and landed on my wrist with a nervous chirp. I rubbed a finger against his chest feathers and he cocked his head, staring at me with his little glinty black eyes. The poor bird looked rather worse for wear: his feathers were all dusty and disarrayed. Goodness knows what he had been through. "You're safe now, Mort. There's a good bird." I murmured what I hoped were soothing words, but they came out awkwardly.

"Ow! 'Elp! Murder!" screeched Mort suddenly. "Murder!"

"Grief," said Stone. "He sounds just like Esther."

Mort had Esther's voice to perfection. It was chilling to

listen to him. Were these Esther's last words?

"He's got something wrong with his leg," Stone observed.

Mort made an obscene whistle. "Show a leg darlin'."

I lifted my wrist so I could examine Mort better and saw a lumpy piece of cloth attached to one leg. "There's something tied to it. Can you take it off?" I gently grasped Mort's back to prevent him flying away, plucked him off my wrist, then turned him over in both hands. He nibbled my fingers and protested with a few squawks as Stone began to pick carefully at the cloth and in a few minutes prised off the package it held in place.

He unrolled the layers and found a small cloth bag, folded very small, and a note on a scrap of parchment, which he screwed up his eyes to read. "It's for you, Silke. From Esther."

I put Mort back on my wrist, but he immediately hopped across to Stone's shoulder. I took the attachments from Stone and examined them. The note said:

Silke. 2 drops for ghoulbats. King!! Sorry. E.

I opened the small bag. Inside was a small phial of brown liquid. I unscrewed the top and sniffed at it. It smelled very aromatic and somehow familiar.

"It's one of her herbal concoctions." I handed the stuff to

Stone. "I think I've smelled it before. Can you read anything from it?"

He held the bag and the note in his hand for a moment, then shook his head. "I just get a sense of fear and panic, but I imagine that could be from Mort. He must have been terrified."

"Do you suppose 'ghoulbats' are those things we encountered?" I asked. "They certainly *are* ghoulish. Maybe this is her antidote to their poison!"

Stone made a non-committal noise. "Maybe. I guess she *has* been involved in whatever Sattine is up to. Maybe he got her to produce this stuff for him."

I took back the phial and the note, tucking them safely inside a discreet pocket in my jacket. "Well, it looks as if you were right. She seems to know about the king's illness. If we can get some of this stuff to him, maybe it'll cure him."

"Or send him over the edge."

"No. I can't think that Esther would want us to murder him." There was a sudden cracking sound and some of the flooring fell down from the room above, showering us with plaster and debris. It set us both coughing, and Mort flew up from Stone's shoulder before settling back down again.

"Let's get out of here before we're buried alive!" said Stone, and he led the way back to the street.

We took our seats in the transpo once more and Stone drove away. Mort took up a position on the top of Stone's headrest – he seemed to have taken a shine to him – and screeched a few bird greetings to Juniper. He kept up a constant, distracting chatter until Stone growled, "Shut up, bird!" and Mort went silent.

"We should have made inquiries about the fire," I said. "Find out if Esther was hurt and where she is now."

"I can check with the Fire Department as soon as we find a public comm-booth," said Stone. The traffic was denser now, and he had to concentrate on his driving. "I'll try to contact Vyktor as well."

"You'll have to be careful. They'll be monitoring all communications with the palace."

"I know, but I won't leave a name. Vyktor will know it's me." He was silent for a while, and I watched the streets gliding slowly by, lost in my own thoughts. Then he said quietly, "How are you feeling, Silke? That must have been quite a shock for you."

I thought about that. I was sorry and angry about the shop being torched, but I couldn't believe Esther was *dead*. Perhaps the brain needs to see a corpse in order to be convinced that someone isn't there any more. "I don't know," I replied. "A bit numb I guess. I can't believe she's gone. But I can believe Sattine might be holding her somewhere. We don't know whether he got what he wanted from her, for one thing. He's not likely to kill someone who's useful to him." I remembered his conversation with me at Blackstone Keep, how he'd tried to recruit me to his cause.

"There's a booth!" I said, pointing across the street.

Stone swung the transpo to the side of the kerb and stopped. Blares of angry horns sounded behind us, but he ignored them. He opened his door to get out and the smell of the river wafted inside. It was stronger than before, because we were much nearer, and once again my senses went into overdrive. I suddenly knew, beyond reason, that I had to get to my apartment.

I opened my own door, narrowly missing a passing vehicle, and slammed it shut behind me. I barely registered Stone's surprised shout, but took off fast, weaving through the traffic and disappearing down the first alley I came to. An irrational fear was driving me: my apartment was in terrible danger and I must get to it at all costs! Images of Esther's torched shop tormented me. Faster and faster I ran, dodging vehicles and pedestrians, taking no notice of shouts and curses and shrugging off the hands of angry passers-by who plucked at my jacket.

Home! I must get home! Hurry! It's almost too late!

The docks came in sight. Still I ran.

My lungs heaving, I reached the door to my building and stopped to catch my breath. The next minute, I was being attacked by feathered fury, as Mort suddenly dived at me, screeching abuse. I threw my hands up at my face to try and fend him off, but he was relentless. His beak and claws gave me spiteful little nips and scratches.

"Mort! Stop! . . . Ow . . . ouch! Mort!"

"*Silke!*"

I tried to turn, but it was difficult with Mort throwing himself at me.

"Silke . . . ! Come away from there!" It was Stone's voice, but he sounded very breathless. He must have chased after me when I took off.

"*Mort!*" I yelled at the stupid bird. "I have to get inside—"

"No. No you don't," said Stone, behind me. "It's not real, Silke. It's a trap."

I shook my head. "You don't understand, Stone. I *have* to get—"

He shook me roughly. "Don't you see? It's a spell, Silke. They're waiting for you! They're *compelling* you to come to them."

My brain hurt. Voices in my head were still insisting that I had to get to my apartment at all costs, but Mort had distracted me from them. And now Stone was making me question my grasp of reality. Fortunately, Mort had stopped his wild attack and was back on Stone's shoulder, his fierce little eyes watching me.

I rubbed my ears and ran my fingers through my cropped hair. *Think, Silke, think.* There was a numbness about me: that heavy, blanket feeling I experienced in Blackstone

Keep. Something was blocking my perceptions. I took a few deep breaths and then gently summoned power into my hands. I placed my palms flat on the door of the building and then I felt it: a compulsion spell. My head fell forward and rested on the painted wood while I drew the words of the counterspell from deep in my subconscious and breathed them into the fabric of the building like a long sigh. The insistent voices left me.

Wearily, I turned to face Stone. "I can't believe that just happened."

He reached out and pulled me away from the door. "Come on. Let's get out of here before they come for us. You said yourself Sattine's powerful. He must have found a way to put some kind of a block on you, so you couldn't detect the enchantment."

"How did you know?"

Stone shut his eyes and gave a little huffy sigh. "Well, the way you took off like a maniac, for one thing. It was too sudden and unwarranted, and twice transpos almost killed you as you careened down the street. Your aura was scrambled, and I could sense your desperation to get into your apartment at all costs. It just wasn't rational. And then when Mort took off after you, I guessed what might be happening." He stopped to give the bird on his shoulder a scratch, and smiled. "You told me yourself that spells could be worked out with a bit of logical thinking."

We were walking at a leisurely pace now, back towards where he had left the transpo. I still couldn't believe I had come so close to succumbing to a compulsion spell. "Yeah," I muttered. "Logical thinking just doesn't seem to be my strong point at the moment. What a stupid, stupid idiot."

"You can't possibly blame yourself, Silke. He's your brother. Who better to understand how to take advantage of you?"

He opened the passenger door of the transpo for me and I slumped into my seat, feeling decidedly depressed. Esther was missing, her shop destroyed. The king was dying, his children prisoners. And what possible help had I been to any of them? None. Sattine was working to some hideous, mysterious agenda to take over the world, involving mythical gems and creatures of nightmares, and now I was losing my grip. And with it, my confidence. I was falling into a black well of despair. And to cap it all, I probably wouldn't get to collect one *onik* of my fee. Some investigator *I* was.

Stone was saying something to me. ". . . Promise not to move for the next five minutes. I'll go and make those calls."

I stared numbly out of the window as he used the comm-booth, watching the dumb-show of his conversations, seeing him glance towards me with a frown, then nodding or shaking his head in response to the things the comm was saying to him.

Juniper leaped over the back of the seats and down into my lap. He kneaded me with his paws, then turned round and round to make himself comfortable. I absently stroked him, but I wanted to cry.

Then Stone was walking back to the vehicle.

He slid behind the controls and almost immediately gunned away from the kerb, slipping easily into the ragged stream of traffic. For a while he concentrated on navigating the city streets and said nothing. I just sat in miserable silence.

"I rang the Fire Department," Stone said eventually. "There was no one in the building when it was on fire. They didn't find any animals either."

Well, that was something. Esther was doubtless a prisoner somewhere.

When I didn't say anything, he continued, "The prince and princess have been taken away from the city. 'For their own safety' is the official line. The king's no worse, but no better either. They must be keeping him alive for some purpose of their own."

I thought about it. "He's taken them to Blackstone Keep, hasn't he? It's the obvious place," I said, turning to look at Stone. Then a horrible thought struck me. "Do you suppose he's got one of them to tell him where the vault is?"

"We have to assume he has."

"Stone! We must stop him somehow!"

"I agree. But first we're going to go home, have something to eat, do a little planning and kit ourselves up for storming the keep. No point going at it in broad daylight."

And although I chafed at the idea of all the delays, I had to agree he was right.

"OK, but first drop me at a utility clothing store. I need a change of clothes."

FIFTEEN

When Trace opened the door, his brows shot up and he did a comical double take. We must have looked a bit of a sight. As well as our shopping parcels (Stone had bought more takeaways) I was carrying Juniper and Mort was still on Stone's shoulder.

"I thought the cat was going home," Trace said.

"Change of plan," said Stone. "His home got torched."

"And the bird?"

"This is Mort," I put in. "He belongs to Esther, too. We found him in the ruins, so brought him with us."

Trace nodded and shut the door behind us.

"Ding, dong!" said Mort. "Mornin' darlin'!"

Trace closed his eyes briefly, but said nothing. A man of restraint.

We ate lunch, then I went off to have a nap, so I'd be properly rested before we set out for the keep. I kept forgetting I was supposed to be a convalescent, but the others reminded me. I left Stone poring over charts, and Trace had disappeared into a makeshift lab, where he was eagerly dissecting the ghoulbat we'd brought back with us and analysing the contents of the bottle Esther had left me. I had taken only the briefest of looks at the ghoulbat: enough to see that it had long fangs like a snake, extraordinarily large, multifaceted eyes, and membranous wings. "A bat from hell" described it perfectly.

Two hours later I rejoined them, napped and showered and decked out in my new black combat gear (and fresh underwear) that I'd picked up at a military surplus store. Of course, I'd have preferred some of my own clothes from home, but that hadn't been possible.

Stone was all in black, too. He had a utility belt round his waist and was busy snapping various weapons and gadgets on to it. There was more stuff spread out on the floor. I could identify various stunners, knives, stars, coils of fine rope and what looked like an ice pick, but there was other stuff that was new to me. It was quite an arsenal, and I doubted Stone had a licence for most of it. Not bad for someone who reckoned to be a mere psychic investigator. I sensed there was much more to him than I had discovered so far.

"Pick what you want," he told me.

"I don't think I'd know how to use half of these things," I said. I couldn't help remembering that it wasn't so long ago I'd insisted on working alone. There were times when you just had to swallow your pride and admit that it was good to have help.

I settled for a couple of knives, a stunner and some wire-rope.

Trace came into the room. He glanced at all the weaponry and his mouth set in a hard line. As a medic he totally disapproved of anything designed to kill or maim, but he kept his opinions to himself. Instead, he asked me if I was still having bad dreams. The question took me totally by surprise.

"I . . . er . . . well, now you mention it . . . Yes, I am," I told him. "But they're not as bad as they were."

He nodded, as if he expected as much. "I've done an analysis of the creature you brought back with you. I won't bore you with the details, but the sample of venom I was able to retrieve suggests that it contains hallucinogens. It corrupts the blood and targets the brain, causing all kinds of illusions and hallucinations. It's virulent stuff."

He held up Esther's phial, which was now empty.

"This one was pure silithium. I've put it in a handier bottle for you."

Stone and I exchanged a glance. Then we both asked, "What's silithium?"

"Well, it's got several uses, actually," Trace replied. "It's a brain stimulant. In small doses it's used to help patients with mental disorders. An overdose would blow your mind completely. You'd probably never come down to earth again. But often it's mixed with other drugs to heighten their efficacy."

"What's it made from?"

"Distilled silith root." He handed me the silithium bottle and I stashed it in a pocket. "It's a very expensive drug. You'd need a large quantity of the root just to get what's in there."

I looked at Stone. "Lord Joslin must be producing his own supply."

"But why?"

"Can you tell if this stuff is an antidote to the venom, Trace?" I asked.

"I don't think it's an antidote exactly," he said carefully. "But I think it could be added to the venom to dilute it, or harness it, to control its effects. I'd need to do a great many tests before I could say for certain."

"We don't have time," I pointed out. "Our priority must be to recover the Darkstone and get Veelya and Vyktor – and maybe Esther as well – out of Blackstone Keep."

"Why don't you just notify the Enforcers?" asked Trace, with a touch of irritation.

"Notify them of what?" I asked. "That the king's right-hand man is plotting with an outlawed Ellanoi to take over the kingdom? They'd wet themselves laughing, Trace. We have no evidence to give them."

He frowned unhappily. "Very well. I'll stay with Marcus until you get back."

If we got back.

"If there are any complications, Trace—" Stone started to say.

Trace waved his hand. "Yes, I know. All the documents and instructions are in the drawer."

"Right." Stone rolled up the map and picked up a black canvas kitbag. "Let's go," he said to me.

SIXTEEN

It was early evening when we finally parked the transpo deep in a wooded area within hiking distance of the keep. Stone had chosen to go by terrain, rather than fly, as he said flyers could be tracked more easily and we didn't want to alert Sattine to our presence. We covered the transpo with some leafy branches to camouflage it a little from casual glance. I could have worked a concealment spell on it, but the magic might give us away.

The air was crisp and fresh, and redolent with earthy, woody smells that seeped into my skin somehow. I was glad that it was getting dark: all this outdoors stuff might be good for the lungs, but it creeped me out. Give me polluted city streets any day.

I walked behind Stone, who had no problem at all negotiating the landscape. I could see where I was going all right – Ellanoi have very good night vision – but I just couldn't seem to judge which ground was firm and which would turn out to be boggy and swallow up my foot. I felt clumsy and awkward, and my mud-covered shoes gave testament to my lack of skill. Stone's shoes, of course, stayed clean.

We were following a small river that would lead us, so the map suggested, right up to the keep. It looked very much as if the river flowed under the keep, giving it a natural source of water and waste disposal, and we were banking on the conduit being our way in. Stone was a lot more confident about the prospects than I was, but then it *was* his element. I was already feeling the dampening effects of the combined power of Earth and Water around us.

The trees thinned and we got our first sight of the keep, rising dark and solid ahead of us in the evening light. It was a lot bigger than I remembered from our previous encounter, and I felt the first misgivings about what we were attempting to do. It looked vast and impenetrable, having endured for hundreds of years, and likely to be around for another millennium after Stone and I were long forgotten. This side of it was sunk deep into the hill. The ground rose steeply towards the front of the keep, so that the gate and entrance courtyard were considerably higher.

We advanced cautiously. Grassy banks gave way to stone as we approached the massive walls. I glanced up, but saw no sign of anyone on watch. The only sound I could hear was that of the river tumbling over rocks. I guessed no one was expecting us on this side.

Stone tugged on my sleeve to get my attention. Ahead I could see white foaming water and a low iron grating covering the drain outlet from the castle. I grinned at him and gave him a thumbs-up sign. Our elation was to be short-lived, however. As we climbed up towards the opening, I heard a low, snuffling wheeze and almost at the same time caught a nauseating whiff of rotting carrion. I put out a hand to caution Stone, but he had noticed it, too, and stopped.

Something large was lumbering along the base of the wall on the other side of the narrow channel of water not far ahead of us. I heard the clink of chains and the unmistakable sound of a tail dragging. My heart sank.

There was a dargbeast guarding the conduit.

I already had my knife in one hand and the stunner in the other, but if the beast was a large one it was going to be difficult to subdue. They had tough, armoured hides. More importantly, they were savage fighters, with strong jaws and talons that could rip you to shreds. It helped that it was chained up, but we still had to get rid of it before we could enter the conduit, and the best way to kill it would be to stab it from behind, just behind the foreleg, where the skin was softer.

"You draw it away," I whispered to Stone, "and I'll come at it from behind."

He shook his head. "Too dangerous," he whispered back.

At the sound of our whispering, the beast snarled and lunged towards us. The chain snapped to its full extension and I inadvertently jumped back. *Just our luck.* It was the biggest brute I'd ever seen.

Stone meanwhile was undoing his kitbag and taking things out of it.

"Here, take this," he said, and handed me a small package. "Toss it well over to the left when I say so."

"What is it?" I asked, imagining it must be some kind of explosive device.

"Bacon sandwich."

Stone unclipped one of the weapons from his belt and disappeared into the gloom to the right. I worked my way to the edge of the water and heard the dargbeast moving parallel to me, no doubt hoping I'd get close enough for it to snap a chunk out of me.

"Now, Silke!"

I heard the words clearly in my head and flung the food as hard as I could. The dargbeast gave a snort and lunged after it. As it turned, a bright flare of light caught the beast behind its foreleg, and I saw it drop heavily, as if its legs were suddenly cut from under it. But it didn't stay down. With grunting effort, the creature staggered to its feet again and turned its attention to where Stone was positioned.

"Stone!"

The beast charged, and without thinking I ran to

intercept it. But I'd never have reached it in time. Stone fired again, straight into its eyes. The dargbeast squealed, turned a clumsy somersault and rolled down towards the channel of water. It might have slipped further, except that the chain was not long enough. There was an audible crack as its neck broke.

I reached Stone. "Nice shooting. You OK?"

"Yup. The mechanism jammed. Took me a couple of seconds to fire the second charge."

"If you will buy these cheap forgeries."

I saw his teeth gleam in the dark.

"Come on," he said. "Let's get inside."

The low grating was embedded into the stones of the wall, but we made short work of it with a small explosive charge. The noise was muffled by the thickness of the walls and the noise of the water, so we weren't too worried about being heard. We were at the back of the great round tower, so there were no ramparts or lookouts on this side. The early builders obviously put too much faith in inaccessibility.

Scrambling through the hole, though, was a wet, mucky process. The water wasn't deep, but I didn't like to think too much about what was in it. We were soon through and into the dark tunnel that led under the heart of the great keep that was towering over our heads. It was cold, damp and smelled of mildew and decaying matter.

Once away from the exterior walls, the tunnel widened and had narrow access ledges each side of the water channel, presumably for maintenance crews. We lit flares and followed the walkway along until we came to an opening off to the right. Stone was leading the way. With my powers becoming duller by the minute, I was relying on his telepathic skills to give us early warning of anyone approaching.

We reached a flight of steps and made our way up them to the door at the top.

Stone listened for a moment, then quickly picked at the lock. The door opened and we were into one of the cellar corridors. We knew from Stone's research that they were constructed in a spiral, around the circumference of the tower and working their way upwards, with side corridors leading off into the heart of the fortress. All we had to do was follow the right ones!

We didn't speak. Cautiously, we made our way into the labyrinth. While Stone was focused on finding Veelya and Vyktor, I was trying to stay alert to possible danger. It wouldn't have surprised me to find a dargbeast wandering loose down here.

It didn't take us long to find the royal twins in a cell on the second level. As luck would have it, the key hung on a hook to one side of the door, so we had no trouble opening it up. The only light in the room came from two sputtering candles in wall sconces, but it was enough for me to see

Veelya crouched on the floor next to Vyktor, who was lying on a low pallet. He looked sick: his face was pale and covered with dark blotches.

"Stone!" I whispered. "They've poisoned Vyktor!"

Veelya's face was haggard, her clothes soiled and creased, but as soon as she saw us she cried "Silke!" and pulled herself from the floor. She threw her arms around me. "Oh, Silke! I knew you'd come!" she sobbed into my shoulder. "It's been so awful. Joslin kept asking us about the vault. You were right: Sattine wants the Darkstone, Silke. And they gave Vyktor this horrible stuff to drink. He's been delirious and rambling. And I think he's told them where the vault is."

She pulled away then, as if suddenly collecting herself.

"Are you sure?" I asked.

She nodded miserably and wiped her face on her sleeve.

Stone was already examining Vyktor and talking to him quietly. There was nothing princely about the boy now: he looked dirty, very weak and somehow smaller.

"Should I give him some of Esther's serum?" I whispered.

Stone shrugged. "I doubt it could make him worse. He won't last long like this, Silke."

"OK. Give me a hand."

Trace had sensibly transferred the serum into a bottle with a pipette in the cap. I filled the pipette, and while Stone held Vyktor's mouth open, put two drops of the serum on his tongue. Then I replaced the cap and returned the bottle to my pocket. Vyktor gave a shudder and lay back on his pallet.

"We can't wait to see if it works, Stone. We must find Esther."

Stone smoothed Vyktor's hair away from his face and rested his hand on the boy's fevered forehead for a moment. "I know," he said.

We gave Veelya the key and told her to lock herself in once we had left. It might keep the guards out, but that was about all. She didn't want us to leave her, but we had no choice.

"We'll be back as soon as we can," I promised her, "then we'll get you out of here. Just be brave. Try and keep Vyktor warm."

There was an eerie quietness to these lower levels that put a chill in my soul. Stone and I went quickly to every door we came across, but Esther was behind none of them. I kept expecting guards to appear, or – worse – a patrolling dargbeast, but it was just as if everyone was celebrating a public holiday. The place was deserted.

"She's not here," Stone said quietly. "I think we should make for the vault room. It's in the centre of the tower."

Just at that moment there was a muffled booming noise and I felt the floor and walls rock as if there'd been an earth tremor or explosion.

"Something's happening," I said. "Sattine may have the stone already. Come on!"

We ran. Down corridors and up flights of stairs we raced, changing direction time and time again, but all the while moving closer to the heart of the keep. And as we got nearer, so I started to feel the magic at work. Powerful magic.

I began to feel very afraid.

Stone suddenly stopped dead in front of me. He put his finger to his lips, then went forward very cautiously. I guessed we were very near to our goal, but although my ears were buzzing, I couldn't hear or see anything in the gloom ahead of us. My knife was in my hand, ready for anything, but I wasn't prepared for a door opening suddenly and the figure that stepped into our path.

Dervan.

"Stop right there!" he commanded. "Let's get a look at you."

We obeyed. Probably because he was holding a very formidable disrupter: aimed at us.

"Well, well, I am impressed," he sneered. "The little Dragon Tamer has not only returned from the dead, but she's brought the Ice Warrior with her. What a pity we won't have very long to get properly acquainted."

He raised the weapon towards Stone, but I flung myself at him with a yell. Dervan turned his attention to me and threw up an arm to protect himself from my impact. Stone immediately dropped into a fighting stance and lashed out with his foot, connecting with Dervan's ribs and forcing the air from his chest in a rush. The disrupter clattered away down the corridor.

Dervan recovered sufficiently to knock me to one side, and fling out a disabling spell towards Stone. Stone ducked and rolled out of the way, and the spell hit a door instead, lifting it off its hinges. I aimed a spell of my own at Dervan, but it was sluggish and heavy, the way I was feeling. Dervan laughed and wrapped it up neatly in a ball of light, tossing it away from him.

"You'll have to do better than that, Silke," he jeered. "I guess you're out of practice."

Mortified, I tried to draw up more of my magepower, but large, clawed hands suddenly gripped my arms from behind me and lifted me off my feet. I gasped, struggled and kicked out, but the Taurug that held me was impervious to it all. Beside me, Stone had the clawed hand of a second guard round his neck. We'd been so focused on Dervan that neither of us had been aware of them coming up behind us.

Dervan laughed again. "Don't kill them, Ghall, will you? I think Sattine would like to decide what to do with them. Bring them along. First, though, I think we'll take their toys away." He disarmed us of all our weapons, dropping Stone's utility belt and kitbag on the floor and taking time to run his hands over me thoroughly and offensively for anything concealed.

Then he turned and went briskly up the corridor. Our guards marched us behind. I could hear Stone struggling to breathe, and I was afraid the Taurug might strangle him by mistake.

Dervan threw open a small, plain door and we were pushed roughly inside. We had reached the heart of the keep.

SEVENTEEN

I couldn't believe what I saw.

I was expecting the room to be small, dark and enclosed; to fit with my idea of a secure vault. But instead, it was huge and full of light from hundreds of flame lamps, which reflected off incredible mosaic work on the floor, ceiling and walls. Gold and silver leaf, and countless jewels sparkled and winked from every aspect. This really was a treasure room, but where the treasure was kept was not immediately obvious.

In the very centre was a wide, dark, oily pool. Standing at its edge, his arms outstretched, was Sattine. He was just completing what I recognised to be a spell of opening. As he spoke the last words, the room rocked with another blast of magic, making the rest of us stagger. If I hadn't been held so tightly, I would have lost my balance completely. I realised then that he still hadn't acquired the Darkstone, but was trying to access the vault.

The room remained unchanged. The surface of the pool moved with wavelets from the vibrations, and the lamps flickered wildly, but of the vault there was no sign. Vyktor may have been coerced into revealing its location, but it would seem that he had not given away the password that would unlock its secrets.

"Give up, Sattine," I said, "before you bring the whole keep down on our heads."

He turned to me and I recoiled a little inside when I saw the fierce look in his eyes. He was very angry. He stared at us as if trying to comprehend who we were, and then his face softened a little and he moved towards me.

"Silke."

I stared at his handsome Ellanoi features and the grace with which he moved, and suddenly felt overwhelmed with sadness and a great sense of loss. How could my own brother have become so corrupted? For just a moment I imagined how wonderful it would have been if I had been able to love him and look up to him in my younger days when I desperately needed love and security. What memorable times we could have spent together, if only he had been different.

"Sattine," I whispered. "Don't do this. Whatever it is you want, it can't be worth all the pain you are causing. Please. Let's leave here. I'll go to the Islands with you. We can be together. You can teach me!"

He was standing very close now, but I could not read those violet eyes. Did he regret anything? I couldn't tell. He touched my cheek with his hand.

"I've come too far, Silke," he said at last. "You cannot comprehend just what this means to me."

"What have you done with Esther?" I asked.

He frowned for a moment, as if he was trying to remember. "Esther? Ah, yes. She is here. She has been a valuable asset to me, but I think now that she has outgrown her usefulness. She made up the serum that harnesses the power of the ghoulswine."

Ghoulswine. I remembered the word from my nightmare. "Is that the venom from those nasty little crawlers in my cell?" I asked.

Sattine gave a short laugh and then suddenly grabbed my hair and tilted my head back roughly. "That's right. Clever little creatures, aren't they? I bred them myself to provide me with just the kind of venom I required for my purposes. I had planned to give you the serum, to see how well it worked on Ellanoi metabolism, but unfortunately you left before we could give it to you. By rights, little sister, you should be dead, as their venom is very toxic if not controlled." He tipped my head to one side, then the other, as if looking for evidence of the poison still in my system. "Remarkable. I suppose Esther gave you the serum herself."

"What does it do?" I asked him.

232

"Ghoulswine? On its own, and for a mere mortal, it's just an unpleasant, slow poison that leads eventually to death. But with the serum, it becomes a powerful catalyst. It enhances magepower. I can reach out to new dimensions and call on the creatures of the otherworld so they obey me. And once I get hold of the Darkstone, I will be invincible. I will have control of all four elements. I will be able to move through worlds and have whole armies at my beck and call. There will be nothing I cannot do."

"Is that why you are poisoning the king? Were you hoping he'd give up the password for the vault?" As soon as I said it I knew I had made a serious error. Sattine gave my hair another painful wrench. His eyes flared bright violet.

"What do you know of the password, Silke?" he spoke right into my face and I could feel his breath against my skin. "Tell me now, or it will not go well for your friends. Unfortunately the prince lost consciousness before he could tell me himself, but I still have the girl."

"Let go of me," I gasped. "I don't know what the password is – I only know there is one! The king is the only one who knows it!" It was a lie, of course, but it might buy us time. I saw him glance towards Dervan and nod his head.

"Be so good as to bring the girl, Dervan, and ask Joslin to join us." Sattine let go of my hair and stepped back. He then went over to Stone, who was standing rigidly in the vicelike grip of the Taurug guard.

"I underestimated you, young man," he said. "Silke did a convincing job earlier of making me believe she did not know you. And yet here you both are, working together. Hmmm. I wonder just how much of a nuisance you are going to be." He tapped his finger to his mouth, as if trying to figure out the best way of dealing with Stone. Remembering what happened last time, I was beginning to dread what imaginative punishment Sattine might be dreaming up.

"He's just a private investigator hired by Vyktor," I said, trying to sound bored. "I found him useful, that's all."

Sattine looked at me, then back at Stone. Stone did not look away. For a long minute they silently assessed each other, then Sattine turned to me again.

"You are going to help me, little sister," he said. "You will persuade your friends to tell me the password and I am going to raise the Darkstone."

I told him graphically what I thought he could do with his idea.

"Don't make me angry, Silke," he warned. "You wouldn't want to be responsible for . . . something *unpleasant* happening to this young man, or the girl and her brother. And there is Esther too, don't forget. She is still alive, but need not remain so."

There was a commotion at the door and then Dervan returned, pulling Veelya roughly into the room with him.

The locked door obviously hadn't posed too much of a problem for him.

They were followed by Lord Joslin, carrying a small tray with a glass on it. Immediately my hair lifted at the roots and my ears started their buzzing again. This guy was so not what he seemed. I heard a quick intake of breath and turned to look at Stone. He had gone very pale and was staring at Joslin with a look of horror.

What? What is it, Stone? Just for once, I hoped he could read my mind.

Snake!

Snake? What did he mean? I could readily believe that Joslin was a slimy creep, but then anyone who worked for Sattine qualified in that respect.

Veelya lay crumpled at Dervan's feet, sobbing. She looked even worse in this bright, glittering room, and seeing Dervan's contemptuous glance at her, I felt really angry on her behalf. She didn't deserve any of this. When she looked up and saw Stone and me, I saw the despair in her eyes.

"Veelya," I said. "It's OK. Don't say anything."

Sattine stepped between us. "Princess," he said soothingly. "I'm sorry your brother was unable to tell me what I need to know. I would have liked to spare him all that pain. But you can help instead. And there is still time to give him the antidote to the poison. He does not need to die."

Liar, I thought. I felt Ghall tighten his grip on me.

He waited, giving Veelya time to assimilate what he was saying to her.

"I know the vault is here, Princess. All I need is the word that will open it for me. Will you give me that word? I only want the Darkstone, you understand. You and your brother can keep the rest of the treasures. And Joslin here will undertake to be your guardian, as it were, until such time as Vyktor can be king. Or you can both rule, if you prefer. It does not matter to me. I am only interested in the Darkstone."

There was a hypnotic quality to his voice. He almost had me believing that this one small request would set everything to rights and harm no one.

"Don't listen to him, Vee."

Veelya just sat on the floor and shook her head. Then Dervan crouched down close beside her and ran his hand up her arm, whispering something in her ear. She snatched her arm away and recoiled from him. "No! No!" she sobbed.

In a lightning move, Dervan yanked Veelya's head back, even as she was still protesting. He snatched the glass from Joslin and began pouring its contents down her throat. She gagged and coughed and tried to resist.

I had never felt so helpless in my life. I thrashed and bucked in Ghall's grip, kicking and struggling to get free, but I might as well have spared myself the effort. He was an immovable rock.

But Stone's guard must have been distracted by the action in front of him, for Stone suddenly twisted out of his grip and launched himself at Dervan. He kicked the glass out of Dervan's hand and knocked him to the floor. He then turned to tackle Sattine, but Sattine immediately flung a firespell at him.

"*Stone!*" I screamed.

There was a *whumph*, and Stone was engulfed in blue flames. He dived straight into the pool and disappeared from sight, nothing but the hiss of extinguished flames and the smell of scorched clothing remaining in the air.

We all stared at the water in shocked silence, but it went glassy smooth. It seemed as if it had just swallowed Stone up completely.

"Joslin!" Sattine snapped.

My mind could barely comprehend what had happened. I felt as if a knife had been plunged right through me. But there was worse to come. Joslin threw off the robe he was wearing and began to . . . melt. His face became elongated and smooth. His limbs seemed to be sucked into his body, which became long and thin as I watched. I thought I might throw up any minute. His skin turned a greeny brown colour. Then the rest of his clothes pooled on to the ground and Joslin crawled away from them. Except it wasn't Joslin. It was a huge snake. Stone's word suddenly became clear to me. Joslin was a shapechanger! Mesmerised and appalled, I watched the creature glide forward to the edge of the pool and slide into the water with barely a ripple. Then it, too, disappeared, no doubt to search out Stone and ensure he did not return alive.

"Sattine!" I cried. "Don't do this!"

He looked steadily at me. "You can stop it, Silke. I can tell Joslin not to harm your young man. I can give the girl here the antidote to the poison. I can restore Esther and even give her a new shop. It's up to you."

I was in an agony of indecision. I did not want to give in to his blackmail, but I could not be responsible for letting all these people come to harm. The heavy weight of defeat settled over me, but I figured that stalling for time might give me a little edge of opportunity. "What do you want me to do?" I whispered.

Sattine gave me a beautiful smile. "It's not so much, Silke." He held out his hand. "Let me show you."

The guard dropped his grip on my arms and I stepped away from him. Reluctantly, I went towards my brother and slowly put my hand in his.

EIGHTEEN

His grip was cool and firm. As our hands touched, so the magefire within us both met and kissed and flared, vibrant and exciting. It was a shock to feel so wonderfully energised after all the other tensions and emotions I had felt in the last hour or so. But before I could really appreciate the sensation, the glittering treasure room of the keep disappeared, and I found myself weightless and bodiless on a sickening roller coaster in space and time.

Sattine took my spirit to the place of my nightmare: the black rock in a roaring, sulphurous sea of molten lava and spitting geysers, bubbling and churning all around us. Multi-coloured flames, fifty, a hundred metres high leaped and curled in fantastic shapes and patterns. I gripped his hand in a mix of terror and exhilaration. It might only be an illusion, but that did not lessen the effect of the flames and the heat. They were powerful and magical. I could feel my blood sing. The magefire caressed my skin and lifted my hair. In a whispered breath, I was ten feet tall and invincible. Heat, light and noise surrounded me. It was like finding the heart of myself.

"This is our power, Silke," Sattine shouted at me over the noise. "The heart of the magefire. We can control it, draw from it, use it. It's ours. It's in our blood. Can't you feel it?"

Oh, yes. I was giddy with it. But it was raw power. Primeval heat. Beyond my control. It would devour me if it could.

"Yes," I shouted back. "I can feel it. But it's your power, Sattine. Not mine."

"You're wrong, Silke. You've just never used it. I can teach you how."

"What? How to destroy people and homes with firebolts?" I said. "I've done with that. I've grown up. Elginagen and Ysgard are my world, Sattine. I want to live there. Not raze it to the ground."

"You don't have to. You can use the magefire to heal. You do know it can heal, don't you? Fire burns out impurities. It forges strength. Imagine having the power to meld and mend and *restore life*, Silke."

He made it sound enticing. I suddenly thought about Marcus Stone and his wasting illness. It would be incredible if I could make him whole, and maybe others like him. That was the least I could do, since we had lost Lucius. A lump came to my throat and I had difficulty swallowing: Lucius was beyond my help. But then I remembered Esther. Flawed as she was, she was still able to heal, and she didn't use omnipotent power to do it. She worked with nature. Balance and harmony, she was always telling me. I didn't need invincibility: I could work with the power I already had.

"No, Sattine." I shook my head. "You're wrong. We can't use this kind of power for anything but destruction. Look at it! Everything this fire touches is consumed. Is that what you want?"

He laughed. "Yes! Don't you see? Power lies in control. You and I can take this power and use it however we want to. It is enough to know we can. Let me show you something else."

He raised his arms then, and shouted a command over the fiery wastes.

At first nothing seemed to be happening, and then I heard that rhythmic beating sound that put a chill in my heart. Louder and louder it grew, until I could see a dark cloud of winged creatures flying towards us. I might have been back in my dream again, but it was Sattine calling the demons.

"No! Don't!" I gripped Sattine's arm in terror, but he laughed and ignored me.

"We come!" A thousand hissing, spitting voices answered his call.

The air was thick with their thin, disgusting bodies. I remembered only too well the wings, claws and teeth; their foetid breath, their scabrous skin. I turned my head from them, but could not shut out the sounds or smell of them.

"See my armies, Silke!" said Sattine. "I can send them anywhere and they will obey me without question. No one will be able to make a stand against such legions."

I shuddered, but had no voice to scream. My throat was already raw.

Sattine stepped to the edge of the rocky precipice on which we stood. His outstretched arms seemed to encompass the hordes gathered before us.

"Faithful ones!" he shouted. "See, this young woman. She is of my blood. We are kin. You must give her your allegiance! Just as I have claimed you, so will she! Where she commands, you must obey! Give me your assent!"

There was a great roar of sound from the host of demons. I felt faint.

"They are yours now, Silke," he said. "Yours to command."

"What have you done?" I screamed hoarsely at him. "I don't want them! They are unnatural. They don't belong in this world. Send them back, Sattine. They will destroy you. You cannot form an alliance with creatures such as these!"

"Don't be foolish. This is just the beginning. Once I have the Darkstone, all things will become subject to me. All things will be possible. I will have dominion over *all* elemental creatures, not just these. I am inviting you to share it with me, Silke."

"Never! Take me back. I want to get out of here. Take us back, Sattine."

His eyes darkened with impatient anger, but he said no more on the subject. Instead, he took my hand again and to my great relief the fire and the demons vanished. "I have one more thing to show you before you decide."

We spun in the vortex of time and space once more. I shut my eyes, fighting the nausea, and when we stopped moving I opened them again. We were standing on a balcony in a magnificent house made of marble. After the noise of our last location, this one was extraordinarily quiet. It was also full of light and fragrant with the scent of flowers. A blissful contrast to the previous horrors. Then I heard voices and looked down to see three young children running into an exquisite garden below us. They all had Ellanoi features: two girls and a boy; bright, healthy and happy.

I couldn't help grinning at them. "They're beautiful. Whose children are they?"

"They're yours."

"*What?*" I turned to Sattine. "What game are you playing now?"

"I am showing you your future. Look."

As I watched, a man and a woman emerged from the house. Stunned, I recognised myself in the woman: a little older, perhaps, but still unmistakably me. And then the man turned and I saw his face. *Dervan!*

"What does this mean?" I demanded.

"Silke. The Ellanoi are a dying, scattered race. I want to build them up once more. Make us strong again. Dervan is loyal to me. Despite what you think of him, he would make you a perfect lifemate. You are not exactly strangers, after all. And you liked each other once. Together you could have children just like these. It's what I want for you, Silke. What I want for our race."

I think my jaw may have dropped in astonishment. I wanted to laugh out loud at the absurdity of what he was proposing, but then I saw the look in his eyes and realised that there was nothing humorous about it at all.

"You can't possibly be serious? Me and *Dervan*? Have you gone completely mad? Whatever once was, is long finished. It died along with the street gangs we both used to run with. I was very young and very impressionable then. Times change, Sattine. Besides, we're not even pure Ellanoi. Neither are you if it comes to that. Our mother was human, remember? And Dervan is more Romish than Ellanoi. I'm afraid you'll have to look further afield for your pure-blooded breeding pair."

He ignored my sarcasm. "Genes can be manipulated.

244

That's not a problem. See what I achieved with the ghoulbats. If you prefer, you could just be a surrogate mother and Dervan could donate—"

I had never felt so angry or appalled.

"Absolutely not! How dare you! How *dare* you imagine you can manage and manipulate me like I was some . . . brood mare! I'd rather die with my friends than ally myself to you and your disgusting schemes. Take us back *now*, Sattine. I've seen more than enough, thanks."

He stared at me long and hard. "Very well. If that's your decision. But don't forget, Silke, you had it in your power to save the others."

He gripped my hand once more and we entered the vortex a final time. When the world stopped spinning, I opened my eyes to find that nothing had changed in the treasure room. The tableau was frozen in time: the two Taurug guards stood by the pool, and Dervan leaned over Veelya, lying shivering on the mosaic floor. They probably didn't realise we had left them.

The second I collected my wits, and before he could react, I turned and snatched a stunner from the belt of the nearest guard, and fired at both guards in one swift movement. They went down without a murmur. I pivoted on my left foot and whipped the stunner right into Dervan's face as he lunged for me. He staggered a moment, dazed, and I fired at him, but the charge wasn't strong enough to keep him down. It only disabled him briefly, but gave me enough time to snatch a knife from his belt with my left hand and throw myself on to his chest. I felt the air gush out of his lungs with the impact. Then Sattine's roaring voice penetrated my brain.

"*Silke!*"

Holding the knife at Dervan's throat, I looked up and saw Sattine had Veelya in his arms. She was sobbing hysterically. Blue and green flames licked over her skin.

"Put her down, if you want Dervan to live," I said.

"No. You put your knife down, Silke, if you want Veelya to live. She is seconds away from being consumed by fire. Do as I say."

It was an impasse.

But just at that moment, the waters of the pool began to roil and heave. Something very large was thrashing about under the surface, causing waves and splashes that covered and soaked us all. A battle seemed to be in progress, but as yet we couldn't see the combatants. Then two heads broke free of the surface for a moment and my heart leaped when I saw that one of them belonged to Lucius Stone. But the other was the serpentine head of Lord Joslin. Over and over, they twisted and turned around each other in a bizarre dance of death. Stone's hands were gripping the snake's throat, forcing it away from him, but the lethal-looking fangs were only centimetres away from Stone's face and coils of its body were wrapped around Stone's chest and arms. Then they both sank beneath the water once more.

I felt Dervan move under my grip. But I wasn't about to be distracted by his struggles. I simply pushed the stunner to his head and fired. At such close range, even a low charge was effective. Dervan's eyes rolled back into his head and he collapsed unconscious on to the tiles.

I got to my feet, but Sattine warned me away, stepping even closer to the edge of the pool with Veelya.

"Put your weapons down, Silke."

I slowly bent down to put them on the floor at my feet.

For a long moment we watched each other. Veelya was making small whimpering noises, then I saw her head loll back limply. She had probably fainted.

The surface of the pool moved again. We both turned to look: the churning water was turning dark red with blood. Too much blood.

For once I was too afraid to move. I went cold with dread. *Stone!* Had Joslin finally killed him? I stared at the water, willing him to be alive. And then a dark head bobbed up from the surface once more. It was Lucius. He shook the bloody water from his face and looked across at us. One arm hung limp at his side, but there was something dark held tight in his other hand.

"Give that to me!" roared Sattine. He was encumbered by Veelya's inert body, otherwise I don't doubt he would have used his magepower on Stone at that moment. Instead, I heard Stone's voice yell loud in my head: "*Silke! Catch!*" and he threw whatever it was straight at me. My hands went up automatically, like we were playing a child's game, and my fingers closed over something smooth and black that I had no trouble recognising. It had to be the Darkstone.

Vaguely was I aware of Sattine screaming, "*No! That's mine!*" and hearing the loud splash as he callously threw Veelya into the pool to reach out towards me, his beautiful face twisted with hatred and rage.

I felt his magic surround me, but he was too late. The instant I held the stone the most incredible feeling had washed over me from the roots of my hair to my toes. I felt its magic and power pour into every part of me: every atom of my being. And my own magepower rose immediately to meet it. The magics coalesced with the vestiges of ghouls-wine and serum in my blood, and I could feel the one enhancing the others. My blood was afire with power. This was an intoxicating cocktail indeed. Not only was my own power opening up in ways I had never even imagined, but I felt the surge of power from all the other elements – Earth, Air, Fire and Water – and the essence of that ancient mage whose petrified heart I now held in my grasp. *Belàthiel.* I even knew his name. The whole cosmic energy lay open to me: I knew I could ride the wind, fly far into space, touch ancient dragons asleep in their lairs deep in the earth, dive into the depths of the oceans with Leviathan and burn with the roaring energy of the volcano.

I looked into the eyes of my brother and saw his despair. I saw the years of loneliness and anger in his exile, the driving force of his hatred for those responsible for his humiliation. And I understood how he had hungered and lusted after the power offered by the Darkstone; his dream of world domination, his thirst for revenge.

It would not do.

Even as he reached for me with his magic, I batted him aside with a mere thought. I could have annihilated him in that instant and scattered his atoms across the universe. But I knew then that I could not destroy him. He was my brother. All I could see were his hurts and frailties. I could not condemn him for being flawed.

Instead, I reached out with my consciousness to that turbulent heart of our magepower and the teeming, loathsome creatures of the underworld that he had summoned even now to his aid. I sent them back with a command, just as I had returned the dragon to its long sleep. *You do not belong here*, I told them. *An-athewata! Be gone!* They scuttled away, cringing, into the darkness, as if I was too bright for them to look upon, and I sealed the hole in the fabric of the universe that had allowed them through in the first place.

I brought my focus back to the keep. A battle was in progress up at ground level, along the battlements and around the gatehouse. Sattine's forces were locked in combat with an army of Enforcers and soldiers from the palace at Ysgard. Someone must have finally realised that the prince and princess had been taken prisoner, and mobilised a rescue force. That was why Stone and I had not encountered any resistance when we arrived: the guards were already preoccupied on the higher levels. I reached out with my power and sent a curling wisp of enchantment through the ranks of combatants, sending Sattine's people collapsing into sleep and sweeping away all the weapons. There was no need for any more bloodshed.

Part of me was aware of Stone hauling himself and Veelya awkwardly from the water. They were safe, if exhausted. But before I returned to the treasure room, I had one other mission.

I sent my thoughts through every layer of the keep until I found what I was seeking.

Esther.

She was sitting on the floor of a small, cramped cell, her arms locked around her body, shivering and weeping with fear and remorse. My heart went out to her. I unlocked her cell and touched her with my magepower. She lifted her head and I saw the tears coursing down her haggard face, and heard her whisper my name, even though she couldn't see me.

It was time to go home. I drew back into myself and faced the awestruck group gathered in the treasure room. Stone was holding Veelya, rubbing her arms and legs to get her warm. Dervan and the two Taurugs were still unconscious. I left them that way for the Enforcers to find.

Only Sattine stood, watching me hungrily, warily.

"Silke . . ." he whispered. Magic trickled over my skin and set my ears ringing. "Give me the Darkstone. It is mine by rights, you know it is. I have earned it. Do you not see? You cannot possibly know how to use it. It will consume you, Silke."

His rich, seductive voice stole over me. Had I not had the Darkstone in my hand, I know it would have enchanted me and I would have done anything for him.

"No, Sattine," I said. "Your heart is set on revenge and destruction. This stone does not belong to either of us. Its powers are seductive, but I know it is much too powerful for me. And you are much too greedy and ambitious to have control of it."

There was a small noise behind me and I saw Sattine's eyes shift to something in the doorway and grow wide with alarm. Stone, too, looked up, pale and horrified. I turned.

Vyktor leaned against the doorframe, weak and sickly but with a murderous look in his dark eyes. He held a disrupter with both hands as if it was almost too heavy for him to lift.

"The Darkstone is ours," he said, with enormous effort, and before I could think to stop him he fired straight at Sattine. There was a blinding burst of flame and light, a smell of burning and acrid smoke. A voice in my head screamed, but when I opened my eyes my brother was gone.

The world went dark, and I knew nothing beyond the cold stone of the mosaic floor coming up to meet me. Powerful though it was, the Darkstone could not prevent me from fainting with shock.

NINETEEN

A large woman was leaning over me when I next opened my eyes. She seemed vaguely familiar, but my brain couldn't quite sort out the relevant facts in my head. Her face was sweaty and smudged with dirt and blood.

"Are you hurt?" she asked.

I considered her question. I felt no pain except an aching grief in my heart, for the loss of the brother I never truly knew. But I shut the lid quickly on that thought. I would mourn for him later. For now, I had to marshal my wits.

"Who are you?"

"I am Astrid. Princess Veelya's personal bodyguard."

Ah yes. The Adamanté Salon. My gaze automatically dropped to her finely-manicured hands with their gemstone fingertips, currently cradling a formidable-looking weapon.

"Nice nails," I said, and she blushed. "Help me up, will you?"

She pulled me upright with a powerful one-handed thrust and I rocked a little on my feet while looking around to get my bearings. We were still in the treasure room, but it was rather crowded with black-clad Enforcers and palace militia in combat camouflage. They seemed to be arguing about who should be in charge of the prisoners.

"Where is everyone?"

Astrid looked as if the question amused her. But I knew what I meant: I couldn't see Stone, or Veelya and Vyktor. Then I caught a glimpse of Dervan shuffling out of the room between two Enforcers, his hands and ankles in silver restraints that would prevent him using magic to escape.

"Their royal highnesses are being examined by our paramedics," said Astrid. "Your friend Stone is with them. He explained about the poison they were given, but thinks you will be able to help them better."

"Yeah," I said, and was then aware that I was clutching something so tightly in my hand that my muscles were cramping. It was the Darkstone. I slipped it casually into my jacket pocket. "You'd better take me to them, Astrid. Has anyone seen a rather scruffy-looking witch called Esther?"

Astrid shook her head. "I don't think so. But there are many levels in this place and our soldiers are still searching them for renegades. We have not found Lord Joslin, either."

"No, I'm afraid what's left of him is almost certainly lying at the bottom of that pool."

"I see. Well, that will save us one trial."

So much for *his* epitaph. I guess that being a bodyguard makes you pretty callous about these things.

We moved out of the treasure room and Astrid led me down the corridor.

"So who finally rang the alarm at the palace that all was not quite as it seemed?" I asked.

"We did. The personal bodyguards. When Lord Joslin went off with the prince and princess, leaving the king alone, I could not understand it. I have been at the princess's side since she was old enough to walk. She would not go anywhere without me, or one of her other guards. I'm sure you are aware that things are not *easy*, shall we say, between the members of the Royal Family, particularly while the king is ill. And since the threatening notes and practical jokes, Veelya has been very worried about her safety."

"I know. That's why she hired me."

Astrid's lips tightened. "I did not approve of her action."

"Well, no. I can imagine you felt you could handle anything yourself. But you wouldn't have been much use against a mage, Astrid. And I doubt you knew that Lord Joslin and the ambassador's nephew were working against you."

"No, you are right," she conceded. "I'm a bodyguard, not an investigator. In here." We had stopped outside a door and Astrid leaned forward to open it for me.

"Silke!" A wobbly chorus greeted my entrance and I grinned to see Stone, Veelya and Vyktor all looking at me from various pallets and chairs around the room. None of them looked particularly healthy. Veelya and her brother were still yellow and blue from the ghoulswine and clearly weak; Stone was white-faced and drawn. His left arm was heavily bandaged and in a sling. He and Veelya were wrapped in thermal blankets because their clothes were soaked. Various medics were fussing over the royal pair and tut-tutting about the best way to treat their symptoms. I figured I'd better intervene.

"Here, I can help. If you'd just like to move out of the way and give me some room."

There were some vociferous arguments. Medics just love to put you in your place, but Astrid was at my back and made sure they all got out of my way despite their protests. I fished out the bottle of serum, which miraculously was still safe in my pocket, and gave Veelya a couple of drops on her tongue. It showed how ill she was that she didn't make any complaint at all, but then she *had* almost drowned as well.

Vyktor, I knew, would probably be able to fight the poison now, and wouldn't need any more of the serum. But I remembered the Darkstone, and thought I might try a little home remedy of my own to give him some strength back.

I wrapped my hand around the stone in my pocket and

rested the other on Vyktor's chest, gently calling up the magefire. Immediately I felt it singing through me, stronger than I had ever known it, pouring out through my fingers and palm into Vyktor. I felt it course through him, like water in a dry valley: a slow trickle at first, then gushing stronger and stronger. It burned away the impurities in his blood, healed his damaged systems and internal organs, and gave new strength to his heart. When his eyes snapped open and he looked at me in astonishment, I couldn't help laughing. It was a good feeling: I just knew he was well again.

"What was *that*?" he asked.

"Oh, just a little something I kind of had up my sleeve," I told him, a bit smugly. I felt a little bit guilty, too, as I hadn't yet confessed to having the Darkstone – but I wanted to hang on to it a little longer.

"Well, you ought to bottle it. You'd make a fortune."

The medics rushed back to his side to examine him again, but he waved them away impatiently. "I'm fine. Go away and help somebody else."

As I turned away, he caught my arm.

"Silke. I don't know how to say this. I'm really sorry about Sattine. I didn't know he was your brother. I'd never have—"

"It's all right, Vyktor," I said. "You did what you thought was right at the time. I'm not angry with you. Sattine was very dangerous. He may have been my brother, but we were never close, unfortunately. I wish it had been different." I shrugged, not really wanting to say more.

There was a light touch on my shoulder and I looked up to see Stone standing close to me. I could see by his expression that he knew exactly what I was feeling.

"Hey," I said softly.

"Hey yourself," he said.

"Are you OK?"

"I will be. You did good back there, Silke."

"So did you. You'll have to tell me how you managed to avoid drowning, find the stone *and* slay the sinister serpent!" I grinned at him.

He shuddered and turned even paler. "Don't. I never told you about my phobia of snakes, did I?"

I stared at him. He was serious. "I think, Stone, that there's quite a bit you haven't told me."

He gave me something like his old smile and adjusted his glasses. A gesture of habit. "I suppose not. Well, there'll be time for us to catch up. You need to go and check on Veelya."

I looked down at the arm in the sling. "How about your arm?" I asked. "I could probably—"

"It'll keep. It's nothing."

I nodded. It would probably look too suspicious if *everyone* suddenly got better all at once. I went to Veelya's side. She looked at me wanly and tried to say something, but was too overcome. She squeezed her eyes shut and tears trickled between her lashes. I held her hand and sent my power gently through her, cleansing her blood, healing her damaged lungs and quieting her heart.

"Oh, Silke!" she whispered. "It's been so awful."

"Sssh! I know," I said. "But it's all over now."

There was a sudden commotion at the door of the room. Two burly palace guards – one of them with the epaulettes of a major – pushed their way in awkwardly. Between them was a small, dishevelled, roundish person dressed in grimy skirts and hugging a shawl tightly around her chest, loudly protesting about being manhandled.

"Just you take your filthy hands off me before I turn you into a maggot. Don't you know who I am? Where's your respect? Silke will tell you, you'll see. She knows me. I'm a respectable tradeswoman, I am."

"Esther! Are you all right?" I ran up and gave her a hug, making her beads and bracelets rattle.

"Silke, darlin'! There now. There's nowt a wash and an iron and a nice cup of my tea won't put right. But tell these brutish bullies who I am, for love's sake, dearie. They think I'm one of *them*."

"It's OK, Major," I told the soldiers. "I know this woman. She's not one of the renegades."

"We found her wandering the corridors on the fifth

level," said the major, his distaste visible in his expression. "You do know she's a *witch*?"

"You watch your step, young man. I don't like your tone!"

I squeezed Esther's shoulder to quieten her. "Yes, I know. She has a herbal shop. Well, *had* a herbal shop, in Lepp Street. She's fully licensed. You don't have to worry. I'll answer for her."

"And you are?"

Before I could reply, Astrid stepped in front of me. "Excuse me, Major. These two are private investigators, hired by Prince Vyktor and Princess Veelya. As the princess's personal bodyguard, I must ask you to arrange a fast escort for their royal highnesses so they can return to the palace immediately. They need to be with their father."

With a jolt I realised I had forgotten about the king. We needed to get back to see if we could do anything to help him. That is, if it wasn't already too late. Even with the help of the Darkstone, I doubted I'd be able to bring him back from the dead.

The guards nodded, snapped Astrid a salute and promised to see to it right away.

"Do you think they'd let us squeeze in with them?" I asked Stone. It was going to take us ages to drive back in his transpo, besides I wasn't sure he could drive with his injured arm. I'd have to see if I could heal it first.

Astrid heard me. "That won't be a problem. We have three flyers on site, so there'll be plenty of room for you. We're leaving a division behind to clear up and secure the keep."

"Oh." I hadn't thought about flyers. Suddenly the long drive in the transpo didn't seem so bad.

Stone explained about his vehicle and Astrid promised to get one of the guards to drive it back to the palace for him. He gave her his ignition disk.

The major appeared in the doorway again. "If you'd all like to follow me, we'll take you back to Ysgard now."

Veelya and her brother went out with Astrid. Stone and I followed, and I felt Esther behind me give a tug on my shirt.

"What is it, Esther?"

"Are we going in one of those fancy flying things?" she whispered.

I thought perhaps she was nervous, like I was. "Yes, but it's OK. It's not a long trip and you'll hardly know you're up in the air," I reassured her, thinking *Liar, liar*.

Her eyes shone. "Oh, no, dearie. Esther doesn't mind. She's just never been in one before. It's so thrilling."

I clamped my mouth shut. There was nothing I could usefully add to that. But I did catch Stone with a smirk on his face, the rat. I nearly mentioned snakes, but thought it would probably be childish of me.

261

As we made our way up to ground level, I put my arm round Esther. "I'm sorry about the shop, Esther," I said. "But we've got Mort and Juniper safe for you."

"Oh, that's nice. I did worry about them. I daresay the others aren't too far away. I did tell them all to make themselves scarce, you know. Did you find the creature in the jar? I bespelled it so it wouldn't get destroyed. I wanted you to find it."

There was still guilt and remorse in her old eyes. "Yes, we found it. And the message on Mort's leg, thanks. It was a great help."

She gripped my arm with trembling fingers. "Believe me, Silke, I didn't want to help him, but he threatened such terrible things—"

"I know. It's OK. Tell us all about it later."

"Will you rebuild your shop?" Stone asked.

"Oh, yes. That shop's been in Esther's family for generations, it has. There'll be insurance money, you'll see, and it will be good as new again."

If anyone could squeeze compensation out of an insurance company then a licensed witch ought to manage it. I daresay she had ways and means of persuading them to be generous, but I didn't ask.

We reached the entrance hall of the keep, where Stone and I had made our escape only days ago. The place was littered with groups of prisoners under guard. Some of them were still sleeping or groggy, and I remembered with a flush of guilt that I had put them all into a sleep to stop them fighting. Well, it seemed a good idea at the time.

The major pushed open the big double doors and we went out into the crisp night air. I was glad it was dark. I wouldn't have to see how fast and high we were flying.

Veelya and Vyktor were being led to a separate craft with a fancy royal crest on its fuselage. Before climbing up the steps, Veelya turned back and ran towards me, still clutching her blanket around her and clearly feeling a lot better.

"Silke, I didn't thank you for what you and Stone did for us. We're both really very grateful."

"That's OK, Princess," I said cheerfully. "Wait till you see our bills."

She grinned. "I daresay we'll be able to afford them. You'll be coming back to the palace, won't you?"

"Oh, yes," I said. "We've some unfinished business to sort out, including removing some rather unpleasant pests that are currently living in your basement."

TWENTY

The flight back to Ysgard wasn't as terrifying as that first experience. For one thing, the craft was much larger, so it wasn't so obvious that we were in a confined space dicing with the elements, and I didn't have that constricting webbing locking me into my seat. Also, I was sitting between Stone and Esther (who wanted desperately to sit by the window) and there were rows of seats in front of us, so I didn't have to watch the dawn lighting up the clouds beneath us. Besides, I had a zillion questions I wanted to ask Stone, which distracted me nicely.

"When you disappeared into the water like that and then never came up again, I really thought we'd lost you for good," I told him.

"You forget, Silke. I have an affinity with water. It would be almost impossible for me to drown. Just as you'd never get burned by fire."

I could understand that. "So what did happen when Joslin went after you?"

He shuddered. "I was terrified. I never could stand snakes, and he was big enough to have been the grandfather of all of them."

"He was a mage, too," I pointed out.

"Don't remind me. I think while he was in snake form, though, he could only be a snake, if you see what I mean. He tried to sink his fangs into me first, and then he tried crushing me. My arm got the worst of it."

So that accounted for the bandage.

"Is it broken?"

"No, just mauled about."

"What happened next?"

"Well, as you know, the vault lies at the bottom of the pool. It's constructed on the same principle as a diving bell, only on a huge scale. Once you swim underneath it, you come up inside into a pocket of trapped air. It's filled with stacks of ceremonial stuff – you know, crowns, jewels, regalia – all arranged behind glass on shelves above water level. I just smashed one of the cases and grabbed a ceremonial sword. Chopped his head off with it."

"If you can swim up inside the vault, what's the point of having a password to open it?"

"I didn't try it, but my guess is that the password causes the vault to rise up out of the water and become more accessible. Not many people are going to want to dive down far enough to be able to access the treasure underwater, are they?"

"I suppose not. So, you obviously found the Darkstone easily enough."

"Not quite. I was looking for something pretty spectacular, since Veelya said about how priceless it was. In fact, it turned out to look pretty dull and ordinary amongst all the other glittery stuff in there. Then I wondered if I'd have trouble taking it out of the crown, but I just touched it with my fingers and it fell into my hands. Weird. It was almost as if it had been waiting for me."

I had to ask him. "Did you feel anything when you held it?"

"Yes."

I waited for him to say more.

"Just, 'yes'?"

He sighed. "Silke, handling that stone was probably the hardest thing I have ever done in my life. I'm an empath. That stone is the petrified heart of a great mage. It was forged deep inside a volcano, just as the legend says. Can you imagine the images I picked up from it? Believe me, if you felt and saw the things I saw, you'd never want to touch it again as long as you lived."

"Oh." If it had been anyone else but Lucius, I would have given his hand a comforting squeeze. But I knew I couldn't do that. "I'm sorry," I said, instead, and thought about the effect the Darkstone had had on me. It was still in my pocket. How easy it would be to take it in my hand and have the power to do anything I wished. I thought of Sattine's dream of being the greatest mage of all time and how I might have kings eating out of my hand; dragons at my beck and call; mages carrying out my every whim.

"What are you thinking about?" Stone asked me.

"Don't you know?"

He gave a sad smile. "All I know is that your mind is grappling with something difficult and emotional. I think I can guess what it is, but if you don't want to talk about it, that's OK."

I glanced at Esther with her nose practically glued to the window, even though there wasn't much to see.

"Not now," I replied quietly.

"Esther," I said.

"Yes, dearie?" She turned away from the window.

"Will you come into the palace with us and see if you can help the king?"

Her face clouded a little. She was doubtless thinking of her own unwitting part in the king's demise. "Yes. I probably should. But you don't need Esther, you know. You can put him right yourself. As long as he's still with us, poor man."

"How can you be sure?" I asked. "I've never tried healing anyone that sick before. I don't really know what to do."

"Ah, but you haven't had that mix of ghoulswine and Esther's serum in your blood before, or the Darkstone in your hand." I flinched and felt my face colour. "Yes, dearie, I know it's in your pocket. It's hard to hide something that powerful from feyfolk. For a short time, darlin', you will have a great deal more healing power than ever Esther had."

"How do you mean, 'a short time'?"

"Don't you see? The three things work together. But blood is constantly being renewed, so once the toxin and serum are eliminated, you won't have the same heightened abilities. Like any drugs, to keep up the effects you'd need them for the rest of your life. Take it from Esther, they wouldn't do you much good in the end."

This was a surprisingly long and wise speech for Esther. It gave me a deal to think about.

"So when Sattine thought he'd found the source of omnipotent power, he hadn't thought quite far enough. There was a catch to it."

"Oh yes, dearie. But Esther told him that. He didn't care. He thought it was a small price to pay for being the greatest mage of all time."

"But what about the Darkstone? Doesn't it have any effect without the ghoulswine?"

"The Darkstone is *elemental* magic, dear. It's wild and strong. It will enhance your own elemental power as a fire-mage, but you won't always have as much control over it as you do at the moment. Eventually it will take over. It was once the heart of a great sorcerer, remember, so along with all his magic, it carries his greedy ambitions. And believe Esther, humility is not usually a strong point in a sorcerer."

"So why was it put into the Imperial Crown? Why not destroy it?"

"It's a symbol of power, dearie. The monarchs of Elginagen can never be taken over by magic as long as they have the Darkstone. It keeps them safe from people like Sattine."

"But the king *wasn't* safe."

"The king was being *poisoned*. Not magicked."

Hmmm. I suppose that was true. I was curious. "Would you want the Darkstone yourself?" I asked her.

"Oh, my word!" Esther laughed and clutched her clothes over her heart. "What would Esther do with such a thing? No, dearie. It's not for the likes of me. And you be careful with it, too, Silke. Don't keep it too long or you won't be able to give it up."

The flyer gave a lurch, which caused my stomach to drop to my boots, and I realised we must be coming down to land. I felt the blood drain from my face. I shut my eyes and clutched at the armrest of the seat as if my life depended on it.

"Oooh, look!" said Esther. "I can see all of Ysgard from here. Who'd have thought it! And look! There's the palace. We must be landing in the grounds. Whoooo! We just missed that tower!"

Gah. Shut up, Esther!

There was a light bump and the flyer mercifully rolled to a stop.

I stayed as I was, trying to breathe deeply and take command of my nerves.

"Uh . . . Silke?" Stone's voice, sounding very strained.

I opened my eyes and looked at him. There was perspiration on his face and he was extremely pale. He glanced down at his bandaged arm and I realised then that I had been crushing it in my panic. Mortified, I lifted my hand off him.

"Oh, Stone. Sorry. I didn't realise . . ."

He was taking some deep breaths himself. "It's OK. Don't worry about it."

"Here – let me fix it." Before he could refuse, I curled my fingers round the Darkstone again and lightly touched Stone's damaged arm with my free hand. Immediately, I could sense the healing warmth coursing through damaged muscle, tendons and bone.

"Wow!" Stone flexed his fingers. "That's some trick, Silke." He began ripping off the bandages, just as the major came briskly down the aisle towards us looking very concerned.

"We've had a communication from the king's aide," he said. "The king hasn't got very long. We must hurry."

TWENTY-ONE

There was quite a crowd in the king's bedroom by the time we got there, and even though I'm fairly tall, I couldn't even see the bed. The major tried to clear a path for us, but in the end I tugged on his jacket and said in his ear, "You must clear the room, Major. We can't do a thing with all these people here."

He sensibly got hold of a couple of senior palace people and together they physically moved everyone out of the door, leaving Veelya and Vyktor standing anxiously at the royal bedside, an elderly gent in black medical garb I imagined was the Royal Physician, Baracleth, and one other person who introduced himself in a subdued voice as Marlot, the king's aide. Astrid and Vyktor's PBs stood by the door keeping people out.

I went up to the huge bed with its golden canopy, feeling distinctly awed. It's not every day you get asked to save the life of the king, after all. But one look at that wasted, fragile body lying still beneath the shroud-like sheets and I forgot my nervousness. His face was that of an old man, but I knew he couldn't be much more than forty. The smell of sickness and imminent death was almost palpable and I wondered if I had time to wait for Esther to join us: she'd had to follow at her own pace and we'd left her still climbing the many stairs to the royal apartments.

Stone moved up close behind me and touched my arm. "Don't wait. Do what you can, Silke," he said, quietly.

"Please, Silke." It was barely a whisper, but I looked up and saw Veelya on the other side of the bed, pleading with me to help. I sucked in my breath and blew it out slowly to calm myself.

I reached into my pocket and drew out the Darkstone, caressing it with my fingers. It wasn't much to look at: just a heart-shaped charcoal-grey stone with pinkish veins criss-crossing it. But as I focused on the stone, I felt my own magepower coming alive within me, surging up to my fingertips to join with the magic of the stone. As the two met, I must have cried out at the incredible explosion of magic within me, and I was distantly aware of hands at my back preventing me from falling.

I could smell saltwater spray, brown earth, green growing things and light airs full of blossom. And warmth. The kind of warmth that makes you feel alive; the heat of the sun on the cool earth bringing forth new life. And suddenly I realised that Sattine had been wrong. My magefire didn't come from the destructive, fiery wastes he had shown me: my fire came from the *sun*! The thought gave me a wonderful feeling of completeness.

Without realising it, I had climbed on to the bed and was kneeling next to the king. I rested a hand over his heart and felt the tiny, weak pulse beneath my palm. Closing my eyes again, I focused the magic and sent the magefire gently into him. Just as it had with Vyktor, I sensed it coursing through his body, burning up the ghoulswine that had all but ruined every part of him, sealing broken internal blood vessels, cleansing his systems. I felt the elemental magic of the Darkstone combining with mine to put his mind and body once more in balance. When I was sure I had done as much as I could, I gave him restful sleep.

"Silke!"

I opened my eyes to find that Stone was holding me. Doctor Baracleth had pushed Veelya and her brother aside and was fussing over the patient in the bed. I felt unutterably weary and drained. The Darkstone was still pulsing in my hands, I just had enough presence of mind to tuck it away in my pocket again.

"The king?"

Stone smiled. "He's OK. Asleep, but already looking better. His heart's stronger and Doctor Baracleth thinks he's going to be fine."

I shut my eyes with relief.

"Give the girl a chance to rest, why don't you? Here, put her in that chair and give her some cordial. I suppose you *have* alomel cordial amongst your fancy medicines. Working that kind of magic is exhausting, don't you know?"

Esther had arrived. She was organising everyone and I could tell she was hugely enjoying ordering around all the nobby medics, as she'd call them, and palace staff. If I weren't so weak, I'd have laughed. I just had time to see the doctor scowling across at her, before Stone lifted me from the bed and helped me over to an elegant chair.

"Madam," said Baracleth, "kindly don't try and tell me my job. I have been the Royal Physician for thirty years."

"Well, you 'asn't made much of a job of it then, is all I can say," Esther retorted. "It took my Silke here to make the king better, bless 'im. And don't you forget it. Now, have you got this cordial or shall I have to go and make it myself?"

The doctor looked about to burst a blood vessel, despite Vyktor's calming hand on his arm.

"Esther, I'm fine now," I said. "I don't need any cordial. I think we ought to go with Stone and sort out those . . . *creatures* . . . of Sattine's. They can't be allowed to survive. Do you know how to get rid of them?"

She looked huffy for a moment or two as if she would

have liked to take on the doctor a lot longer, but then she shook her head and turned back to me. "They don't live long, anyway, dearie. I daresay they're already dead. Sattine had to clone them all: they can't breed, you know."

"Well, let's be sure. They're too dangerous to leave in the palace. Can you take us down there, Stone?" I didn't want to go at all, but I couldn't leave this place without making sure the nasty things were gone.

"Sure. Maybe we'll take a couple of guards as well, just in case?"

I got to my feet with his help and we made our way down to the cellars. The major gave us two of his guards to accompany us. They each carried disruptors.

Stone located the cell and stood for a moment with his hands against the door, concentrating. "I can't sense any life in there," he said.

"I suppose they would have all been in this one room?" I asked. I realised then that I was shivering with dread and tried to get a grip.

Esther nodded, her expression pained. "They used to experiment with prisoners," she said quietly. "See how long it took them to die."

"But we don't know where he did his experimental breeding," Stone pointed out.

"At his house in the Southern Isles, I expect," I said. "That will have to be investigated at some point, but I've no idea where it is." I stood back from the door, flexing my fingers in case I had to suddenly use my magefire. "If we're going to do this, let's get on with it."

The guards stood either side of the door. Stone and I stood in front, but well back against the far wall of the corridor. Esther watched calmly to one side of us. I'm sure she thought we were all being paranoid.

One guard pulled open the door quickly, the other ducked down and swept the inside of the room with his disruptor. There were no squeals or flapping sounds as far as I could tell. Both guards moved cautiously into the cell.

"It looks clear in here," one said.

"You stay here," Stone said to me. "I'll go in and check."

I nodded and waited while he went inside. He wasn't gone many seconds.

"A few rotting bat bodies, that's all," he said. "I think we can be sure they're gone."

"Well, there's just one thing I want to do before we leave it," I said. "All of you stand well back."

I didn't need the Darkstone for what I wanted to do. I stepped inside the doorway of the cell, raised my hands and called up my magepower. I sent searing, cleansing flame throughout the entire room, burning away every vestige of evil corruption and smell of death. By the time the last embers had died, there was absolutely nothing left in the room but bare walls, ceiling and floor. It was sterile, without even the ghost of a memory of all the pain and horror it had seen.

When I turned away from the door, I saw that the others had all shielded their eyes from the brightness. Slowly they lowered their arms.

"Very nice, dear," said Esther, mopping her face with a large handkerchief. I realised, then, that I had covered them – and myself – with fine ash.

"Oops, sorry," I said, and brushed guiltily at Stone's sleeves while he shook ash out of his hair and then wiped off his glasses. Mind you, his clothes were such a state from his ordeal at the keep that a little ash didn't make much difference.

"No problem," he said dryly. "I plan to bin this outfit anyway."

I linked my arm in his. "Let's go home, Stone."

"Just what I was about to say myself. You must be a telepath."

TWENTY-TWO

We had to take leave of Veelya and Vyktor first, of course, and I couldn't just walk out with the Darkstone (although I was seriously tempted). With a great effort of will, I handed it over to Vyktor and he informed us there would be a proper ceremony in due course to return the stone to its place in the imperial crown, once the king was sufficiently recovered. Stone and I agreed to be there.

True to her promise, Astrid had ensured that Stone's transpo was waiting for us in the palace parking lot. As the gates swung open for us to drive out, a few early tourists took photos of us, thinking we must be celebrities of some kind. Esther and I gave them a smile and a wooden wave and then fell about laughing. Stone had difficulty concentrating on his driving.

We dropped Esther at the house of one of her sister witches and then drove back to Stone's place so I could collect my few belongings, together with Juniper and Mort. They were going to stay with me until Esther had her own place again. My apartment wasn't the best home for either of them, but I didn't feel I could foist the responsibility on to Stone and his father.

Unfortunately, the euphoria of being back with our mission accomplished, didn't last long. When Trace opened the door to us I didn't need Stone's gift to see that there was something wrong. The bleak expression on his face told us that much.

"Where is he, Trace?" asked Stone, quietly.

His father.

Dread washed over me. I just hoped we were in time.

"In his room. The doctor's been with him, Lucius, but there isn't much he can do."

Stone took off down the hallway, leaving us to follow.

When I reached the doorway of Marcus's bedroom, Stone was kneeling beside the bed, holding his father's pale hand, his forehead pressed against the bedcovers. I was shocked when I saw just how frail Marcus had become in the short time we had been away.

I no longer had the Darkstone with me, and there was probably precious little of the magic mixture left in my blood now, but I wanted to try and help, for Stone's sake. I moved over to the other side of the bed and focused on my magepower once more, drawing it up from my centre;

feeling it spreading through me and into my hands, comfortable and familiar.

I laid them gently on Marcus. I could count his bones under the thin skin; barely feel his faint pulse and shallow breaths. Closing my eyes, I thought of the healing warmth of the sun ripening wheat, opening blooms, invigorating the earth, and I poured the restoring magefire into him, giving renewed strength to his heart and lungs, soothing his pain and calming his mind.

But it was not like healing the king. This time, my own heart felt leaden, as I knew with absolute certainty that even if I'd had the help of the Darkstone, I would not be able to work any miracle here. The disease had too great a hold on Marcus, and his insides were too badly damaged for me to repair. All I could do was give him a measure of peace.

I looked bleakly across at Trace and gave a tiny shake of my head. He nodded. He, too, knew the score.

Marcus opened his eyes and looked first at me, and then at Lucius, who lifted his head.

"Oh good. You're back," he said with effort.

"Hey, Dad," whispered Lucius. "Yes, we're back. Everything's all right now."

"That young lady friend of yours has a nice touch," said Marcus, with a little huffy laugh in his exhausted voice. "I feel better already."

"That's great, Dad."

"I'll just have a little sleep, Lucius, and then we'll have dinner and you can tell me all about what you've been up to. Maybe I can put it in my next novel." He closed his eyes again, smiling.

"Sure thing." Lucius stood up, then straightened the covers on the bed and leant over to kiss his father's forehead.

I backed out of the room to give them privacy and Trace followed me into the kitchen, where we both wordlessly prepared some fresh kashla for the three of us.

Stone joined us after a while. His face was haggard.

"He's gone."

"Oh, Stone. I'm so sorry. I tried . . ."

He waved his good hand impatiently, then took off his glasses and rubbed at his eyes before putting them back on. "No. It's OK. I know you did your best. He's been ill for too long. I thought I was prepared for this moment, but I guess you never can be fully prepared. You gave him a great gift, Silke. Thank you. He was very peaceful and relaxed, without any pain. I hope I can say as much when it's my turn."

We drank our kashla, saying little, and then Trace helped me put my stuff together. Stone insisted on driving me to my apartment, especially since I had to struggle with Mort and Juniper in wicker baskets, but I made him leave me at my door and return home immediately. He had a great deal to do now, arranging his father's funeral and setting all his affairs in order.

As he put down the last of the bags and stood up, I wrapped my arms round him compulsively.

"Thanks for everything, Stone. And take care."

He hugged me back briefly and gave me a brotherly kiss on the cheek.

"You too, Silke. I'll be in touch."

And then he left.

My apartment was cold and I could tell by the stale smell in the air that quite a few things had gone sour in the fridge, but even so it felt great being home again. My crystal comm was blinking with messages, but I figured they could wait a little longer. I set about doing comforting housekeeping things: tossing clothes and bedding into the washer, fixing the heating and taking two bags of stale food and rubbish down to the recycle centre. It saved me thinking too much about everything. Especially Sattine.

I established Mort on his perch by a window, so he'd have an interesting view, and Juniper made himself at home on my sofa while I went on an errand to buy groceries and pet food. It was all very normal and undemanding, which was exactly what I needed to unwind and to fill the void that inevitably occurred at the end of a complex case.

With the apartment warm once more, and a hot

sandwich in my hand, I lounged next to Juniper, my legs stretched out, and listened to my comm messages. Most of them were too old to be of any use: a couple of hysterical ones from Veelya, for instance, made before they were taken to the keep; a nervous one from Esther (who didn't like using crystalcomms at the best of times) warning me that she might have to go away for a few days. That was before her shop went up in smoke. And then there was a nasty little piece of sleaze from Dervan which sent shivers of dread down me and I had to zap it before it finished. But there were two from prospective clients who wanted to discuss employing my services. I felt a frisson of excitement when I heard those and jotted down the numbers to call them later.

I then set to work on my report and invoice for HRH Veelya Sofania Gloriosa. It took me three hours and was something of a masterpiece, since I had never written quite so much, or had to figure such a complex account before. Satisfied at last, I sealed it in an envelope and dropped it in the mailbox down the street. I just hoped Veelya was prompt with her payment as my financial reserves were badly in need of reinforcement.

I finished the day with a long hot bath, washed my hair and then crashed out in my own comfortable, familiar bed, barely conscious of the warm weight of Juniper curled at the curve of my knees.

TWENTY-THREE

The next few days passed fairly routinely, which means not a lot happened. Esther dropped by to see how Mort and Juniper were faring and to tell me that work had already begun on rebuilding the shop.

"I'm working some spells of my own into the fabric of the walls, this time," she told me. "Better to be safe than sorry. Besides, it gives me a twenty per cent reduction on the insurance premium."

Who said witches couldn't be worldly?

I visited old haunts to catch up with the street news and set up appointments with my two callers.

One turned out to be an aristo acquaintance of Veelya's, wanting me to trace a missing cousin for her. She hoped the cousin was dead, so that she could take over his estate. Charming.

The other was the manager of one of Ysgard's oldest banking establishments, who wanted me to make discreet enquiries about a client suspected of defrauding the bank. Since neither job appeared to involve any kind of magic or sorcery, I felt pretty comfortable about taking them on. I'd had my fill of magic for a while.

Stone called me one morning with the details of his father's funeral. I hadn't known Marcus for long, of course, but I agreed to attend for Stone's sake.

And that same morning, the king's Private Secretary called requesting my attendance at the palace for an audience with His Gracious Majesty. His voice was pompous and patronising, and it sounded as if it was causing him great pain to have to *speak* to lowlife such as I was. It really wound me up, so that when he told me the date and the time, I deliberately made a point of going away to check my diary (which was blank) and pretended to have an appointment with my cat's beautician.

"He absolutely *loathes* it when I cancel," I said, in my best empty-headed voice, "but maybe if I tell him it's for the *king*, he won't mind this time." I gave an inane giggle and when the PS clicked off his comm in disgust, I collapsed laughing. Still, it was good to know that old Vyktor had recovered enough to be holding audiences.

I hadn't received any remittance from Veelya yet, so I figured I may as well chase that up at the same time as visiting her father.

The day of the funeral was fine and warm. I wore my only

good two-piece – a tunic and long skirt – which wasn't the traditional white that everyone wears for funerals, but a pale shade of lavender that looked much better on me anyway. I wasn't a close member of the family, so I wasn't making a social *faux pas*.

Lucius looked stunning in a three-piece white linen outfit, and Trace stood by him, looking tall and elegant as only Narthians can, decked out in white silk under a long, ivory cloak. I had never seen such an elegant pair and I hesitated before going up to them at the door of the temple. I needn't have worried. Lucius smiled, pulled me towards him and kissed my cheek, then Trace lifted me off my feet and planted a kiss on my nose, making me laugh.

"Thanks for coming, Silke," said Lucius. "You're looking well. How are things?"

"OK, thanks. You're both looking pretty good yourselves."

"I'll be glad when today's over. You'll come back to the house after, won't you?"

"Ah . . . " I hadn't planned to. Socialising with a crowd of strangers didn't appeal much. Besides, I didn't have transport. Silly me. Stone picked up on my doubt immediately.

"You can come back with Trace and me, and Trace can run you home when you want to go, or we can get you a cab if you prefer."

That didn't sound so bad, so I agreed and Trace took me inside.

Ha. When we stepped into the circular interior of the temple, I almost changed my mind. It was packed. All the seats on the ground floor – apart from those in the centre reserved for the family – and all three galleries were full. One corner was completely taken up by media people with their cameras and sound booms and as one they all turned, like some synchronised dance routine, and focused on *me* as Trace walked me down to the front. I could even hear someone breathing a commentary into a discreet microphone. I'd forgotten just how famous Marcus Stone had been.

"No, Trace," I whispered, tugging on his arm. "Put me in a dark corner somewhere. I'm not family."

"As good as, Silke," he said quietly. "Besides, I'm not family either, so you can keep me company."

"Does Stone have many relatives?"

"A few aunts and distant cousins, I think. I never saw much of any of them in the six years I looked after Marcus."

I could hear the disapproval in his voice.

"What will you do now, Trace?"

"Oh, there's always someone who needs a private nurse," he replied. It sounded very neutral, but I wouldn't mind betting that he would miss the Stone household a lot.

As my very first memorial service, it went better than I

expected. There was music that Marcus particularly loved. Several famous people spoke warmly about him both as a person and a writer who left his mark on the literary scene, and finally Lucius read an extract from one of his father's books.

The reception at the house afterwards wasn't so bad, either. But I was relieved to be able to slip away eventually and for Trace to drive me back to my apartment. I felt very conspicuous amongst all those friends and relatives of the family, all of whom seemed very human and non-magical. As far as I was aware, no one else in Stone's family had his gifts, but then maybe those of his mother's side had stayed away. I didn't like to ask.

Two days later there was a knock on my door. I opened it to see Astrid standing there, grinning at me.

"I have come to take you to the palace for your audience with the king," she said in her brisk way.

"Right. Thanks, Astrid. Who's looking after the princess while you're doing taxi duty?"

"Oh, she has several bodyguards. Do not worry."

I smiled. I wasn't worried at all, just winding Astrid up a little.

She was looking at me a bit funny. "How soon can you leave?" she asked.

I looked down at myself. My old patchwork leather

jacket and black combats looked pretty clean, and I'd put on my better pair of boots. I didn't think I'd forgotten anything.

"Ready to go," I said, and dangled my keys in front of her to prove it.

She raised a brow. Opened her mouth, then shut it again. "You do not want to change?"

"Nope."

She nodded. "Fine. This way, please."

I locked up, reset my wards and followed her down to the street, where a black palace limo was waiting and beginning to draw a crowd of curious locals. The driver was leaning against the bonnet trying to look intimidating, in case anyone tried to put grubby fingerprints on the shine.

"How is the king?" I asked Astrid as the limo glided smoothly away.

"Good. You will see," she said.

That seemed to be all she was prepared to say. Maybe anything else would contravene official secrets. The rest of the journey passed in silence, so I just stared out of the windows and enjoyed the ride.

The king's audience room was, surprisingly, just a small private sitting room. Astrid announced me and then left, closing the door behind her. I saw immediately that King Vyktor was indeed looking pretty good, and recognised family features that were shared with his children. He was still rather pale and thin, unlike his official portraits, but he came to greet me on steady legs and his handshake was strong enough.

"Thank you for coming, um . . . Ms Silke," he said.

"Just Silke."

"Ah, yes. I forgot. You Ellanoi don't have second names, do you? Please come and sit down."

We went over to a couple of armchairs and sat opposite each other. There was a tray on a small table between us, with a pot and small cups and a plate of tiny biscuits.

"Why don't you pour us both some kashla? Or would you like me to be mother?"

I laughed. Kings weren't supposed to come out with stuff like that. "I can manage fine, thanks."

"First of all, Silke, I must apologise for my family. I'm afraid you haven't seen any of us at our best. I was stupid enough to allow myself to be poisoned, and my two children were too busy bickering with each other to notice anything wrong in the palace. And, of course, you know all about Lord Joslin."

I shrugged. "Every family has problems, I guess. Royal problems are probably just a bit bigger than everyone else's."

"Yes." He paused, as if thinking about that. "But I must thank you for your part in putting things right. Saving my life, for one thing, and saving the lives of my children . . . even if they are a bit tiresome." That last was muttered under his breath and I probably wasn't meant to hear it.

"Ah, well, I didn't do it all on my own. Stone was—"

"Yes, yes. I've already spoken to Lucius. A very presentable young man. So sad about his father. I enjoyed his books."

So, Stone had already been to the palace. I felt mildly annoyed that he hadn't called to tell me.

"I've also had a word with your, um, friend, the . . . er . . . herbalist."

"*Esther?*" How come all my mates were having audiences with the king and not sharing with me? I was beginning to feel I was invisible. Or maybe they were all avoiding me.

"You sound surprised. I needed to find out just what part she played in all this. I think we both have a mutual understanding now. I've asked her to act as a consultant on natural remedies for me." His eyes glinted with amusement. "Advise my regular physician on *alternative* medicine."

I looked at him keenly. *He wasn't quite as daft as people made out.* "Better to work for you than against you," I said.

"Exactly."

I bet Baracleth didn't think much of that idea.

He rubbed his chin and looked a bit preoccupied, like someone in a grocery store trying to remember what was on the shopping list they left at home.

"Ah, yes. The Ambassador of Illithgarten." I may have looked a bit startled. My brain wasn't quite keeping up with his mental leaps.

"The ambassador?" I repeated.

"Yes. You'll be relieved to know that his *real* nephew is quite safe. Master Vander was obliging enough to give my Inquisitor the information we needed to find him."

There was a brief moment when I felt a twinge of pity for Dervan.

"And how are your son and daughter, um . . . sir?" I asked.

"Oh, they're very well, thank you. I packed them off to one of our residences on the coast. To let them convalesce, you know. A bit of sunshine and peace and quiet away from the city ought to do them both some good." He paused and smiled at some thought. "Yes. Their tutors have gone with them. To help them catch up with missed studies while I was . . . indisposed."

I grinned. Poor Veelya and Vyktor wouldn't get much chance to bunk off and enjoy themselves for a while.

The king stood up then and went over to a small desk, where he picked up a leather folder, and came back to his chair again. "Now, I have here your payment for the work you did for my daughter."

Oh, good.

"And I've taken the liberty of adding a little more by way of expressing my own thanks."

"That's very kind, thank you." I did at least know how to be polite to grateful clients.

He cleared his throat. "There was just one other matter I want to mention. It's only fair to tell you that *some* of my advisers thought that it would be appropriate to . . . um . . . question you about how much you might have colluded with the renegade mage, Sattine. I understand you were closely related."

I felt my face go hard and blank. "Yes, we shared parents. But Sattine left me when I was still a child and I neither saw nor heard from him until I began my investigation for your daughter."

He shook his head. "I want you to know that I don't share their suspicions. You can rest assured that I have vouched for your loyalty. And that your friends have vouched for you as well."

So that's why they were called to the palace.

"Oh. Well, that's something." What else could I say?

"But even so, I can't imagine it was easy for you to see him after all these years and then lose him again so . . . tragically. I am sorry for your loss, my dear. There will, of course, have to be an investigation. I have a specialist team searching for his residence. I don't suppose you have any information you could give them?"

"Sorry. I only know that when he was banished he went to live on Farfeld Island in the Southern Isles. I never went there myself or communicated with him. Have you asked Dervan? Sorry, Vander. He worked with Sattine, after all."

"Vander claims he was recruited here, in Ysgard." The king shifted in his seat and leaned forward to put his empty cup on the tray. "No matter. We will find it eventually. I'll make sure you are informed when we do. As his next of kin I imagine you may want to see the place for yourself. After all, it probably belongs to you now."

I hadn't given that much thought, but didn't think there would be much of Sattine's that I'd want to have anything to do with. I said as much to the king. "You might want to warn your team that his place is likely to be heavily warded. Do you have your own mages who could check the place out?"

"Oh, I think we can manage," he said, enigmatically. "Would you like more kashla?"

"No, thanks." I made as if to get up, since this sounded like the end of the audience, but the king put up a hand to stop me.

"Just one more thing." He opened the leather folder he'd picked up from his desk and handed me a stiff piece of parchment, which seemed to have an awful lot of squiggles and fancy decorations all round its margins. "This is for you, Silke, with my thanks. You never know, it might just help your business a little." That glint of amusement was back in his eyes. I took the parchment cautiously, my curiosity piqued.

It took me a while to read the fancy calligraphy and realise just what I had in my hand.

"Is this a Royal Commission?" I asked, incredulous.

"Yes. See . . . it says, 'By *appointment to His Gracious Majesty*,' blah blah, '*his Heirs and Household*,' etc etc, '*Licensed to Investigate*' . . . and so forth."

"So what does it mean?"

He gave a laugh. "It means, Silke, that you can put the royal heraldic device on your business cards now and say 'Licensed Private Investigator, by Appointment to the Royal Court of Elginagen.' I don't know whether it *will* get you a better class of clientele, but it gives your business a little extra social kudos, I think."

I laughed with childish delight. "Hoo! Thanks, sir! I mean, Your Majesty." *Won't that be one in the eye for Mr Lucius Stone!*

We both stood, then, and the king shook my hand again. "I hope you will attend the ceremony to restore the Darkstone. I'll get my secretary to give you the details. I've asked Lucius to attend as well, so perhaps you'd like to travel together. There will only be a small number of people attending, since the location of the royal vault is still an official secret, you understand." He looked at me sharply.

"Oh, yes, I understand."

"Excellent. We'll see you then."

I felt the occasion merited a new outfit. After all, the king *had* given me an astonishingly generous bonus. I toyed briefly with the idea of buying myself a fancy transpo, but I'd have to find a new home as well, since any vehicle parked for any length of time in the docks district was asking to be stripped or nicked. I settled for a state-of-the-art crystalcomm instead and put the rest in the bank, as security for the times when business might be slow. It gave me a good feeling to know it was there.

Blackstone Keep looked less intimidating somehow in the morning sunshine, but that may have been because this time we entered in style, in a cavalcade of official limos and outriders. OK, so Stone and I were in the smallest one, at the back, but it was still pretty impressive.

We'd had to be blindfolded once we were inside the entrance hall, so that we wouldn't know exactly how to find the treasure room. Or at least, *pretend* we didn't know. We'd been briefed about what to expect. The official Keeper of the Treasuries, Lord Farwith, would lead the procession. Behind him would be the king, then Vyktor and Veelya. Stone and I were to bring up the rear, with two royal guards helping us find our way.

We set off on a slow, dignified journey (disorienting for

Stone and myself) through the labyrinth that made up the lower levels of the keep.

Once inside the treasure room we were relieved of our blindfolds. Lord Farwith wore dazzling robes and jewelled regalia that went with his office and made him look as magnificent as the treasure room itself. His family had been Keepers of the Treasuries for aeons, apparently – borne out by his antique outfit, I guess. He handed me the Darkstone on a plump velvet cushion. Stone and I had to give it to the king together, as a symbolic gesture of relinquishing it back into his keeping.

First, however, the vault had to be raised.

The king knelt down at the side of the pool and whispered the password into the water. (No, of course I didn't listen.) Then he stood back. There was a rumbling from deep down in the pool and I could feel vibrations through my feet as gradually the vault itself rose up out of the centre of the pool, water cascading over it. It was a huge, dome-shaped thing made of some kind of non-corrosive metal completely covered with decorative filigree work that sparkled and shone: a masterpiece in itself. As tall as a man at its highest point, its base was at least four metres in diameter. A giant turtle summoned from the sea.

The vault stopped its upward movement once it was clear of the water, then it split open down the centre and I could see what Stone had meant when he described it. Side panels silently moved outwards, displaying row upon row of an astonishing array of jewelled crowns, torques, golden armour, weapons encrusted with gems, and jewellery of every description. The light reflected from the treasure was almost blinding in its intensity. Despite what Stone had told me, I still wasn't prepared for such magnificence. I was the only person in the room that hadn't seen inside the vault before, and I was unashamedly mesmerised by it.

There was further movement at our feet as a wide metal causeway slid smoothly out from the side of the pool, stopping at the open vault.

Lord Farwith gave us a small nod. Stone and I, both holding the sides of the cushion, stepped forward to the king, who stood flanked by his children. He took the cushion from our hands, bowed and then turned and walked along the walkway to the vault followed by the prince and princess. Lord Farwith fell into step behind, then Stone and I.

I couldn't take my eyes off all that priceless treasure. I spotted a jewelled sword lying in a glass case and idly wondered if that was the weapon Stone had used to kill Joslin. I glanced quickly at Stone and he gave a wry smile and a tiny nod of his head.

In the centre of the display was a plain stand holding a small golden crown that looked positively dull amongst all those other fabulous items. It had an oddly-shaped depression in the front of it. Lord Farwith reached out and took the crown in his hands, holding it up to the king, who lifted the Darkstone from its cushion and placed it in the depression in the crown. It fitted perfectly. Immediately, my ears hummed with the sensation of old magic as the stone fused into place, and I felt a sense of completeness. The Darkstone was back where it belonged.

Riding in the back of the limo with Stone on our way home, I couldn't help thinking over a great many things. One thing struck me, however: that Darkstone had been magically welded to the imperial crown. So when Lucius had removed it so easily, it seemed to me that the stone must have *allowed* him to do so. After all, it enabled me to heal the king, so the legend must be right: it did protect the Royal Family from magical harm.

My musings led me to thinking about the future.

Stone and I had worked the case pretty well together. We might be Fire and Ice, but we complemented each other in our skills. Maybe we could do the same again. A partnership, even? *Nah. Maybe not.*

"By the way," said Stone, interrupting my reverie. "I've had some new business cards made." He fished into his breast pocket. "Would you like one?"

There was a look in his eye I didn't altogether trust. I

took the card he held out. It was printed in red and gold, which should have warned me:

Lucius Stone
Psychic Investigator
By Appointment to the Royal Court of Elginagen

And yes, the royal heraldic device was *embossed* at the bottom.

I said a very primitive Ellanoi word that might be politely translated as *bother*.

If you enjoyed *Blood Feud*, look out for the second exciting **Fire and Ice** adventure, *Deadly Encounters*, coming soon . . .

We stared at each other for a nano-second, then started to run back to the office building. The front doors were slightly open – not how we'd left them – and Stone shoved at them with his shoulder. We took the stairs two at a time and, as we reached the landing, two things happened: a firespell erupted in the corridor ahead of us, and a dark figure barrelled into us on its way down the stairs.

"Stone!" I yelled. "Yours!"

I didn't stop to see how he managed, but sped on up to the scene of the fire, which was beginning to catch hold. Taking a deep breath to focus myself, I concentrated on absorbing the flame and the spell that had caused it.

Speaking the Ellanoi words which had come naturally to me since childhood, I raised my arms and stepped into the flames.

They were sharp and acrid, with a distinctive bouquet I did not recognise. Firespells have unique identities, depending on the mage who worked them. I could sense that these flames were greedy for the newly-matured wood used to refurbish the old shell of the bank. I crooned to the fire, calling it to me. At first it resisted. It had its own mission and was reluctant to listen to me. But gradually the flames lessened . . . turned . . . and gave themselves up to me. I gathered them into my hands, like skeins of raw silk, and quenched them utterly.

"Silke? Are you OK?" Stone had come up behind me and wisely hadn't interrupted.

"Yes. What happened to the runner?"

"He was too quick. I got in one slug, but he leapt over the banisters and dropped all the way to the hall. Didn't even stagger when he landed."

"It was a man?"

"The aura was masculine. But it's not an infallible guide." There was a hint of irony in his voice.

"I'll take your word for it. Help me here, Stone." I led the way into the room where most of the spell had been concentrated. Surprise, surprise . . . we found the 'mage' dead behind the scorched desk. His neck was broken.

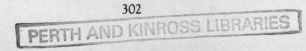